last copy

ENTHUSIAST

Canadian Children's

New York Public Lib

Shortlisted for the Ontario Library Association Silver Birch Award

Shortlisted for the Dog Writers of America Fiction Award

"I was thoroughly entertained by this captivating novel. It is a boy and his dog story, a time travel tale and a grand adventure all rolled into one book ..." VOYA

"... a beautifully resolved ending. *DogStar* is a novel about the great love between humans and animals." VANCOUVER SUN

"More plot twists than a Hardy Boys adventure in cyberspace ... The authors expertly bring to life a time and place for their readers with fully-developed characters and lots of background detail." NORTH SHORE NEWS

"... *DogStar* grows on the reader, and Patsy Ann's doggy grin lingers long after the book is done." QUILL & QUIRE

"A time-travel adventure story with emotional appeal for dog lovers." BOOKLIST

A SIRIUS MYSTERY

JACK'S KNIFE

BEVERLEY WOOD & CHRIS WOOD

Raincoast Books acknowledges the ongoing financial support of the Government of Canada through The Canada Council for the Arts and the Book Publishing Industry Development Program (BPIDP); and the Government of British Columbia through the BC Arts Council.

Editor: Lynn Henry
Typesetting: Teresa Bubela

LIBRARY AND ARCHIVES CANADA CATALOGUING IN PUBLICATION

Wood, Beverley, 1954-
Jack's knife / Beverley Wood & Chris Wood.
ISBN 1-55192-709-8

1. Patsy Ann (Dog)--Juvenile fiction. 2. Juneau (Alaska)--History--Juvenile fiction. I. Wood, Chris, 1953- II. Title.

PS8595.O624J32 2005 jC813'.54 C2005-903302-9

LIBRARY OF CONGRESS CONTROL NUMBER: [to come]

Raincoast Books
9050 Shaughnessy Street
Vancouver, British Columbia
Canada, V6P 6E5
www.raincoast.com

In the United States:
Publishers Group West
1700 Fourth Street
Berkeley, California
94710

At Raincoast Books we are committed to protecting the environment and to the responsible use of natural resources. We are acting on this commitment by working with suppliers and printers to phase out our use of paper produced from ancient forests. This book is one step towards that goal. It is printed on 100% ancient-forest-free paper (40% post-consumer recycled), processed chlorine- and acid-free, and supplied by New Leaf paper. It is printed with vegetable-based inks. For further information, visit our website at www.raincoast.com. We are working with Markets Initiative (www.oldgrowthfree.com) on this project.

Printed in Canada by Webcom Ltd.
10 9 8 7 6 5 4 3 2 1

For my father, Ken Atherley
— Beverley Wood

And my mother, Rosemary Wertheim
— Chris Wood

Table of Contents

One

FISH TALES

JACKSON KYLE reached into his jeans pocket and pulled out his most prized possession. He loved its smooth weight in his hand, the seriousness of it. He admired the cool perfection of the white bone case, the straight steel blade that unfolded from it and locked into place with a sturdy "click." He held it up and the clear morning sunlight split apart on the finely honed blade. A metallic smell lifted from the sheen of sewing-machine oil Al had taught him to use to keep the steel bright and the hinge working smoothly.

This was a real *man*'s tool. One that could do real work — or real damage. Jack's mom hated it.

Somewhere out in the subdivision, a lawn mower started up. A moment later a choking waft of gasoline exhaust blew through the porch, followed by the sweet green smell of cut grass.

Shifting the knife to his right hand, the teenager lifted a green and yellow fish from the bucket beside him. He placed the perch on the sheets of newspaper covering Al's picnic table. Watching the older man beside him, Jackson tried to copy his movements. With his left hand he held the cold, slippery fish down by its head, using his thumb to lift the spiny fin that stuck out just behind the gills. With his right, he ran the knife's blade in a smooth cut from top to bottom.

Gold-and-green scales parted, revealing a line of pearl-coloured meat.

"Now hold it like this," Al said. "Take the knife and run it in *here.*" The older man demonstrated with a fish of his own. With practiced skill, he inserted his own knife blade into the perch just behind the head, its blade aligned with the long dorsal fin. He pressed the knife in and began to slide it back toward the fish's tail. "You'll feel it when the blade hits the bone."

Jackson held his fish so the head was pointed away from him and pressed the point of his knife into the spot where Al had put his. The skin of the fish puckered but didn't break.

"A little harder," Al said. "Like this." Stepping behind the boy, he placed one callused brown hand over Jackson's, trapping the fish securely. Reaching around, he wrapped the fingers of his right hand firmly around the boy's, directing the knife at the desired point with confidence. With the faintest of twists, the blade slid beneath the scales. "Now, feel that?" Al asked.

Jackson felt the knife blade meet something hard under the flesh. He nodded.

"That's bone, the fish's ribs. We want to run the blade right along those, getting as much meat off it as we possibly can without getting any bones in our breakfast." Still holding the fish firmly by the head, Al guided the boy's hand back along the length of the fish, letting the blade lift and turn as it followed the contours of the creature's spine, rib cage and tail. In a few moments, they had peeled the entire side of the fish cleanly away from the bones.

Al laid the fillet skin-side down on the paper. Taking his own knife, he held it sideways and almost flat against the skin, slicing the tender flesh away from the skin. Finally he placed the palm-sized oval of pure, white meat on a waiting plate.

"Now, do the other side by yourself," the older man said, stepping away and going back to work on his own fish.

Jackson concentrated on the task. But even as he flipped the fish over and once again pressed the knife blade into the scales on the other side, his mind was stuck in the sensation of the momentary closeness. He wondered if that's what a dad felt like, that comforting combination of firmness, confident motion and roughness on the skin. And how come Al McMann still smelled of wood smoke after all these years? *Probably hasn't washed that old shirt since he left the Yukon.*

His first unaided fillet came away from the bone a good deal more raggedly than the one Al had helped with. But it was his very own work, and the old man nodded in approval, saying, "That's it. Now try another."

Fifteen minutes later they had a small stack of fillets and a somewhat larger pile of fish heads, bones and tails. They looked just like the ones cats moon over in cartoons. Fish blood soaked the wet newspaper. Several large blow flies with electric blue bodies buzzed over the gooey mess. Idly, Jack poked around with the point of his knife, separating out purplish blobs — *hearts? livers?* — from the bumpy spaghetti stuff of the yellow guts. A gross comparison hit him and he found himself urgently wishing, *Please, anything but Boy-Ar-Dee tonight.*

Al lifted the plate of cleaned white fillets and turned toward the house. At the door leading to his uncluttered kitchen he paused. "You want to bundle up that mess and get it in the trash before it begins to smell?" he said. "Then we'll see what we can do with these."

Jackson rolled newspaper around the squishy, bony remains of the half-dozen perch they'd plucked from the lake at sunrise. He crossed the lawn to deposit them in the trashcan behind the garage. Jogging back, he felt dew from the deep grass soak coldly through his socks over his new hightops.

In the house, he found Al pulling flour and baking powder from old-fashioned cupboards painted yellow and white. A pie plate now sat beside the one of fish fillets.

"Better wash those knives off before anything else," the old man said over his shoulder. "It's a rule of survival on the trail: whenever you use your knife or your gun, clean it right away. You never know when you'll need it next."

Jackson flushed hot water over the two knives, carefully wiping away the scales that clung to them like flakes of dried rainbow.

And? The teenager waited for the tale of high adventure that usually started about now. Some chance remark would spin Al off into tracking a murderer through snow-filled Yukon passes or fighting the gales off the islands in Alaska's

"What, fishing?" Al's eyebrows shot up in surprise. "They're not in any danger. Not perch. Salmon, maybe. But not perch."

"No, it's not that." Jackson was finding it hard to meet his friend's look. His eyes roamed around the kitchen for a hidden cosmic teleprompter. "It's just that she ... She doesn't think a kid ought to be hanging around with ..." He couldn't finish the thought.

Al's face took on a thoughtful look as he settled back in his chair. He took a sip of coffee and lifted another fillet from the stack onto his plate. "Those won't taste nearly as good cold," he said, nodding his knife in the direction of Jackson's plate.

"She's such a ..." Jackson groped for the right word. The one he wanted to use rhymed with "witch" but he knew Al wouldn't stand for it. "A wuss. Doesn't want me doing anything worth doing. Won't let me even *think* about getting a part-time job. Won't let me get a dog, some *bull* about our lease. Almost went *ballistic* when I showed her my knife." Al had given him the clasp-knife, with its bone case worn smooth by the years, as a birthday gift three months ago. It was one Al had carried in the Arctic. As Jack thought about it, he could feel its hard spine through his jeans pocket. "She treats like I'm ten and I'm almost fifteen!"

"She's only doing what she thinks she needs to," Al said mildly. "It can't be easy on her, trying to bring up a teenage boy on her own ... working two jobs."

Angrily Jackson speared a fillet and brought it whole to his mouth, taking half into his mouth in a single bite. He'd heard the *poor, poor single mother* tune often enough in his life from Mom. He was sick of it. *What was so hard about being a single parent anyway?* he often thought. *Half the parents I know are single.*

"And why's she got this thing against *you* anyway?" he protested, his mouth still full of perch he was no longer tasting. "It's so *unfair*!"

Al was lost for a moment in thought. "Well, I suppose it is unfair," he said at last. "But you know, I don't think it's out of malice, really. In her mind, she thinks she's doing the right thing."

"So? If it's really the *wrong* thing, what does that matter?"

"Jack, sometimes people make mistakes. They think they're doing right, but it comes out wrong — and there's no going back to change it. It's happened to me."

"Yeah, *as if*!" Jackson let his disbelief show.

"The first big case I ever worked. I thought I had the right bad guy. In fact, I was *sure* I had him. Everything lined up, all the evidence. Means. Motive. Opportunity. The whole package. Pretty much everyone else around at the time thought the same. I wound up putting a young man away for eighteen years and left a little boy to grow up without a father."

Jackson looked up. His friend's face wore an unfamiliar sadness. The old man's thoughts seemed to wander somewhere in the past, deep-set eyes haunted by sights he couldn't or wouldn't share.

"Later, I had my doubts, but they came too late. Doing what I was sure was right I'd already ruined three lives: the man I put away, and his wife and his son's. It made me a more careful investigator. But the memory still bothers me.

"So I won't be throwing any stones your mother's way," Al finished. "Now clean up that scone or I'll think you don't like my cooking any more."

Jackson washed down the last buttery crumbs with a mouthful of lukewarm coffee (something else Mom thought wasn't "age-appropriate"). Outside, a car with a cranked-up engine roared into earshot up the street and came to a squealing stop in Al's driveway. With a sinking feeling, Jackson recognized the rusty crunch of the driver's door on his mother's battered Ford Escort. Sharp angry steps sounded around the side of the house and then crossed the porch. The screen door slapped open.

"Here you are!" Carla Kyle shrilled. "What have I told you a thousand times? Out in the car. Now!

"And you!" Her hand shook along with her voice as she leveled a finger at Al McMann. "If I find my son here with you one more time, just *one more time*, I'm pressing charges. Are you hearing me? I don't care how old you are and I don't care how many medals you have on your damn wall. Just one more time!"

Gripping her son by the bicep Jackson's mother pushed him ahead of her out the door.

After a moment, Al McMann stood and began to clear the dishes. He moved slowly, his face clouded and his gestures drained.

THE ESCORT'S worn tires spun as Jackson's mother stamped on the accelerator, then the brake, shifted hard and hit the accelerator again, gunning the car out of Al's driveway and onto the street.

"Did he touch you?" she demanded to know, her voice like metal in its intensity. *"Did he?"*

Oh, jeez ... "Mom! That is so *gross*!" Jackson turned away from her and watched the cookie-cutter housing developments of north Brampton slide by in a blur. He thought about the firm leathery grip guiding his own hand on the knife sliding cleanly through the fresh-killed perch. "Of course he didn't."

Two

DOG ON A MISSION

A SHARP BREEZE sent rolling lines of foam curling and dancing across sparkling blue water. Behind the protective arms of a breakwater, boats large and small rocked restlessly against their ropes. At the very end of one of the longest docks, a tidy wooden sailboat nodded to the white clouds scurrying overhead. Brown ropes slapped time against the varnished timber of its two masts.

Untouched by the chilly fingers of wind playing around the harbour, a dog lay stretched out along one side of the sailboat. With its back to the sheltering wall of a low cabin and all four legs stuck out straight like toothpicks in a sausage, it took up the full width of the narrow deck. From its black nose to the tip of its unremarkable tail it lay in sunlight, as though it had precisely measured the spot between the shadows cast by the boat's handrail.

With each gentle rock of the boat the sunlit deck rose and fell, lifting the dog up and away from the weathered wooden dock, then dropping it back down again. Just as regularly, the not-entirely-clean but otherwise white side of the dog rose and fell in deep steady breaths. At one end of the creature, black nostrils flared from time to time. At the other, the tip of its whip-like tail did the same. Now and again all four legs jerked as though the animal was chasing some dream squirrel through a forest of sleep. Whuffles and grunts emerged from the dog's soft muzzle (as white as the rest of it, although no cleaner).

Suddenly the broad head shot up and two black eyes opened brightly. Sharp pointed ears stood at attention. A pink tongue lapped out, licking the air that smelled of salt and iodine and, unmistakably, rotting fish.

The dog scrambled to its feet and gave itself a shake that started at its heavy head and worked its way in a thorough fashion down the well-rounded sides to grimy white haunches and finally to the very point of the skimpy tail. With a confidence that spoke of ample practice, the animal crouched at the edge of the deck, watching the boat's roll bring it down close to the dock. Then it stepped off with a neatness that might almost have been called ladylike.

Immediately it set off down the dock, trotting steadily. It held its muscular head low, sharp eyes and pointed ears trained ahead and tail straight out behind. It seemed to be on a mission, stepping aside only to avoid a metal toolbox, coil of rope or pair of salt- and grease-stained rubber boots.

Only once did the white dog slow down. Where one dock joined another, it stopped long enough to bestow a lick on the hand of a tall man. He wore shiny brown leather shoes and the sun flashed off a silver badge pinned to his plaid bush shirt. His fingers tasted of salt. A moment later the dog was off again.

It paused again where a steep gangway led up from the floating docks to a seawall of tarred timber. For a moment the animal crouched low, forepaws resting on the foot of the gangway. Then it launched itself up the ladder-steep planking, taking its full length in one scrambling a rush. At the top, the dog paused to give itself another quick shake and set out again.

Five minutes later the dog trotted down a graveled path between a paved road and a wide expanse of blue water flecked with whitecaps. A strong breeze carried the smell of foam and cedar and fir trees off the water and the black nostrils twitched. Suddenly the dog made a hard right across the empty road and trotted through a gate in a fence almost entirely hidden by green vines.

Inside the gate, another gravel walk led to the front door of a house. Before reaching it, the dog turned off the path and walked down the side of the white-painted building into a small backyard. Still moving steadily, it waded through the exuberantly overgrown patch of grass and disappeared beneath a tangle of tall green canes, where bees buzzed among sprays of white flowers and clumps of heavy red berries.

Moments later, the dog emerged on the other side, between green branches that flourished almost to the height of a wooden fence behind them. There it paused again. The black nose twitched and snuffled as the thick head and pointed ears turned this way and that. A ray of sun caught the small black eyes, momentarily striking an answering spark in their depths. Then the dog set off once more.

Ten minutes later the white dog came to a broad expanse of green lawn and slowed its pace. The air was sweet and thick with the wet smell of freshly cut grass. Over toward the far side of the lawn, glimpses of brown dirt, a high fence of wire mesh held up by tall poles and two sets of low wooden bleacher seats provided evidence of a baseball diamond. Just in front of the dog, the smooth turf of a well-tended outfield gave way to taller stands of unmown grass. The tallest fronds reached the dog's moist black nose.

The white dog shouldered its way into the high grass. Once inside the sheltering stalks it turned several times in a complete circle, pawing the dry grass matted close to the ground and flattening living stems and until it had fashioned a round nest exactly its own size. Only then did it drop down onto the ground with a heavy sigh, white muzzle and black nose positioned right at the edge of the meadow with a view out over the mown grass.

Small black eyes gazed steadily out as the sun and clouds chased each other across the heated green of the playing field.

Three

HIGH FLY

THE BATTERED green Escort pulled to a hard stop at the curb. Carla Kyle leaned across the seat and pecked her son on the cheek.

Jack groaned inwardly.

"Have fun darling. Be a star!" his mother said with that brittle brightness she had. More and more these days it set him seething. Not that it took much today. He was still pretty steamed from the scene this morning.

Pulling his cap down low over his eyes and burying his left hand in the stiff leather of a baseball glove, Jackson pulled himself out of the car and shoved the door shut with one knee. A flash of sunlight on the window glass hid his mother from view as she popped the car into gear and shot back out into the street.

"Give her a break," Al says, Jack thought as he walked toward the dugout. *But, jeez, she could ease up a little. It's like every little thing I do she's marking me on. Either that or she's telling me how I'm gonna ruin my life if I do it.*

Baseball had been a rare compromise between them. Every since her only son was little, Carla Kyle had enrolled him in one supervised "play" event after group activity after another. Jack knew his Mom needed to work to meet the rent and car payments, to feed and clothe a growing boy. But especially lately he'd begun to chafe at the predictability of it all — and feel there was something more going on for Mom. If he wasn't doing something that involved signing up for rule sheets and nametags and some kind of babysitters, it seemed Mom was sure he'd get into some kind of trouble ... trying drugs or falling in with bad company or breaking his arms and legs doing something stupid down at the old quarry.

Like I'm some kind of idiot. Maybe if there was a guy around the house to do guy stuff with ... But that was a thought he'd learned to push away whenever it came to him. He couldn't remember there ever being a guy around the house and Mom refused to talk about his real dad. Now and again some "date" would come to pick up Carla, struggling to say two words to Jack before making his getaway with Mom, but none of them appeared more than once or twice,

Carla Kyle thought baseball was "well structured." It had "good supervision." And besides, "you'll be with boys your own age." That awful bright note in her voice again. And the unspoken message that anything was better than hanging with a ninety-year-old guy who'd actually been out there in the real world. *Jeesh!*

By the time Coach Aseem ticked Jack's name off the roster, his stomach was working overtime again and he was just itching to take a swing at *something.*

"Star" might have been overstating it, but there was no

doubt that Jackson Kyle was one of the Brampton Home Store Bullets' stronger players. A year or so past his last growth spurt, he was the tallest kid on the team and Coach had put him at center field for his ability to field the ball reliably with an arm strong enough to reach the plate.

Today he played with resentful energy. He got a piece of a couple of pitches, making it to second base twice and all the way round once, off Miguel Somoza's sacrifice bunt. When he kept his mind on the play all those other thoughts somehow shut up, at least for a while.

His mind strayed only once or twice — when he made the mistake of looking up at the Bullets' bleachers. He knew Mom wouldn't be there; her second shift at Denny's didn't end 'til eight. But when he caught sight of Al McMann, the rush of shame over his mother's behavior that morning almost took his breath away. Out of the corner of his eye he caught Al clapping hard every time he came to the plate. But somehow Jackson couldn't bring himself to meet his friend's gaze.

The afternoon humidity was building in towering clouds overhead. Several times in the quiet of the outfield, Jackson heard the distant grumble of thunder. By the time the game ended, with the Bullets ahead of the Dundas Parkside Royals six to three, Jack imagined he could smell the lightning waiting to fire out of them. A wind was blowing dust up off the diamond. He exchanged high fives with the rest of the team at the dugout, but his heart wasn't in it. Breaking away, he ran his eyes over the faces trickling down from the bleachers. Maybe he could at least try to apologize to Al.

But the old man was no longer there.

Crap! Now he thinks I'm as pissed at him as Mom is.

A hot explosion of fury burst out of Jack's gut. Grabbing up a bat and ball, he tossed the ball into the air and watched it fall back. Putting every ounce of frustration and boiling anger into his swing, he nailed the horsehide full-on. *Kr-ackkk!*

High and far it sailed out into the summer sky. A shaft of clear-washed sunlight set the ball glowing against a dark gray thunderhead off over the lake. Jackson watched it soar.

"Lose that ball and it's a five dollar fine," Coach Aseem's crisp reminder broke in.

Oh, flippin' great!

Then something else caught his eye. A flash of white burst out of the tall grass at the far side of the field. *A rabbit? No, way too big. Holy cripes! It's a dog!*

Galloping full tilt across the green outfield, the dog held its head high, its whole being focused on the falling ball. Down, down, down the ball dropped. Playing the angles perfectly the dog raced to intercept its fall. Just when it seemed it would arrive too late, the dog made a final effort, leaping high in the air. From the dugout Jackson saw its jaws close on the ball and, a moment later, across the diamond came the solid *thunk* as ivory came down on horsehide.

Coming to a stop, the white dog stood and shook its head hard around its prize.

"Looks like you're going down for five, guy," Coach said with a sympathetic laugh.

Jack was still absorbing the amazing catch when the dog's

head turned toward the dugout. For a moment, he had the weirdest feeling that the animal was looking directly at *him*. But then it dropped to its belly on the grass and turned its jaws sideways.

Jack began to run. *If I can just get it away from him before he ruins it.* There was enough money in his bank account to pay for the ball. But that would also put off the moment he could buy the *CSI: Crime Scene Investigation* DVD he was saving for.

He began to slow down as he crossed second base. *Don't want to spook it.* But it was too late. The dog was on its feet now, the ball clamped securely in its jaws.

As he got closer, he could make out the animal better. *Ohmigosh, it's ...* The dog's compact body and barrel chest, powerful looking jaws and short white coat all looked to Jack like that dog in *Babe in the City* — the pit bull. He'd heard stories about them on the news. He moved forward cautiously. *Or* is *it?* Something didn't quite match.

"Nice dog," Jack tried to sound reassuring. "Nice boy."

At least it didn't *seem* aggressive. If anything, it seemed to want to play. Looking Jack straight in the eye, it gave the ball another shake, then dropped it to the grass.

Jack took another slow and cautious step toward the dog. It's mouth was open and ... *lookit those teeth!* Then the animal cocked its head, the sun catching the folds at the corner of its mouth. *Looks just like he's smiling.*

Black eyes never leaving the boy's gray ones, the dog bent its head and pushed its grimy nose at the ball. It rolled a few inches over the grass.

"Atta boy ... Good dog," Jack murmured. He bent at the knees and then lunged for the ball.

But the dog was faster. Before the boy's fingers could reach the salty sphere, it was back between the white dog's impressive jaws. The animal's tail waved a cheeky salute as it galloped away toward the tall grass, where copper-coloured tops bent in the wind like waves.

Before the dog got to the high grass it stopped. Turning once more, it lowered its head and gazed at Jack. He could see the wrinkles at the corner of its mouth again. *Almost like it's laughing at me.* The thought seemed goofy, but still.

And something else. It wasn't a *him*. She was a she.

"Good girl," Jack spoke softly. "Bring me the ball. Come on, girl."

But the dog clearly wasn't ready to give up the game just yet. Shaking the ball some more, she trotted off a few more yards. Again Jackson followed. And again the dog moved away, keeping just out of reach.

For ten more minutes she led Jack on a slow-motion chase. The dog would run ahead only to stop, turn and look back at him, tossing the ball back and forth in her teeth as if to tease him with it. Once Jack took to his heels and tried to run her down, but she easily stayed ahead of him.

Finally the dog turned one last time and eyed Jackson closely. Then, seeming to decide that enough was enough, she dropped to the ground and let the ball fall between her front paws. This time she didn't get up as Jack cautiously closed the distance between them. At last he was close enough to make a lunge for the ball.

As he did, so did the dog. But not to bite — or even to grab back the ball. Instead Jack felt her warm tongue lap a coarse wet kiss across the back of his hand.

For the first time he also noticed that the animal wasn't wearing a collar.

A loud crack set off a rolling tumble of thunder somewhere over the subdivisions to the south. He wiping the ball dry against his uniform and looked around for the first time since the chase began.

The pursuit had carried them a long way from the ball field down one of the greenways that divided Brampton's housing developments. In the distance, he could still see the diamond, but it was empty. It seemed that everyone had left, trying to beat the coming storm home. No point in returning the ball now.

He flopped down beside the dog. She was panting heavily, her jaws wide open. Her dental endowment really was impressive. Once more the pink tongue lapped out across his wrist.

No collar. *Hmm.*

Jackson's mind worked. He'd wanted a dog for about as long as he could remember — yet another bone of contention in the Kyle house. "It's in the lease," Mom always said. "We're not allowed." But he suspected she just didn't want to be bothered.

"Maybe if she could only meet you," he said aloud, "then she'd feel differently."

Keeping his movements slow and calm, Jack drew the

belt from the loops of his uniform. He pulled its length back through the buckle to form a loop. In a single quick motion he slid it over the dog's head.

To his surprise, the animal offered no resistance.

Jack got to his feet. "C'mon, girl," he said, giving the belt a gentle tug.

Without hesitation the white dog scrambled to her feet. She gave herself a thorough shake that began at her head and worked its way down to her tail, then looked steadily up at Jackson. She still seemed to be smiling, those wrinkles at the corners of her wide mouth deeper than ever.

"Let's go." Jack gave the belt another soft tug and began to walk. The first heavy drops hit his shoulder as just as the dog fell into step beside him.

Four

BANISHED

THE POWERFUL marshy smell of wet dog overrode even the fake floral emissions of the chemical air fresheners Carla Kyle kept plugged into every room of their townhouse.

Jack turned another illustrated page in the book that lay in front of him. "Ah-hah! I *knew* it," he burst out over the sound of his hand slapping the counter in satisfaction. "You're not a *pit* bull, you're a bull *terrier!*" He looked from the picture in the book in front of him to the animal at his feet.

Some time ago he'd bought the guide to dog breeds, hoping to find one Mom might let him have. That hadn't worked. But now the pictures made it clear that this wasn't one of those aggressive breeds raised to fight. The high arch of the dog's muzzle — what the book called a *Roman* nose — and those tall pointed ears marked it as a member of a different family entirely. Bull terriers, the book said, were best known for being loyal and attentive companions. *I could use that,* Jackson thought.

At the moment, though, this particular Roman nose was smeared with patches of strawberry pink. After getting back to the narrow townhouse where he'd always lived, Jack had made them both peanut butter and jelly sandwiches. He had ripped one into chunks and served it to the dog in a cereal bowl. After nosing it curiously — transferring a considerable amount of jam to her face in the process — the dog had wolfed down the meal. Now she was using her long tongue to explore as much of her muzzle as she could reach for the last of the jelly.

It was comical sight and Jack couldn't suppress a smile. "You look pretty well-fed for a homeless dog," he said. *But she doesn't have a collar or tags. That's gotta mean she doesn't have a family either.* He began to think about what he could name her ... *Hobo? Freedom?*

From beneath his feet he heard the garage door grind open, then the gunned engine and squeal of brakes that meant Mom was home. *Jeez, can't she even go a little easy on the* car?

Steps sounded on the stairs. Carla Kyle came into the kitchen and dumped a takeout bag from the restaurant on the counter. "Hi, hon ... *OhmiGodwhatISthat!?*" It all came out in one long shriek as Jackson's mother stepped sideways around the room to put the table between herself and the animal.

Jack almost laughed out loud. "Aw, c'mon, Mom, she's just a dog. She was at the ballpark."

"It's a *stray*? You brought it *home*? Are you *crazy*? Just look at it, it's *filthy*! Can't you *smell it*?"

From its place beside the cereal bowl the dog looked up at the woman with calm interest. It seemed entirely unmoved by the attack on its character.

"She doesn't have tags or anything," Jack tried, "so I figure she needs a home. Maybe..."

"No, no, no, no, you *canNOT* keep it. No. No way. Absolutely not. God *knows* what diseases it's got. For sure it's just *crawling* with fleas. I mean, *smell* the thing, I bet it's never had a bath in its life."

Carla's eyes never left the dog as she sidled sideways across the room, one arm groping behind her. Finding what she sought by touch, Jack's mother reached back and fumbled open the door to a narrow closet. When her hand reappeared it held a broom.

"Mom!" Jack rose from his chair in protest. But it was no use.

Holding the broom ahead of her like a shovel, Carla prodded the dog until it got to its feet. "Out!" she ordered. "Get out of my kitchen! Go! Go! Shoo!" Keeping the broom as far in front of her body as possible, she swept the dog back toward the stairs. It went reluctantly, its scanty tail tucked between plump white hams.

At the top of the stairs it stopped for a moment and looked back past the woman. Boy and dog locked eyes. Jack tried to let it know this wasn't *his* idea. "I'm soooo sorry, girl," his eyes said. But the dog hardly seemed upset at all. The dark eyes were bright and alert. The wide mouth still wore its wrinkled smile.

Suddenly the skimpy tail came up and whipped back and forth hard. Once again Jack got that electric charge up the back of his neck, the same one he'd felt at the ball diamond.

"GO!" his mother shrilled again, shoving hard with the broom. This time the dog had no choice but to start down the stairs, the broom prodding it at each step.

Jack followed behind his mother, his gut a knot of conflicting emotions.

Carla drove the dog in front of her to the garage. A last shove with the broom forced the dog inside. She slammed shut the door and turned on her son.

"What in heaven's name were you *thinking*?" she demanded. "That thing could be *rabid* for all you know! It could have distemper. It ..." Running out of possibilities she changed gears. "Get out of those clothes right now and take a shower. A hot one!"

Jack rolled his eyes. "Jeesh, Mom, she's not any of those things. She's just a dog!"

"Don't argue with me. Get moving, now!"

Jack was happy enough to get away from her. He headed for the bathroom.

When he came back into the kitchen, his hair was wet and he wore fresh jeans and a faded *Free Willy* T-shirt. Carla had the phone book open in front of her, the handset in the crook of one shoulder.

"Nothing but a recording," she grumped. "What do they think, stray animals only show up during business hours?" She banged the phone down. "The moment I get through to them tomorrow, those animal control people are hauling their butts over here to dispose of that thing. Here," she pushed a restaurant bag across the table. "Your burger's cold but you can nuke it."

Dispose. The word had a horrid, final sound to it. Jackson glowered at his mother as he listened to the microwave hum and count down the seconds.

He was hungry but the hamburger tasted like sawdust. When his mother went to the living room and flicked on the TV, Jackson wrapped most of it, along with a fistful of French fries, back up in its paper wrapper.

He kept the paper package balled in his hand and out of his mother's sight as he skirted the living room on the way to the stairs up to bed. Above the sound of the TV, he could hear rain rattling heavily on window glass. He looked across the room and the world beyond the windowpanes briefly flashed purple and white. Thunder came rolling after it a moment later.

"G'night," he said. Even he could hear the grudge in his voice.

But somehow Mom seemed to miss it. "Good night, darling," she chirped in that maddening voice that bugged him so much. "And honey," she called after him. "Don't be mad. You know it's the rules. And you *know* you can't look after a dog."

No. No, I don't *know that. You just think this 'cuz you don't think I can do* anything! But he kept that thought to himself, along with the others already taking shape in his mind.

Five

JAILBREAK

JACKSON AWOKE in the darkness from a deep sleep. His bedside radio glowed 4:44 in red numbers and was singing softly, "... never settle for the path of least resistance. Living might mean taking chances ..."

He rolled over in the dark and pushed on the bar that turned the alarm off. For a moment he lay in silence and held his breath, listening. *Nope ... nothing.* Carla Kyle was a heavy sleeper. She hadn't woken up yesterday either, when Jack had snuck out early to go fishing.

He dressed quickly in the dark, pulling on a fresh T-shirt and jeans by the dim glow of the streetlight. Patting his pockets he ran through a mental checklist, hearing one of Al's favorite bits of advice come back to him: "Fail to plan, and you plan to fail!"

From the box in his sock drawer he pulled his entire cash savings: two bills and some coins — *check*. There was still the school prize money in his bank account, forty dollars he'd won for an essay on whales. But he'd promised Mom to treat that as the start of what he'd need some day for college.

Front-door key — *check*. His knife — *check*. He did up his sneakers and shrugged into his denim jacket. Then Jackson picked up the four pairs of shoelaces he'd tied together last night into a makeshift leash and eased open his bedroom door.

He had only crept down the first few stairs when he remembered the half-eaten burger. He turned back.

Jack was still in the middle of the small upstairs landing when a sound froze him in place. It came from his mother's room: first the creak of bedsprings, then a shuffling noise like feet looking for slippers.

Hastily Jackson stepped back into his room and pulled the door almost shut behind him. He hardly dared to breathe and his pulse seemed like thunder in his ears.

Through the crack he heard the muffled sound of footsteps on carpet, then saw a glow come from the direction of the bathroom. It was quickly snuffed out as his mother shut the door behind her.

Grabbing the squishy paper package from his desk he again slipped out the door, drawing it nearly closed once more behind him. By the time he heard the toilet flush, he was already at the foot of the second flight of stairs, standing stock-still just outside the door to the garage.

He listened as his mother's footsteps shuffled back to her room and her bed creaked gently. The house settled back into silence. Heart pounding, he began to count in his head. *One thousand and one, one thousand and two.*

Beyond the door he heard movement, moving, the scratch of canine toenails on the concrete floor, a rippling riffle that might have been the white dog shaking itself, then the unmistakable *flump* of something soft but heavy hitting the ground. *One thousand seven-hundred and forty, one thousand seven-hundred and forty-one.* In the silence, the sound of the fridge motor kicking on in the kitchen upstairs made him start. He could smell the dust and salt dried into the winter boots still piled next to the door from the garage.

One thousand, one hundred and seventy-nine ... one thousand seven-hundred and eighty. Three minutes ... *that ought to be enough.*

Very slowly he began to turn the door handle. From the far side of the door came the scuffle of paws on concrete and a sort of *thrippp*-ing sound he thought must be the dog shaking itself awake. *Please, pleeease, don't bark,* he breathed.

He eased the door open. The dog did not bark. He slipped into the garage and crouched in the darkness. On his open palm he held out the remains of the takeout burger. He felt a cold nose, followed by a warm muzzle. He could hear the dog snuffing the air, then a little grunt and the burger disappeared from his palm with a wet lap of a rough tongue. He slipped the shoelace leash over the dog's ears.

"C'mon, girl," he barely breathed the words aloud. She followed him out into the short hallway without hesitation and stood patiently while he worked the key carefully in the front door lock.

The rain had stopped and the night was warm and smelled of earthworms and night flowers and new green leaves opening to the air for the first time. Jackson stepped outside, the dog at his heels. He tugged the solid door closed behind him and the latch shot home, sending his heart leaping at the heavy *foomp* and sharp *snick*.

Stepping back from the door he looked up, but his mother's bedroom window remained dark.

Then they were on their way. Over toward the city, the inky blue sky along the eastern horizon was showing the first pale gleam of a coming day.

When they reached the corner of the second block he felt safe enough to let the dog in on his plan. "I'm going to take you to meet a friend of mine," he said to the animal trotting at his side. "He'll know what to do so you don't go to dog jail." *Or, worse, get "disposed" of.*

The dog just kept on walking as though he hadn't said anything at all.

TWENTY MINUTES later they turned onto the street where Al lived. His house was the oldest among hundreds of newer ones, a holdover from a time before subdivisions had spread lawns, driveways and convenience stores across former farmland. By now the sky behind him, over the distant city, was a lemon yellow. At the point where the sun's fire was about to break free of the horizon it was rapidly brightening.

The sky over Al's house was still dark. But there were lights of a different sort in that direction. Pulled to the curb in front of Al's trim lawn was a boxy vehicle painted mostly white. Red and white lights strobed brilliantly from each of its square corners. A figure in blue overalls was just closing the back door, then they stepped along the side of the vehicle and got inside.

A cold fist closed around Jackson's heart. He broke into a run. The dog seemed to sense the boy's urgency. Suddenly it was galloping out ahead of him, pulling him forward by the makeshift leash.

They closed the distance fast. But not quite fast enough. They were still several houses away when the ambulance pulled abruptly out from the curb.

"Nooo! Wait!" Jackson shouted. But his voice was drowned in the eerie wail of a siren as the flashing red and white lights receded down the street, then turned sharply around a distant corner.

Al's house was dark when Jackson and the dog finally reached it. There was no answer when Jack pushed and pushed again on the bell. Turning away he felt tears sting his eyes. Dejection swept over him as he sank down on the topmost concrete step.

The dog dropped to a sitting position next to him, leaning heavily against his leg. Jack found its warm presence unexpectedly comforting.

In a sudden blaze, the bright rim of the sun lifted above the horizon.

IT TOOK Jackson a while to think it through and decide what to do. The closest hospital was not that far from Al McMann's house.

By the time he and the dog reached it thirty minutes later, the sun had pulled itself fully above the horizon. It was still low enough that the hospital's concrete bulk cast a chilly shadow over the emergency entrance.

"Wait here," he told the dog, knotting the free end of the shoelace leash around a bicycle rack. She lapped his hand once, then stood and watched him trot across the small parking lot reserved for ambulances. Wide doors sighed open automatically and he walked through.

Inside, several people sat in ones and twos on vinyl benches. Facing him was a row of small cubicles where chairs faced other chairs across low counters equipped with computer screens. In some of these, people in white sat behind the counters. He walked up to one of them.

"Umm, I'm here to see Mr. Alan McMann," he told the woman in the white uniform.

She punched the name into her keyboard. "Uh-huh, and are you family?" she said.

His heart sank. "Almost."

"Almost?"

"He ..." Jack struggled to find the right words. "He's ... just like my dad."

"But he is not your father, not actually *family*?" She fixed him with a stern look.

"No," he admitted.

"Then I'm sorry, we can't release any information. Hospital policy," she said with finality.

JACKSON RETRIEVED the dog and began to walk again. He walked slowly and without any particular destination in mind. The white dog trotted ahead of him with an energy that kept a gentle tension on his shoelace-leash. Jack didn't mind letting her lead. His own brain seemed to be taking a coffee break. His only real plan had been to ask Al what to do with the dog, but that problem now seemed have been swallowed up by his worry for his friend. He tried to think what Al would do, but nothing came.

Jeesh, maybe Mom's right after all. Maybe I really can't *manage anything on my own.*

With a mild jolt of surprise he looked to his left and recognized the same winding green space where he'd first slipped his belt over the dog's neck.

"Maybe you're better off without me after all, girl," he said. Glumly, he reached down and pulled the loop of shoelace off her neck. "Go on, beat it!"

But the dog didn't budge. Instead it snuffed heavily at him, nuzzling that arched nose, that *Roman* nose, hard into his crotch. Then it sat back on its haunches and looked at him. The mouth with its impressive teeth was open wide. Wrinkles showed at the corners — *smile wrinkles,* he thought again. The small dark eyes held his and for a third time he felt that weird electric charge.

The sound of a truck engine broke the spell. Looking to his right he got a jolt of a different kind. The sound came from a blue van. White letters on the side read CITY OF BRAMPTON ANIMAL SERVICES. In the cab, he could see a face turned his way. The van slowed to a stop.

Ohmigosh. "Beat it!" he told the dog again, more urgently this time.

She didn't budge. In fact, she didn't look as if she had even heard him.

"No, really! You've got to get out of here!"

The van turned around. Now it was coming back toward them.

"GIT!" he almost yelled. *Stupid dog.* Desperately he flicked the shoelace leash at her, trying to scare her into motion.

Deftly the dog dodged the laces but still she would not leave. If anything, her wrinkly smile seemed to be getting even wider.

Oh, jeesh. "Awright then. C'mon!" he yanked hard on the oily fur of the animal's grimy, uncollared neck and started to a run. Finally, the dog responded and together they bolted away from the street and out into the green expanse of parkland.

The sun was fully up now, warming the denim on Jackson's back and bringing up a peppery green smell from the newly mown grass.

Snatching a look over his shoulder, Jack got a double shock. The blue van had not abandoned the chase. It had climbed the curb and was now closing the distance along a paved path that snaked through the greenway. Worse still, Jack could see another vehicle beyond it, a white car with the red and blue stripes of a police cruiser. As he watched, the light bar on its roof flickered into red and blue life.

The car turned up onto the curb to follow the van.

Jack's foot caught on something and he stumbled. He got his hands out in time to break his fall and push himself back up instantly from the grass, palms stinging. He looked ahead and for a moment felt a fresh confusion. *Where'd she go?*

A sharp bark snapped his attention to the right. *There!* She stood near a thicket of green shrubbery, her profile turned to the bushes, head lowered and looking directly at him. Another sharp bark rang out.

Jackson cut sharply toward her. Somewhere behind him he heard tires slide to a stop on gravel and a vehicle door opening.

He was a stride or two away from the wall of shrubbery when the white dog turned and disappeared into the dense branches. Without a second thought or look back, Jackson threw himself to his hands and knees and followed.

Inside the shrubbery the light was dim and lemony green. He could smell leaves breathing overhead and the moist dampness of earth under his hands. Twigs plucked at his hair and jacket. Ahead in the dimness, he could just see a flash of white through the stalks and trunks.

Suddenly she vanished. *Eh?*

But, no, she hadn't vanished. There was a fence, a wooden fence of broad vertical planks. And in it, one broken plank left a hole just big enough for a dog to get through.

Or maybe a skinny kid.

Falling flat on his stomach Jackson pushed himself forward between the broken boards.

Six

GIRLS IN A GARDEN

THE BUSHES and green light, now even dimmer, continued on the other side of the fence. Only now the grasping branches were sharper — *much* sharper! *Ow!* And they smelled different: *sweeter*, but also somehow acid. Something on the ground was wet and squishy.

Jack broke his scramble long enough to lift one hand and look at the palm. *Yikes!* Surely he hadn't bled *that* much when he fell back there.

Ahead of him the white dog suddenly disappeared again. But now the dim light was getting brighter even as the stalks around him seemed to be getting even thicker and their spines more dangerous. A moment later Jackson crawled free from the clutching branches and stood upright in bright sunshine.

He found himself at the edge of a coarse lawn, uneven and most of it much taller than the manicured space on the other side of the fence. His heart was racing and he could feel the adrenalin pumping in his arms.

Then ... *Ohmigosh!* Not only was he in somebody's backyard but the somebody was in their yard, too!

Two somebodies, in fact. Two girls of about his own age

sat on wooden steps leading to a back porch that reminded him a lot of Al's. For a long moment they stared back at him in a surprise matching his own.

Jack found himself taking a second to make sense of the scene: The girls wore dresses, which wasn't so odd on its own. He knew several girls who wore long dresses instead of jeans to school. But they usually also wore headscarves and their complexions reflected their parents' roots in Africa or the Middle East. These two looked more like girls in old TV shows, like that Lucy lady.

His surprise grew when he focused on the two large bowls sitting between them. One was partly full of thick green pods like overweight green beans. The other held a much smaller pool of peas, like bright green pills. Piled at their feet were the split husks of pods he guessed they had already emptied.

Back-to-the-landers ... in Brampton?

The girl on the left had reddish brown pigtails. The other had blonde hair cut straight over her eyes.

Pigtails broke the startled silence first. "Why, Patsy Ann." She ducked her head and smiled at the white dog, "Who's this?" The girl leaned down and held out a handful of peas to the dog. Her keen green eyes stayed on the tall boy gaping in front of her.

Jack felt a pit open in his chest. "This is *your* dog?" Then the emotions of the morning boiled over. "Then you shouldn't let her run around without a collar," he added hotly. "She could get lost, get picked up, maybe even get *put down.*"

The girls burst into laughter as though this was the funniest thing they'd heard all day. Jack felt the blood rise to his face.

"Patsy Ann's *everyone's* dog," the blonde girl said. "And everyone knows she won't wear a collar." The blue eyes looking out from beneath straw-coloured bangs clearly added, *Are you a total idiot? Don't you know anything?*

"Yeah, well, the dogcatcher almost got her," Jack said, his voice rising as a defensive note crept into it. But this only set off new peals of laughter.

"Are you right off the boat?" the blonde one finally got out. "The dogcatcher knows better than to arrest Patsy Ann."

As if to emphasize the point, the dog flopped down and pressed her not-entirely-clean white back against the blonde girl's legs. From that position she gazed up at Jack, a wrinkled grin at the corners of her mouth. Sunlight danced in her black eyes.

Jackson felt the electricity thing again, only much *much* stronger this time. For the first time since he'd scrambled out of the bushes he looked around ... and felt a strange sensation, as if a wave had suddenly rocked the ground under him. It was the same feeling he'd had when he stepped for the first time into Al's boat and the floor dipped abruptly under his weight. Something was definitely not right about this picture.

The bushes he'd crawled through were raspberry canes. *That's why they were so scratchy*. And beyond them he could see the top of the weathered gray fence. But that wasn't the freaky part.

Beyond that there should have been blue sky, maybe the tops of one or two tall trees in the green space and then the angular high-rises towering over by Highway 10. Instead — Jack closed his eyes and shook his head *hard.*

When he looked again they were still not there. Instead, beyond the fence a green wall of dark evergreen forest rose almost vertically toward wispy clouds high overhead.

Jackson suddenly felt sick to his stomach.

He spun back to the girls. They were no longer laughing. The blonde girl looked at him apprehensively. "Are you all right?" she asked, concern in her voice.

Pigtails said nothing. Her face wore a deeply thoughtful expression as she seemed to examine him closely for the first time. As Jackson watched, her intent gaze ran him up and down. Her eyes came to a stop at his feet and rested there for a long moment before coming back up to look searchingly in his face.

"You're not from Juneau, are you?" she asked him, her voice now quiet and unexpectedly serious.

Where?

All of a sudden, the thought of explaining himself to the police didn't seem so awful. *Heck, maybe they'll even give me a ride home.* Not even the idea of facing Mom seemed all that bad at the moment.

"Um ... listen," he stammered, "I don't mean to be rude or anything, but I think I'll just go back the way I came in. Sorry for the intrusion and all. It was nice to meet you. And you ..." He stepped quickly forward and scuffled his fingers a moment behind the white dog's erect ears. "Patsy Ann, or whoever you are. Thanks for an interesting time and everything, but maybe you'd better not go picking up any more stray kids, okay?"

Before the girls could say anything, Jack turned and took five steps across the small yard. He dropped to his hands and knees and shouldered his way back into the green cave under the berry canes. Once again he felt scratching pain as barbed branches caught in his hair and clothes. A faint "*Yikes*" escaped him as his bare hands and knees came down on petrified spines of dead stalks that lay on the ground. The sweet acid smell, the odour of earthworms and damp things living in the shade made his head swim, bringing a formless fear that sometimes haunted his nightmares.

But ahead of him he could see the fence now. And there was the hole, green light shining through it. *Just let me get through that and back into good old Brampton*. His ears were singing with a sound like mosquitos. He dropped flat once more and wriggled through the ragged hole.

He emerged into more leaves. *But these aren't right.* Instead of shrubbery, bushes and small trees, the foliage blocking Jack's way had fleshy stalks, like oversize red celery, and was topped in floppy leaves, dark green and as large as elephant's ears.

Almost immediately he could scramble back to his feet.

He stood again in broad sunlight. Only this wasn't the early fresh early morning light he had been running through only minutes earlier, slanting across a clipped expanse of municipal lawn buzzing with summer insects. Nor was there any blue van, white police car — or even a paved pathway they might have driven along.

What was there was a narrow dirt footpath, overgrown on each side with weeds. Beyond that, a thicket of knotted gray branches fringed with shiny leaves and beyond those ... a steep wall of deep green fir trees, broken by planes of bare rock. He leaned back to look up, but could not find a summit. Trees, moss and rock seemed to go up and up forever, to where he lost sight of them in wispy white clouds hovering in a deep blue sky.

Instead of the hot, dusty smell of grass baking in the summer sun, damp and misty air flowed down from the heights above, mixed with the sharp scent of evergreens.

Oh ... my ... God ... It's a mountain! *A flippin' mountain*! Jackson swayed on his feet.

Running feet sounded off to his right. Looking, he saw the white dog ... *Patsy Ann* ... coming at full rabbity gallop toward him. Then the two girls appeared around the end of the fence, running just as hard.

He opened his mouth to say something, but nothing came out.

Now Patsy Ann was at his feet, jumping about in tight, manic circles. Her hard little body bumped heavily into his knees, almost knocking him over. She wore her wrinkled grin and as he tried to fend her off she deposited sloppy wet tongue kisses all over his hands.

Well, she *seems glad I'm still here. Wherever* here *is.*

Now the two girls were at his side, faces flushed and

breathing hard. Patsy Ann dropped her tail to the ground and looked up, her eyes flicking from Jack to the two girls and back.

Pigtails spoke first. "So who are you anyway? I haven't seen you in school."

"My name's Jackson ... Jack." He held out his hand awkwardly and immediately pulled it back. He rubbed the palm hard on his jeans, trying to rid it of grass, dirt and berry juice. It wasn't much cleaner when he stuck it out again.

"Hi, Jackson Jack," Pigtails said, her smile taking the sting out of the tease. Her hand was firm and cool in his. "I'm Rose Baker and that's my backyard," she nodded over the fence. "This is Miranda."

"Hi," he said. His stained, sticky paw seemed especially crude in her clean fingers.

"Hi," Miranda murmured with a good deal less enthusiasm. She took her hand back and dusted it discreetly on her skirt.

"Are you new in Juneau?" Rose asked.

Eh? That's what he'd thought she said the first time. But that wasn't possible. Juneau was in Alaska, away up somewhere north of British Columbia. *What? Four or five thousand miles* from where he'd woken up this morning.

That would sure be a "yes" then.

Except that was not possible... NOT POSSIBLE, he reminded himself. He looked up at the mountain wall to his left. *Then again*, that's *not very possible either.*

He looked back to the two girls waiting for him to reply.

At last he said, "Uh-huh. I'm from Brampton. That's in Canada."

That thoughtful look returned to Rose's face and her eyes dropped again to his feet. *What's with that?* Jack couldn't help wondering. *Hasn't she ever seen sneakers before?*

"Did Patsy Ann bring you here?" the pigtailed girl asked.

"Yeeahh," he said, a little cautious now. He didn't really want to get into *how,* exactly. *She'll think I'm on drugs or something.*

But the girls didn't seem especially surprised. "Patsy Ann brought another boy here from Canada one time," Rose said. Then, in a low voice, she added, "He had funny shoes, too."

For the first time Jack noticed the girls' shoes. They were a little scuffed, but nothing he hadn't seen on classmates at school. Carly, who shopped for retro fashions at secondhand stores, wore shoes just like them. Then again, who got that girls-and-footwear thing, anyway?

Rose tilted her head and looked up at the tall boy. She seemed to be considering something a moment. Then she apparently reached a decision. "I think there's someone you need to meet," she said.

Does he come with a magic wand to send me home?

Jackson felt a warm lap as Patsy Ann licked his hand. Looking down, his gaze met shining dark eyes. Once more he got that funny feeling. *It's like you're trying to communicate with me,* he thought. He wondered if this was a normal dog thing. This sure didn't seem like a normal dog!

"Okay," he agreed. "Who? Where?"

"C'mon," Rose said, "I'll show you." She turned back down

the path in the direction she and her friend had come. Jack followed her and Patsy Ann fell into step beside him. Miranda brought up the rear.

Where the fence ended they turned and walked along a green hedge. Through gaps in the branches, Jack could see Rose's house over to the right. By now it hardly fazed him when the hedge ended at a road he had never seen before ... or that beyond it spread a wide body of deep blue water flecked with white. Beyond that, another mountain loomed in the distance.

Nothing in Brampton looked even remotely like this. Or smelled like it. The stiff breeze coming off the dancing waves was fresh and bracing but nothing at all like the air at the lake where he and Al had fished yesterday. This was stronger. Saltier. Fishier. *Wilder*.

"Let me grab my books," Miranda broke in, stepping ahead of them.

She crossed the end of the hedge and turned up a gravel path that led back to the front of the house. This was a boxy, two-storey affair with a steep roof and plain painted wood siding. Windows framed the narrow front steps. But Jack couldn't see where the garage was. *There's not even a driveway. That's weird.*

"You can come in, too," Rose said. Inside, the house smelled of baking and wood smoke and furniture polish. The walls had the same kind of floral wallpaper Al's walls had, except that this looked fresh and bright.

With Patsy Ann getting in the way, butting at their shins,

the three teenagers made their way down a short hall into a kitchen. This managed to be even more old-fashioned than Al's. Linoleum covered the floors and the counters were bare scrubbed wood. To one side, an immense stove dominated half of the room. A black-painted pipe, as big around as Jack's head, rose from the back of the stove and disappeared into the wall.

Then Jackson felt his gut give the hardest lurch of this whole bizarre morning.

On the wall beside the stove hung a calendar. It had a bright colour painting of what looked like a pioneer town, with false fronts extending above the rooflines of stores and a trio of painted totem poles sprouting from a street corner. The caption beneath the picture read: JUNEAU — ALASKA'S FUTURE STATE CAPITAL.

That wasn't what had made his stomach churn. He blinked his eyes several times to clear his vision. But when he focused again at the date printed in red block letters above the picture, it had not changed.

It still read JULY 1935.

1935?

Seven

PORT IN A STORM

"OKAY," Miranda said brightly, snatching up a small stack of heavy hardbound books from the kitchen table. "Let's go."

Jack's mind was still spinning as they walked back through the old-fashioned hall. Trying to be discreet about it he shot glances through the open doors he passed to left and right. One room held armchairs, lamps and a table with a wooden box shaped like a church window with knobs and dials. But he could see no television or anything that looked like a computer, not even a bookshelf stereo like the one they had at home. The books on the shelves were serious-looking hardcover volumes like the ones in Miranda's arms or in libraries, not the gaudy paperbacks his mother tore through.

Outside again Jack squinted into the clear sunlight breaking like glass off the waves in the deep blue channel. A strong wind chased the waves up the dark water. A medical smell mingled with salt and rotting fish in the air. He had that same queasy out-of-body sensation he remembered from when he'd run a temperature of a hundred and three and Mom rushed him to the emergency room.

He put his hand to his forehead. He didn't *feel* hot.

At the road they parted ways. Rose and Patsy Ann went left,

Miranda off to the right. "I have to see if you-know-who's going to be home for supper," she explained to Rose. "Maybe I'll see you later."

Miranda's voice was bright, but Jack thought he detected an edge of something else. Then again, *anything* was possible this morning. He wasn't at all sure how far he trusted his own senses, let alone his hunches. He raised an inquiring eyebrow at Rose.

"Her father," said Rose. "He ... works a lot. She's always hoping he'll be home but he almost never is. Mostly she eats with us."

"That's a drag."

Rose gave him a puzzled look and Jack tasted shoe leather. "I mean about her dad."

"A ... 'drag'?"

"I mean, that's too bad. About her father." *Jeesh, now I can't even* talk *right.*

Rose shrugged in the matter-of-fact way she seemed to have. "There are worse things."

Ahead of them the road swung around in a broad curve past a graveled parking area. Several trucks were pulled up. They looked old enough to star in a vintage car parade, if they hadn't all been so beaten up, scuffed and dented. With Patsy Ann in the lead they filed between two battered pickups to a platform built entirely from large beams of squared timber that gave a view out over the water.

Jack stopped. Spread out below him was a sheltered boat harbour. It reminded him of the marinas down on Lake

Ontario. Only here were none of the sleek speedboats and gleaming white sailing yachts he'd seen there. All these boats were tough and chunky working craft, with sturdy little cabins at the front, no-nonsense black- or white-painted masts, and behind them unfamiliar, oversized reels and tall rods mounted over broad low-slung decks. The breeze coming off the water carried a strong smell of salt and well-aged fish.

A wooden bridge that was more like a ladder dropped steeply down to the docks. Patsy Ann took it at a scrabbling run; the two humans, a little more cautiously.

At the bottom, the bridge rested on a wooden raft. It was the first in a maze of wooden floats rising and falling on tall upright pilings sticky with black tar. Rose and Patsy Ann headed confidently off down a row of swaying floats. Their route led them between the dipping prows of heavy wooden boats as big as buses, most with pairs of tall poles pulled up on either side of stubby cabins with glassed-in fronts. A few had huge spools set on low decks that seemed to hang just inches from the water.

Jack followed along behind Rose and the dog, staggering on the unsteady surface and raising his arms to keep his balance. The tipsy effect added a new element to the mounting sensation that he was far outside his usual comfort zone.

Five minutes and several turns brought them to the very edge of the boat basin. Only a narrow channel now lay between Jack and the seaweed-covered boulders of a breakwater. Ahead was a boat not like the rest. A low cabin nestled behind one soaring wooden mast and just ahead of a stubbier one. Jack supposed that the long bundles of heavy fabric trailing from the masts must be sails.

The boat's name was lettered across its stern in a flowing script: *DogStar*.

Jack felt a first faint glimmer ignite in the dark confusion of his thoughts. *The dog brought me here. Now Rose has brought me to a boat named DogStar. I sure hope this isn't just a coincidence.*

He could almost hear Al's voice: *"Most 'coincidences' aren't."*

Patsy Ann pulled up beside the boat and gave a short, sharp bark. A moment later a man's face appeared behind the small window in the low cabin door.

The face wore a grizzled gray beard and a faded blue peaked cap. It looked well worn the same way Al's face was, as though it had spent a lot of time outdoors. But this man, though definitely older than Jack's mom, was at the same time clearly younger than Al. At sight of the white dog the deep eyes crinkled and an angular smile broke out below the brown face.

"Permission to come aboard, Captain?" Rose called out.

The smile broadened. "Aye, Miss Rose, of course. And hello to you, too, old girl."

Patsy Ann crouched, eyeing the edge of the deck. As it rolled down toward the dock her stocky white body tensed. It uncoiled a fraction of a second before the deck hit the bottom of its roll, sending her plump little body in a tidy leap onto the boat's narrow side deck. She deposited a lick on the old sailor's extended hand and disappeared inside the little cabin.

The old man turned to look at Jackson and the crinkles disappeared from his deep-set eyes. His brows lowered, as though the gray gaze were searching a hazy horizon for hidden squalls. "And who have we here?" he asked, concluding his examination with a long, thoughtful look at the teenager's feet.

"He says his name is Jack," Rose said, gripping the boat's wooden rail. In a smooth movement she pulled herself up to stand beside the cabin door. "He says he's from Canada. And," her voice dropped to a conspiratorial whisper, "he's got the same funny shoes. *And* Patsy Ann brought him!" She raised her eyebrows meaningfully at this last point. Then she turned sideways on the deck and leaned against the cabin wall so she could look again at Jack.

Standing unsteadily on the rocking float Jack felt like a used car being checked for rust spots and bad tires.

"Canada, *eh*?" the old sailor said, with what might have been a twinkle of humour in his clear eyes.

Jack swallowed his inward groan. He raised his hand and said firmly, "Yes, sir, from Brampton, Ontario. Jackson Kyle. Pleased to meet you."

"Well, my name's Harper," the man said, gripping Jack's firmly. "And you may as well come aboard, too." Without warning he heaved and a moment later Jack, too, was standing on the narrow deck.

The added weight made the boat rock and Jack only just in time grabbed the rail for support.

"This *Brampton* of yours is no seaport, I take it," the old man. But once again Jack thought he detected a hint of warmth under the wry remark.

"Uh, no, sir. Though sometimes we get ocean ships in Toronto."

The gray brows furrowed at that and Jack wondered what he'd said. The Captain glanced over the boy's shoulder for a moment at Rose, then his eyes came back to Jack. "And how do you find yourself in Juneau, then?"

Okaaay. Uh-huh. Tough one. "I guess, sort of ... by accident. That is, I met up with Patsy Ann and, well, here I am." *Thin, waaay thin. Al wouldn't buy it for a second.*

It didn't look like the Captain was buying it much either. Jack glanced back at Rose in time to catch another "see-what-I-mean?" look.

"You're not in trouble with the law by any chance?" asked the Captain, his eyebrows lifting.

"No, sir." *Not unless you count the dogcatcher and my own mom ... back in 2005.*

Once more the old sailor looked down at Jack's shoes, his gray brows coming together again.

What IS it with the shoes? Hasn't anyone here ever seen a pair of Air Jordans?

"And you brought him here, did you?" The Captain addressed this question to Patsy Ann. In answer he got a short, sharp bark, then two more.

"Well, this is something to think about all right," he said as if to himself. Inside the boat a bell struck two clear notes.

The sound seemed to shake the old sailor out of his reverie. He turned to Rose.

"You'd best be getting along miss. Your mother will be home any minute and you'd best be waiting for her. I'll be along in a bell or two."

Rose's mouth opened and for a moment Jack thought she might fight this dismissal. But then it closed again, and Rose gave the Captain a knowing nod before turning back up the dock.

"Oh, and if you would," the Captain called. Rose turned, her face a question. "Kindly convey my regrets to your mother for the short notice but beg her to lay an extra plate. I think *we'll* be along for dinner."

Rose answered with a curt nod and a half smile and set off sure-footedly along the rocking floats.

"LET'S GO BELOW," the old sailor said to Jack. He moved aside and motioned for the teenager to step into the cabin.

Jack ducked through the low door. Standing erect again inside, he saw the Captain give a long searching look around the boat basin before following him.

The deckhouse had no more room than was needed to steer the boat. Glass windows swept across the front and both sides. A ship's spoked wheel stood beside something like a tin can made out of brass and hung inside metal loops. Beside that, narrow stairs led steeply forward. There was an oily scent of diesel, the sour musty smell of trapped water and lingering traces of tobacco smoke.

The Captain gestured for Jack to go down the stairs.

These were very steep, like a stepladder, and Jack had to lean back to avoid cracking his head as he descended. But there was a handrail of polished brass to hold onto on the way down and room to stand up at the bottom.

He found himself in a tiny but warm and welcoming space. A built-in sofa hugged one wall, facing a table with odd little fences all around the edges. Woodwork gleamed, and coloured spines in tidy bookshelves glowed in sharp circles of brilliant sunlight. These moved around playfully as the boat rocked on its moorings.

"Sit yourself down," the Captain indicated the sofa.

Before Jackson got there, the boat dipped in a roll deeper than any yet. He reached out again to keep from falling, finding another handrail just above the sofa. Gratefully, he pivoted and dropped down onto the long, cushioned bench.

A moment later he had to sciffle over to make room for Patsy Ann. The dog had followed them below. Now she settled heavily beside Jackson. Her grimy white hams pushed hard against his hip. Her head rested on her paws.

The Captain drew the only chair in the room closer to the table and eased into it. "Now, tell me again, how did you say you came to be here?"

Soooo, he didn't buy it.

Jackson looked down at Patsy Ann, but she was no help. Her dark little eyes were half closed and even as he considered how to answer this question her breathing slowed to a sleepy rhythm. *Oh, great. You've picked a fine time to check out on me.*

He looked back at the Captain. The old man sat watching him. Not impatiently. But not letting the question drop either.

"Well, sir, it's like this," he started. *"Always stick with the truth," Al says.* He began again: "I was at the ball field and Patsy Ann caught a ball." The old man acknowledged this much with a smile. "So I chased her for it. When I caught her, she didn't have any tags. I figured that meant she was a stray and I wanted to keep her.

"But Mom was going to call the dogcatcher. I couldn't let her go to the pound. So this morning we lit out. But then we saw the dogcatcher and he saw us, and then, well, Patsy Ann headed into some bushes and I followed her. And when we came out, we were in Rose's backyard." *So far, so true.*

"*When* was this ball game?" said the Captain.

Yeahhh, well ... "Just yesterday." *Sort of.*

"And *where* was it?"

Jackson swallowed hard. "Uh, it was at the diamond."

The Captain's head came down and his heavy brows rose skeptically. "Here in Juneau?"

"Well, actually, no. It was ... it was in ... "

"In, where did you say, *Bramtown*?"

Jack glanced down at Patsy Ann. All he got back was a low snore. At a loss and unable to meet the old man's eyes, he looked around the small room for inspiration. None came.

"And what would you say if I told you that no ship has arrived in Juneau in the past twenty-four hours with passengers from *anywhere*?" the old man asked. This would make nonsense of Jack's story. Yet he could have sworn once again that underneath the stern words, there was a warm ripple of amusement.

Jack said nothing.

The Captain rose suddenly to his feet. Stepping across the cabin he reached beneath a small, built-in desk and pulled out a drawer. After a moment's search he found what he was looking for. When he returned he had something in his hand. He offered it to Jack.

It turned out to be an ordinary travel brochure printed on glossy paper. On the front was a bright, full-colour photo of a gleaming modern cruise ship. Inside were splashy ads for whale-watching tours, heli-skiing adventures and McDonald's. Near the bottom of the back page someone had drawn a circle in pencil around the words, "Copyright 1998, Inside Passage Cruise Lines Ltd."

Jackson felt the room swirl in way that had nothing to do with the waves outside.

"Today is Wednesday, the tenth of July, 1935," the Captain said quietly. "I'm guessing that whenever your ballgame was, it wasn't on Tuesday, July the ninth. Or, indeed, in 1935." He dropped back into the chair and fixed his unwavering gray eyes on the teenager across the table.

The icy ball in Jack's stomach was taking some time to melt. As it happened, the ball game *was* on the ninth of July — *Saturday*, the ninth of July, *2005*. He let out a long, slow breath.

"That wee book came into my hands through another ... *guest* of Patsy Ann's," the Captain was saying now. "As it happens he came from Canada, too — and had some difficulties explaining just exactly how." A ghostly smile played over the grizzled features. "What say you, Mr. Kyle ... has something the same happened to you?"

Jack looked once again at the sleeping dog, then back to the Captain. Now he saw nothing in the calm gray eyes but an open invitation to what was clearly not possible. *This cannot be,* CANNOT *be. But still ... I'm here and it sure doesn't* feel *like some hallucination.* "I don't know," he started to say. "I don't know how ... It shouldn't be. It doesn't make any sense. But ... yeah, I guess it must have."

"Well, I won't pretend it's *usual* exactly, and maybe it's not even *natural,*" the Captain smiled. "But sense is something else entirely."

The old man leaned forward. "Patsy Ann's no ordinary dog. She doesn't do anything for no reason. As it turned out, there was a very good reason for her to bring that other young fellow here. It may not be clear right now, but I'll wager there's a reason she brought you as well."

Jack felt as though his head might explode. This was like being dropped into a video game in real life — *slay the worgs, find the treasure and rescue the princess. Or die trying. And do I get multiple lives if the worgs get me first?*

"What happened to him? That other guy?"

Now the Captain was flat-out grinning. "Oh, he found his way home. Eventually."

With a lurch, the dog beside Jack got to her feet and arched her back in a deep stretch. Then Patsy Ann turned carefully on the narrow sofa to face him. The black nose butted hard on Jack's chin.

In the dark, shining eyes Jack thought he saw something more than a simple reflection, something like a deep and sure promise. *Is that the deal? I do whatever I'm here for, then I get to go home — back to the future?*

The warm pink tongue lapped out and slapped wetly across his chin.

Eight

BOARDING HOUSE RULES

"MEANWHILE," the Captain was saying now, "you may be here a spell. We'd best figure out what to do with you. You'll be needing a roof and rations."

Oh, great. Mom's always saying I'll wind up homeless if I'm not careful.

"Mrs. Baker may be able to help with that," the old sailor went on. "But first we'd better find something else for your feet."

Again with the shoes! "What for? I only got these for my birthday. They're practically brand new."

"A mite *too* brand new for these modern times, I'm afraid. They look like they walked off the cover of *Amazing Stories*. Wear 'em downtown and you'll find yourself on the front page of the *Empire*, with some reporter wanting to know where you got 'em. Better for you to blend in a while, 'til it's clearer why you're here."

"Won't people notice me going barefoot, too?"

The Captain got up and disappeared toward the front of the boat. Jack could hear him rummaging. A moment later he reappeared carrying a pair of heavy black rubber boots with thick soles.

"Give these a try," he said.

Jack took the boots doubtfully. They looked like something a fisherman would wear and smelled of rubber and ... *Don't even go there.* He tugged at his sneakers and slipped them off. Nose wrinkling, he slipped his left foot into a boot. It was stiff and felt strangely hard and cold, but it didn't seem to be crushing any bones. He tugged the other boot on. "I guess," he said. *As long as I don't have to try any ten mile hike.*

"What about these?" Mom would kill him if he showed up home without his major birthday present.

"I can find a spot to stow them. They'll be here when you need them again."

When ... Jackson noticed.

"Now let's see what we can do about finding you room and board."

Jack got to his feet, feeling as strange in the unfamiliar boots as he had felt all this strange day. Ahead of him Patsy Ann scrambled up the short stairs that led outside. Clumping awkwardly in his borrowed footwear, he followed her.

They wound back through the maze of docks to the bridge leading to shore. For some reason, it didn't seem quite as steep as it had been earlier.

That out-of-body sensation hit Jackson again. *Could I just be dreaming all this? Maybe I've been in an accident and hit my head. Or was there something in that hamburger Mom brought home? Jeez, if I'm imagining all this, I hope I imagined the ambulance at Al's, too.*

Experimentally he pinched his arm — *hard*. He didn't wake up. All it did was raise a red welt. Anyway, while all this felt more than a little strange, it didn't have that peculiar slippery feeling dreams do, where one scene slides into another that's completely different. Nor, despite the unfamiliarity of everything, did he feel that horrid nameless terror he sometimes struggled to awaken from in nightmares. This all felt perfectly real, even pleasant.

It just wasn't possible.

Patsy Ann butted him suddenly from behind. She sure didn't *feel* like a fantasy. A moment later a curl of wind brought a strong waft of salt and old fish to his nose. Jack couldn't remember any dreams that came with smell-o-vision.

They turned in where green vines covered a white-painted gate with fragrant cream and pink blossoms. The Captain opened the door to Rose Baker's house, called out "Ahoy there!" in a foghorn voice, and stepped inside.

A slender woman in a flowered dress and floury apron met them in the hall. She seemed older than Jackson's mom but younger than the Captain.

"How's my favourite lady today?" the seaman asked, removing his blue cap and leaning down to plant a kiss on the woman's cheek.

"Oh, go on with you," she gave him back, batting her apron playfully at him. Then she looked past the Captain and asked, "Is this our dinner guest?"

"Aye," the captain nodded. "This is Jackson Kyle. Mr. Kyle,

meet Mrs. Sylvia Baker. You already know Miss Rose Baker, of course."

Jack didn't miss the woman's sharp look at this last observation. He got the impression it was news to Rose's mother — not necessarily welcome news.

All she said was, "Indeed?" And then, "Well, dinner's ready. Go on through and wash up and let's sit."

Scrubbing his hands clean at the deep kitchen sink, Jackson gazed at the Juneau calendar and its date — *1935*. He suddenly wondered what his own mother was doing right at this minute — if that even made any sense. Had she called the police to report him as a runaway? Or did everything that was happening "then" simply stop and wait for him to get back to the future? A wilder thought struck him: was this what really happened to people who went missing and were never found? Did they drop through some hole in time and just never find their way home?

He was still thinking about this when he followed the Captain back into the hall. Through a door to the left, one of those he'd passed earlier in the day, was a room almost entirely filled by a large dining table. Rose sat near one end and beside her sat Miranda.

"Hi," Jack murmured, not entirely sure it was a good idea to admit he already knew the two girls.

"Hi," the blonde smiled back at him. Rose merely bobbed her auburn head.

He and the Captain sat opposite the two girls and Sylvia took the place between them at the head of the table.

The big table could easily have served as many people again.

Before anyone began eating, the others closed their eyes and bowed their heads. Jackson followed suit.

"Great Creator," he heard the Captain say, "bless this food and this company with your divine grace. Amen."

Sylvia lifted the lid from a large china bowl in front of her and a rich, meaty aroma floated out over the table. Suddenly it seemed like a very long time indeed since Jackson had forced down half a nuked-over burger the night before — *or was it, let's see, seventy years from now?* He helped himself with enthusiasm to steaming chunks of pot roast and a small mountain of mashed potatoes. Even the peas, not usually his favorite green thing, had a fresh and delicious taste. *Is this what getting them right out of the garden is like?* Sort of the difference between fresh-caught perch and Captain High Liner's frozen fish.

A question from Sylvia brought his attention back to the conversation around him. "So, you're from Canada?"

What was it Al said about working undercover, pretending to be someone or something you're not? *Oh, yeah ...* keep your answers short and sweet. Don't rattle on. The less you say, the less chance you'll get caught up in a lie. "Yes, that's right."

"And where will you be staying while you're in town?"

Darn good question.

The Captain rescued him. "As a matter of fact, Sylvia, I was going to suggest he board with you. With those miners gone, you've got extra rooms not earning their keep."

Rose's mother hesitated, looking from Jack to Rose and

Miranda and back. "Well ... Forgive me, Mr. Kyle, but we really don't know you."

"There's not much we know about anyone who washes up in Juneau," the Captain said mildly.

Sylvia appeared to examine Jack with a new intensity. "Have you been in a scrap?"

"Eh?" Jack reached up and ran his fingers over his face. There *did* seem to be some rough patches on his cheeks that weren't there this morning.

A sudden burst of laughter erupted across the table. "Those are *raspberry* scratches, that's all," Rose said.

"He got them crawling through the canes out back," Miranda added.

"And what were you doing crawling through my raspberries?" Sylvia seemed a long way from being mollified.

"I didn't know they were your raspberries, ma'am. In fact, I didn't know there was going to be raspberries at all. I just followed Patsy Ann through the fence and there they were." *Well, that was certainly true.*

"You know, my dear," the Captain put in, "you'll never get your boardinghouse off the ground if you keep turning away tenants."

From beneath the table, a muffled *woof* sounded. Sylvia leaned sideways in her chair to exchange a look with Patsy Ann. A rhythmic *thump thump thump* sounded as the white dog's thin tail drummed the floorboards. Sylvia's resistance seemed to waver and at last she said, "I charge five dollars a week." She made it sound like a warning. "Breakfast, dinner and one change of bed things a week."

"I can do that," Jack agreed. *For awhile, anyway*. Reaching into his pocket he pulled out the savings he'd pulled from his sock drawer that morning: a purple Canadian ten-dollar bill, a blue five and a pair of two-dollar coins with bronze bull's-eyes inside nickel rings.

Miranda and Rose craned their heads for a better look at the colourful money. But Sylvia's brows shot up with renewed doubts. Too late it occurred to Jack that the coins, at least, had dates stamped on them that would be hard to explain here in 1935.

"Put that away, lad," said the Captain, reaching out a callused hand to close Jack's fingers around his cash. "I'm afraid your Canadian dollars are no good in the Alaska Territory."

"I can't take a boarder on credit," Sylvia sounded alarmed. "Especially not one with such a hearty appetite," she added, eyeing his plate.

Jack felt a sudden twinge of guilt over the hearty second servings he had just helped himself to.

"Tell you what." Again it was the Captain who came to his rescue. "There's plenty of work around town for a strapping lad like Jack. He'll pick something up. Meanwhile I'll put up a week's board on his account. He'll pay me back when he gets paid. Sound square to you, young man?"

"I ..." *A job? Mom doesn't even trust me to babysit.* But surely the Captain knew what he was doing. And, anyway, it wasn't like there were a lot of other options right now. "I mean ... sure. You bet."

The year 2005 might still be far off in the future according to the calendar in the kitchen, but suddenly this morning felt like a very long time ago to Jack. Far, far too much had happened in the hours — *or was it years?* — since then.

Jack's vision swam and he felt his head snap sharply upright. He felt both warm and heavy at the same time. He blinked to clear the fog and tried again. "That is, thank you, Captain. And thank you, too," he added, ducking his head in Sylvia's direction.

With that settled, Mrs. Baker appeared to relax a little. The two girls rose to change the plates and returned carrying a homemade pie. The floury smell of crust done to perfection filled the room, giving way to the sweetly acid scent of baked raspberries when Sylvia cut into it.

At first bite, Jackson realized he would never feel the same way again about the day-old slices that Carla sometimes brought home from the restaurant. Compared to this, they tasted like cardboard.

When everyone was done Sylvia rose from her chair. "If you two will clear the table," she said to the girls, "I'll show our new boarder his room."

This turned out to be a space off the kitchen hardly larger than the laundry closet back home. A bed in an iron frame filled one wall. The comforter that covered it was bright and inviting. A night table big enough to hold a shaded lamp and a plain chest of drawers left just about enough room for Jack to stand up and change his clothes. A window above the bed let in the night smells of nearby fir trees and damp earth. What Sylvia Baker called the "facilities" were in an even tinier closet-sized room on the far side of the kitchen.

Miranda left to walk home as soon as the last plate was dried. Jack was sorry to see her go. There was something mysterious about the blonde girl that teased at his emotions.

A few moments later Sylvia shooed her daughter toward the stairs. "See you in the morning," Rose called back to Jack as she went.

Shortly after that the Captain also said good night. Before going, he shook Jack's hand once more. Locking eyes with the youth, he spoke softly: "There's a reason you're here, Jack. Stand fast, keep your mind open and it will come clear." Then he stepped out into the lavender dusk of the northern summer evening.

From a spot beneath the big iron stove Patsy Ann watched the old sailor go. Sylvia held the kitchen door open and leaned down to address the dog: "And what about you, girl? Want to be off about your rounds?"

Patsy Ann got to her feet and shook herself briskly. But instead of going outside, she ambled over to where Jack stood by the door to his new bedroom.

Sylvia's face registered her surprise. "Well, I'll be! That's a first." She shook her head and laughed. "Well, as long as you stay on the floor." Nodding a good night to Jackson, she followed her daughter toward the stairs.

For the first time in what felt like a week Jack was alone. He closed the door, scuffed off the heavy black boots and dropped backward onto the iron bed.

The comforter was as deep and soft as it looked. Surrendering to its welcome embrace, Jack closed his eyes. Fractured images whirled around in the darkness behind his lowered lids. The boat. The calendar. Miranda. Sunshine through green raspberry leaves. Shiny paper in a callused brown hand. Flashing lights on an ambulance.

Did he complain only yesterday that Mom wouldn't let him grow up? Now it seemed he was going to have to — ready or not. Somehow, now that it was right in front of him, the idea seemed a lot less appealing.

Something heavy landed on the bed, bringing a muted shriek from the springs. Jack opened his eyes long enough to confirm that Patsy Ann had ignored Sylvia's edict. A warm wet tongue lapped over his face and a moment later the solid white dog was curled into the crook of his body. Jack tried to push her back onto the floor but his efforts were halfhearted and no match for the dog's stubborn weight. Soon he gave up. The warm white presence felt too irresistibly comforting. Instead he reached over and turned off the lamp.

At last, he slept.

Nine

ON THE DOCKS

JACK WOKE with a jolt and a momentary panic. His stomach felt sour with an unpleasant test-day knot. *Where the heck ...?*

Nothing was where it ought to be. Where his favorite poster of whales underwater should have been, facing the foot of his bed, was a blank wall. Instead of his familiar desk with its usual clutter of comics and dirty clothes, he saw a plain chest of drawers. This didn't even *smell* right: wood smoke and coffee instead of mom's chemical air "fresheners" and his own stinky sneakers. In a dim haze he remembered leaving the townhouse yesterday, heading for Al's. *Is that where I am?* Had he stayed overnight?

Through the door he heard the light skirfing sound of metal sliding over metal and the hubble-bubble of something boiling.

Something heavy shifted beside him in the bed. A triangular white face topped with pointed ears lifted above the jumbled comforter and fixed a pair of small, dark eyes on him. The dusty, musky smell of unwashed dog reached his nostrils and it all came back to him in a tumbled rush.

Holy time machine! It wasn't *a dream.* It really was 1935, and Jack was stuck here for some reason that the Captain had promised he would eventually discover. Until he found out what it was, he'd need to find some kind of job to pay for this soft, warm bed and whatever he ate.

Oh ... my ... God. The knot in his stomach tied itself in an extra loop.

Once more Jack pinched himself hard — just in case this was one of those dreams where you think you're awake. But nothing changed. He didn't wake up. He just developed another red welt on an arm that, he noticed, was still tracked with tiny scratches from his trips through the raspberry patch.

"What have you got me into?" he asked the white dog in bed beside him. For an answer she delivered a wet lap of her tongue and a waft of bad dog-breath. *Whew, talk about "morning mouth."*

The little dog stood, stretched, shook herself thoroughly from nose to tail and dropped heavily to the floor. Steps sounded, coming to the door, followed by a sharp rap on the wood. "Breakfast's up," a woman's voice called out. "And we don't wait on lie-a-beds!"

The moment he left the bedroom, Patsy Ann vanished out the back door.

BREAKFAST TURNED out to be thick, sticky porridge with milk and dark brown sugar. To drink there was a choice of milk or coffee. But no OJ and Cocoa Puffs in the Thirties, it seemed. *Guess that means no Pop-Tarts, either.*

Rose appeared, gave him a sleepy "G'morning" and

dropped into a chair on the far side of the table.

Jack sipped at a mug of milky coffee and considered the day ahead. Fast-food places always seemed to hire lots of teenagers. "Where's the McDonald's?" he asked Rose.

"Who?"

"Golden Arches? Egg McMuffins?"

"Huh?"

Oh-oh. "Wendy's? Pizza Hut? Burger King?"

"What *are* you talking about?"

"Don't you have *any* restaurants in Juneau?"

"Of course, we do! There's the Baranoff, where Ma used to work. There's the Alaska Hotel and the Gold Dust Cafe and the Gastineau. Why? Don't you like Ma's cooking?"

"No! No, it's fine! I was just thinking about finding a job."

"Well, there might be a place for a dishwasher at one of the hotels," Sylvia Baker offered as she came into the room with her own breakfast in hand. "But mostly they hire cooks from the camps or off the ships."

Yuck. Washing up, on the rare occasion when the dishwasher was on the fritz, was Jack's least favorite chore. "I guess that means there's probably no 7-Eleven either, huh?"

"What?" Rose gave him a what-planet-are-*you*-from look.

This was definitely going to take some mental adjustment.

"Variety stores?"

"We have a couple of general stores," Rose answered. "But Howie Hamm's got so many kids of his own he doesn't need anyone else. And Amory's, well ..."

"No one seems to last very long at Amory's," her mother finished the thought.

This wasn't looking good. Jack tried to think where else his classmates held part-time jobs back in Brampton.

"Golf courses?"

Rose laughed out loud into her glass of milk, spraying a mouthful of white spray over the table in a most unladylike manner. "This is Juneau, Alaska!" she gasped when she'd caught her breath again. "Not New York City."

"Most able-bodied young men who come to town find work in the mine or on the boats down at the waterfront," said her mother. "Of course, lately the mine hasn't been hiring."

Down the mine? A minor miner? I don't thiiink so!

That left the waterfront.

AFTER BREAKFAST, Jack left Rose up to her elbows in soapsuds and followed the Bakers' directions: "Just go out the door, turn right and follow the road."

The day was bright and smelled of wind and salt. The sun, though low in the sky, felt warm on his back. Off to his left as he walked, white crests rolled down blue waves. A dozen boats drew darker blue chevrons of wake behind them as they crossed this way and that over the inlet. A larger ship glided in slow motion a few hundred yards offshore, following the center of the channel in the same direction Jack was going. In the distance blue mountains came to soaring peaks so white his eyes hurt to look at them.

This looks like Al's country, he thought. Yet now he was actually in the middle of it, Jackson's appetite for high adventure on the Klondike trail wasn't what it had been over hot scones and blackcurrant jam in his friend's kitchen. The breeze coming off the water was cool and carried a faint smell of antiseptic. The hospital and the strict woman at the computer screen came back to him like a bad dream. *"But you're not really family."* If only he'd got to Al's just a little sooner. *Please, God, let him be okay.*

Ahead of him, a row of big, boxy structures with corrugated metal roofs lined the shore. From a distance, they looked like so many gray shipping containers against the green mountainside rising up behind them. But the scale was deceiving. It took longer than he expected to come up to the first building, and when he did, it was a lot larger than he had expected.

The knot was back in his stomach, too.

So how does this go, he wondered. *Do I just walk up and say, "Hi, I'm from the future. Got work?"*

Now the road was following the edge of a graveled work yard. Huge wooden spindles stood on their rims in a row, like so many wheels waiting for some giant wooden car. In another area, wooden pallets were stacked five and six deep. He passed the end of the first of the huge sheds.

From somewhere nearby a sharp bark rang out. Following the sound, Jack spotted Patsy Ann standing near the door of what looked like a garden shed attached to the larger building. On the gray weathered wooden planks above it, faded white letters identified the building as the BERING AND PACIFIC STEAM FISHERY CO.

Patsy Ann watched Jackson approach, her head low and small black eyes fixed on him. As he reached her side, Patsy Ann turned and with her head butted open the door to the small shed with her head. Glancing back at the boy, she stepped confidently inside.

"B'JOUR, YOU," a deep voice said from the semidarkness of the small room. *"Viens manger?"*

Stepping to the door, Jack looked cautiously inside. As his eyes adjusted to the gloom, he made out a room not much bigger than his own back at the Bakers' boarding house. This one was almost entirely filled by a workbench along the back wall. It supported a long gray metal cabinet with yellow dials that glowed above black knobs in various sizes. In front of the cabinet a microphone, one of the large, old-fashioned kind, hung suspended in a sort of metal cage by rubber bands. Off to the right stood a squat iron stove. It gave off a heat that Jackson could feel on his skin.

As he took in these details a man sitting in a swivel chair spun around. Jack had the impression of circles stacked one on top of another, like a kid's bathtub float toy or a snowman — a large round belly surmounted by a nested series of round chins and topped off with a shiny round bald head — except that this fellow was more or less the colour of Jack's morning coffee. The man wore a broad smile and an amused expression in his deep brown eyes. It seemed to be his natural outlook.

Patsy Ann dropped to a sitting position beside the chair. Her dark eyes fixed intently on the man, her skimpy tail stuck straight out behind like a chalk line on the floor. Ever so slightly it quivered.

"Who's this you brought me, you?" the big man asked Patsy Ann.

"I'm Jackson. Jack, if you like." He stepped forward and held out his hand. "I'm looking for work."

"Pontch, me." Without getting up the large man took Jack's hand in a fist the size of a small ham.

At the name Jack couldn't keep his eyes from the man's expansive belly. The merry eyes caught the look and a deep chuckle filled the small room.

"Nope, nothin' to do wit' dat," he laughed. "Pontch is short for Pontchartain. Dat's the place I was born — back in Loo'zian. And any friend of Patsy Ann's is sho' a friend of mine."

A sharp, impatient bark called their attention back to the dog. As Jack looked, Patsy Ann barked again. A little spray of saliva caught the big man's pant leg.

"B'en oui, b'en oui," he laughed again and reached for a large tin. Again Patsy Ann barked. Taking the tin into his lap he pulled off the lid. A deep smoky scent, shot through with something fiery, filled the small room. A big hand went in and came out again holding a peanut in the shell. The big man cracked it and thumbed the two nuts inside toward Patsy Ann. With a small grunt and a louder *chunk,* Patsy Ann's impressive pink jaws snapped shut on the flying treats.

"You?" Pontch held out the can. Inside were more peanuts, though Jack saw now that they were an uncommon tomato colour. "My own recipe, Cajun style. Nuttin' else like it in d'nort'."

Jack helped himself to a few. He broke one open and shook the nuts into his mouth. They crunched softly, bursting with mysterious and delicious flavours that warmed his tongue but didn't set it on fire. "Wow, these are great! What's in them?"

Another deep laugh. "Dat's a family secret. My ol' *gran'-maman*, she'd lay a voodoo on me, I tell you," said Pontch. "Only place you can get 'em is right 'ere." His expression shifted, raised eyebrows making a question of his next words. "You say you looking for work, you?"

"Yes, sir. Anything I can do."

"Dat's d'way to be all right. But who's dis 'Sir'?" He craned his bald head left and right on his thick neck in a mock search for someone hiding in the dark corners of the radio shed. "Nobody here but ol' Pontch," he said. He returned his beaming face to Jack. "But yo' luck, she not running so good right here. D' season be almost done fo' dis year."

"The fishing season?"

"*Oui,* fo' *des grandes peches, b'en sur* — dem bowheads, rights, sperm, too, if dere's any lef' to find."

Eh? With a sick feeling, Jack recognized the names printed on his poster of Great Whales. He'd fallen asleep under those majestic images ever since he was twelve. This man was a *whaler*? He took an unconscious step backward.

"What wrong wit' you? I thought you wanted work? Dis here be a whalin' station. You not know dat?"

"I do!" Jack stammered. "I mean I want to *work*. But no, I didn't know that. I ... I couldn't do that! It's not right. They're almost gone. And even if they weren't ... "

Pontch studied the boy closely for a moment, his smile for once banished from his broad face. "So dey say, some folk. Me, I doan' know 'bout dat. I know I doan' feel good when I see 'em die. Dat's why I keep myself here, doan' go out on de boats no mo', me. But I gotta work, too. Not so much work fo' a radio man in 'dis country." He ate another peanut, then added, almost sadly, "But dey do say *les gran' baleines,* dey runnin' out."

Okay, it's different times, Jackson reminded himself. *But I'll starve before I kill whales for a living.* "Is anyone else hiring, d'you know?"

"Dere's dat bridge dey be buildin' across the water," the big man offered. But then he tipped his head to one side, dismissing the idea. "But dey almost be done dat now. Not hirin' no mo', I doan' t'ink."

Jack cracked open his last spicy peanut.

The big face brightened. "You could try dose longshoremen. Dey always seemin' to need somebody. Too much bendin' over fo' me." Pontch laughed again and patted his broad stomach. "But you come back anytime, you. Have some more of ol' Pontch's Cajun nuggets."

He spun another pair of peanuts in Patsy Ann's direction. She fielded them expertly.

"Thanks, I'll do that." Jack turned to go. "Patsy Ann, you coming?" The white ears did not move and those black eyes remained fixed on Pontch. "Patsy Ann?" he said, louder this time.

"You wastin' yo' breath, you," the big man said. "She doan' hear a t'ing."

"Eh?"

"Dat's right. She stone deaf. Only t'ing she hear is when a big ship comin' in — and no one knows how she does dat."

"You're kidding!"

"Why, doan' you know who dis is? She only be de mos' famous dog west of de ol' man rivah, dat's all. An' our 'ficial town dog. D' mayor, he say so hisself!" Another gust of laughter shook the creaking chair. Pontch held his hands out in front of the dog, dusting them against each other in a "that's all there is" gesture.

Patsy Ann delivered a generous lick to the thick brown fingers, stood, gave herself a quick shake and then appeared to remember Jack's existence. Stepping up to him, she pressed her thick body heavily against his legs as she slipped past and out the door. Outside she stopped, looked back at him and barked.

Weird. Too flippin' weird.

PATSY ANN led Jack back to the road that followed the curve of the shore along the backs of warehouses and boat sheds. Ahead he saw taller structures, some of them four or even five storeys tall. *Beautiful downtown Juneau.*

A few cars passed. All looked like they'd driven out of an old black-and-white movie except that some of them were dark blue or brown. More people were walking than driving. A few girls and women wore loose denim jeans — *no Britney low-riders here* — but most had on skirts or dresses that came down to their shins. The men all wore hats of some sort, brimmed fedoras or low cloth caps with small peaks. Some boys a little younger than himself had on pants that stopped just below their knees, their calves covered by high socks.

Several people stopped to give Patsy Ann a pat on her thick head or slip her something they pulled from a pocket or purse. She took these tributes into her mouth with a surprising gentleness.

"Who's your new friend, Patsy Ann?" one woman asked with a smile in Jack's direction. Even knowing Pasty Ann couldn't hear the question, Jack felt a strange but agreeable new sense of belonging here.

They passed a long block where there were no buildings, just several heaps of some kind of very black gravelly stuff. The sign on the gate said "Peabody Coal, Alaska." Storefronts began to come into view. Jack spotted a green-and-white sign that identified Amory's Outfitters. Beyond that was a drugstore.

A wire display rack stood near the door, its painted tin placard announcing the availability of the *Alaska Daily Empire*. Jackson felt a jolt when he saw the date on the front page of the top copy: Thursday, 11 July, 1935.

A rack of postcards above the newspaper caught his eye. Several were pictures of Patsy Ann! He pulled one out.

It showed the white dog sitting with her back to the camera, gazing out across water toward a distant ship. Jack turned the card over and read the print on the back. "Famous bull terrier dog Patsy Ann is known throughout the Northwest as the Official Town Greeter of Juneau, Alaska. Although she cannot hear, the independent animal appears at the wharf in advance of any steamship arriving in the Territory capital. Juneau's citizens routinely follow her to the dock, a practice they call 'Patsy Anning'."

Holy cow, he smiled to himself, *I'm a friend of* the *Patsy Ann.*

A sharp bark from "the" Patsy Ann herself interrupted his thought. Stuffing the card hastily back into place, he set out again.

Jack hadn't gone far when he came to a long, low structure built out onto a broad wharf of heavy timber. The wharf extended along the shore in either direction for another few dozen yards. Painted on the wooden wall at one end of the building were the words "Longshore and Warehousemen's Benevolent Ass'n." A handwritten sign tacked to a door read, "Hiring – Work Today."

A small group of men and youths stood near the door, talking in ones and twos or leaning against the wooden walls. Some had thick arms and broad shoulders, like men who'd done a lot of heavy lifting in their lives. Others were as old as the Captain but neither so erect nor sturdy looking. Several looked even younger than Jack — and certainly shorter.

So what's the deal here? Do I ask for an application form or something?

Before Jack could answer his own question, the door burst open. A stocky man with the fierce look and battle-scarred face of a human pit bull stepped out. In his hand was a sheet of paper. Without ceremony he began to bellow names in a voice like a foghorn: "Shultz! Krawchek! Miller! Hagen!"

One by one, men and boys stepped out of the crowd and slipped past the man through the door. When he had called out more than half a dozen names the man gave a curt nod of his head, shoved the list into his hip pocket and turned back to the door. With resigned shrugs, those who hadn't been named began to drift away.

Jack's heart sank.

Then Patsy Ann gave a particularly deep and powerful *rrufff!*

The stocky man turned back at the sound, the expression on his florid face unreadable. At sight of Patsy Ann his expression softened for just a moment. But then his glance moved on to Jack and the hard look returned to his eyes.

Now or never, dude. Jack stepped forward. *Arrrghhhmmm,* he coughed, and tried to pitch his voice deeper than it really was. "Sir! Are you sure you can't use just one more?"

The man scowled like he wasn't used to anyone asking him this kind of question.

Patsy Ann barked again — another gruff, tough-sounding bark.

Hard eyes sized Jack up and down. They had the same look a butcher gives a side of beef before he starts cutting. Finally they dropped back to the little white dog sitting at Jack's feet. Thick brows came together as though the brain inside the bullet head was trying to solve an unfamiliar problem.

Somewhere beyond the low building a horn sounded — a long, throbbing note so deep and powerful Jack could feel his insides vibrate.

"That's the *Tyee King*. She's always got a full load and one or two in that lot don't look none too strong." The man seemed to speak to himself — or maybe to Patsy Ann. "This one looks sturdy enough, though."

Now the hard eyes looked directly at Jack. "If you can start this minute I'll give you a try." Once again he gave a little bob of his bullet head, turned and walked through the door without a glance back.

Without another word Jack followed him.

Ten

BLISTERS & BLUSTER

SWEAT RAN down Jackson's face and into his eyes, making him blink. It plastered his T-shirt to his back. His arms ached and the palms of his hands were beginning to sting. Whenever he raised his arms he could smell his pits.

And Mom thinks working at McDonald's is too tough for a kid.

He had learned that the human pit bull's name was Clancy. The *Tyee King* was a freighter ship, as long as three tractor trailers but deeper and very much wider. Its side rose like a rusty steel wall from the edge of the wharf.

Clancy sent some of the men and youths aboard the ship and down inside what he called its "hold." Their job was to attach cables to the items in the ship's cargo — anything from heavy wooden spools like the ones Jack had seen earlier, to bales and crates and barrels, some made of wood, and others of steel. Crates and barrels went onto lumber platforms, suspended at their four corners by cables from above. Gunny sacks were loaded into big rope nets.

Whatever it was, as soon as the cable was attached to it a crane on deck rattled into action. A drum turned and the cable tightened, lifting the load up out of the hold until it swung free over the deck. With a squeal, the crane pivoted until the load was over the wharf. Then, with more rattling and squealing metal, the cable would drop the cargo down to the wharf. There more longshoremen waited to catch or load the cargo onto a "dolly" — a flat square of scarred wood with small iron wheels and a rope for pulling it.

This was where Clancy had teamed Jack up with another young fellow about his own age. His name, Jack learned, was Nils. Copying his more experienced partner's actions, Jack soon fell into the swing of things. Once a load of boxes or a heavy spool of rope sat squarely on the dolly, they pulled and pushed it over the uneven wooden wharf into the echoing warehouse to wherever Clancy directed them. Then they wrestled the load onto the floor (sometimes with help from other longshoremen) and immediately raced back to the side of the ship for another load.

Hour after hour this went on, with Clancy barking directions and urging them every other minute to "Get a move on there. Let's get this done."

Only once did they take a break, for all of fifteen minutes. Then Jack lined up with the rest for a bowl of thick, rich stew served in blue bowls. A vat of the stew steamed on a stove in a partitioned-off corner of the warehouse. Jack had hardly finished wolfing down his meal when Clancy called everyone back to work.

The work wasn't *difficult* exactly, but it sure was *hard.* More than once during that long afternoon Jack felt he couldn't possibly pull one more load. Then he caught sight of someone older or smaller than himself working without complaint. Deep in his weary brain a distant voice — *Al's? Or maybe Coach Aseem's?* — whispered that this was no time to be a quitter. Just *suck it up*. And from somewhere down inside he pulled up enough energy to keep going.

By the time the crane finally wheezed into silence the sun was touching the blue-green mountain across the water. Jack's arms and legs trembled with weariness. His feet inside the thick rubber boots felt hot and swollen and a sharp pain on the left one suggested he was developing a blister.

He lined up with the rest of the crew in the corner "office" to collect his pay. His hand shook as he held it out for Clancy to place six one-dollar bills across his palm. Dimly, Jack's mind registered that this was more than the whole week's board the Captain had loaned him. He looked up and met the crew boss's eyes.

Clancy gave one of his curt little nods and said, "You'll do. Be back tomorrow. Call's at five-thirty."

He tottered out onto the road that led along the shore toward the boarding house. He felt too tired to stand upright let alone walk all the way back to the Bakers'. But inside the fog of weariness was an unfamiliar glow. Whether it was pride at having kept up with the other, older workers to earn his first day's pay or simply that he was light-headed with exhaustion, and despite his aching muscles, Jack had never felt better than he did right now.

With his last reserve of energy he dragged himself through the flower-decked gate and up the gravel path to the Bakers' door.

Sylvia greeted him in the kitchen with a thick sandwich of yesterday's pot roast on soft bread so fresh it was still warm. Even a day old, the slice of berry pie that followed it tasted better than anything Jack could remember coming home with Mom from the restaurant. But it was all he could do to stay awake to finish the last crumbs of crust. He had never been so completely worn out in his whole life.

As the fog closed in around him, Jackson remembered that there was something — *something* — he had to ask Sylvia for. Something to do with the last words Clancy had said.

Oh, yeah!

He was in luck: the Bakers *did* have an alarm clock. Sylvia showed him how to wind a little knob on the back until a hand in front pointed to just before five o'clock.

Ohmigosh, that's, like, six hours *from now!*

In his small room he placed the clock on the bedside table, kicked off his heavy boots and collapsed back onto the comforter. He was instantly asleep.

SUNLIGHT flooded into the small room. Jack opened his eyes, then closed them again. *Oh, yeahhh...* Who knew it could feel this good just not getting up? For the first time in three days the clock's fire-alarm bell hadn't blasted him awake.

That first day on the docks had been hardest, even though the next had been longer. Partway through the second day, they finished taking stuff out of the *Tyee King* and immediately began putting other stuff back in her (everybody called the *King* a "her," Jack noticed). He and Nils spent the long afternoon shuttling dolly-loads of brown cardboard boxes stamped "Alaska Chief Salmon" from the warehouse to the wharf-side. At the end of twelve hours his biggest blisters had popped, smearing his palms with pink-stained wetness. Once again it had been all he could do to stagger back to the Bakers', gulp down supper and collapse into bed.

Day three was more of the same but at least Jack's muscles seemed to be catching up to the new demands he was making of them. Day four had been a mere five hours spent loading steel barrels onto a barge that had replaced the *Tyee King* at the wharf. By the time Jack lined up to receive his pay from Clancy he hardly felt tired at all, compared to the previous afternoons. His hands were sore but no longer shaky and seemed to be developing some welcome calluses at last. He'd also learned a few salty phrases he was pretty sure Mom wouldn't approve of — and picked up a little of what Al called "local intelligence."

The big news in town, he'd figured out, was a radio station that had just opened — Alaska's first. From what the longshoremen said over their bowls of stew during meal breaks, something called the Depression was causing trouble in the rest of the United States. Here in Alaska, or at least in Juneau, there was worry about some gold mine running out of gold, but everyone was looking forward to a good year for "the big fishery" — whatever that was.

A lot of the stuff they'd unloaded from the *Tyee* had been addressed to an outfit named "Eric Ericson & Sons." Jack got the impression the company carried a lot of weight in Juneau. But according to the sarcastic remarks and non-Mom-friendly jokes that flew around the wharf, the "sons" were wishful thinking on Eric Ericson's part. Not only did the wealthy Ericson have no sons, he had no wife. And, since he seemed to be married to his business, the opinion on the docks was that he wouldn't acquire either one anytime soon. "Pity about the girl, though," one or two of the men had added, shaking their heads.

At the end of work yesterday, Clancy confirmed Jack's place on the regular crew. And the next ship wasn't due in port until tomorrow.

That made today a full-fledged holiday!

Jack luxuriated in the thought of a day off. And he was *rich*! — at least by 1935 standards. In the bedside table drawer were twenty-six dollars and fifty cents. Even after he paid the Captain back and gave Sylvia Baker five dollars for the next week's board and bought a few essentials, he would still have substantially more than ten dollars. A "sawbuck," he'd heard Nils call the ten-dollar bill. Judging by the prices he'd seen in shop windows, that had to buy *something*.

One thing he wanted was better footwear. He wasn't the only one wearing rubber boots on the docks, but blisters on his hands were bad enough without the ones on his feet, too.

Then there was that girl, Miranda. He wondered if she'd like to have a soda with him or something.

The smell of frying bacon drifted in under the door. The salty aroma took Jackson's thoughts away from the pretty blonde girl and onto the empty feeling in his stomach. His appetite, he noticed, seemed to be developing extra muscle even faster than his arms.

To his surprise Miranda was at the breakfast table, working through eggs and bacon in a chair next to Rose. *What's the deal?* He wondered again. Did she sleep over? And where was her family?

The two girls greeted Jack politely enough, but as he stepped past them he caught their exchange of rolled eyes. *Eh?*

Sylvia Baker cut his speculation short. "Jack," she began, "if you're not working today, I wonder if you'd run some clothes down to the Captain for me? It's not much, just some shirts and trousers that needed mending. I'd ask Rose but today's our day to wash all the bed things."

"Sure, no sweat," Jack nodded. For some reason this brought a spasm of giggles from the two girls across the table. "I was planning on visiting the Captain anyway," he added, eyeing the duo facing him with a perplexed look.

"Thank you then," Sylvia said primly.

Wiping the last trace of bright orange yolk from his plate with a piece of warm bread, Jack mustered his nerve. "Hey," he began, addressing himself to both the girls. "How about later, when you're done, you guys show me a bit of Juneau? Let me buy a round of ice-cream cones or something."

"Maybe when we're *all* done washing up," Rose answered

primly, rising with her plate in hand. Miranda got up, too, wrinkling her nose at her friend. They disappeared into the kitchen and a moment later Jack heard water running and dishes clinking — and more giggling.

Girls. But he felt his face burn as he tried to decipher Miranda's parting look.

TWENTY MINUTES later, Jack reached the boat docks. In his arms was a bundle of folded clothing, the rough blue wool and soft cotton neatly tied with white string. The sharp smell of laundry soap mingled faintly with the greasy odor of old fish blowing up from below. The combination was not unpleasant. Maybe when he got home he'd try to convince Mom to move to Vancouver or maybe Halifax; somewhere beside the ocean.

And maybe I'll work on the docks. He couldn't help chuckling at the thought. *Just wait 'til they see my resumé!*

The gangway tilted down at a gentle angle toward the floats. After the last few days on the waterfront, this was no longer a mystery. He'd learned that the ocean wasn't always the in same place: tides made it rise and fall. Sometimes the ships' sides towered over the wharf-edge; sometimes he could almost look down into their holds. Today, the tide must be high.

In the distance he could see the twin masts that set Captain Harper's *DogStar* apart from the other boats in the marina. Studying the maze of rocking floats he tried to figure out which ones led in that direction. *Straight, then left, then right ...*

Jack stepped off the gangway onto the first float. It dipped disconcertingly beneath his feet but he found the motion less unsettling than on his first visit. As he turned this way and that, however, working closer to where the *DogStar* lay, he could hear that *someone* was plenty upset.

Through the creak of ropes and the gentle knock of wooden floats against wooden pilings, amid the clear cries of gulls turning overhead, the raised voices sounded harsh and out of place. He turned onto the last stretch of dock. The commotion, he could see now, was coming from a boat slip right next to the Captain's.

A tall man stood on the dock in heated conversation with a suntanned fellow in a boat. The powerful-looking launch was as distinctive in its own way as the *DogStar*. But where the Captain's boat evoked the graceful age of sail, this craft was low, with muscular, swept-back lines and a menacing profile. It reminded Jack of the speedboats on *CSI Miami* except that this one was made of brightly polished wood. The engine was running, sending up a trace of light blue smoke from down near the boat's waterline and filling the warm morning with a powerful rumble.

As he got closer Jack could read the name painted in gold across the back. *Cetus*, it was. *Whatever that means.*

The fellow on the dock was wearing pressed khaki trousers and a plaid bush shirt. A five-pointed star was pinned to the left pocket and a pistol hung in a shiny brown leather holster at his waist.

The man on the boat wore denims, an open green work

shirt and a furious expression on his sunburned face. In one hand he held a rope that ran through a ring on the dock and back to his boat, where it was attached to a shiny brass fitting.

"... then you're no better than one of their goons," the man on the boat was saying, voice thick with anger.

The skin above other man's collar flushed red. "And I'm telling you to keep your distance from them. I know you think you're in the right. But they have the law on their side and no shortage of muscle. Nor a shortage of the will to use it, neither."

"I'm no coward, Marshal."

"I know that, Stanley. But if you won't back off for your own sake, think about that young wife of yours."

"She knew what I stood for when she married me."

"She may have had a choice. Your baby didn't."

"It's for him that I can't back off," the man in the boat said, eyes blazing, "For him and the rest of his generation."

"It's for this generation and the law that I'll arrest you if I have to," the man with the badge replied.

"You'll have to catch me first." Without warning the angry man dropped the rope and yanked hard at the end still attached to his boat. The coarse brown line whipped through the ring, loose end snapping savagely so that the other man had to step out of its way.

The fellow on the speedboat turned and ducked into the low cabin. The engine roared and the boat shot out of the slip, sending a rooster tail of spray high into the air and all over the man standing on the dock. Jackson spun around to keep seawater from soaking the Captain's clean mended clothes.

The man with the badge shook his head and turned toward the shore. As he passed he gave the teenager a wry smile. With a shock, Jackson realized that the tall lawman was really very young. In fact, he didn't look to be much older than Jack himself.

And something else ... But before Jack could put his finger on what it was, a grizzled face popped through *DogStar*'s cabin door.

"What's all the hullabaloo?" Captain Harper asked.

"Beats me," Jack shook his head. "A guy with a badge was arguing with your neighbor."

The Captain gave a slight frown, then nodded Jack aboard. The old man thanked him for the delivery of mended clothes and, when Jack counted out five well-worn dollar bills, commended the prompt repayment of his loan. Then he invited Jackson below.

Lifting a section of the counter next to the boat's small kitchen sink, the seaman produced two green glass bottles and snapped them open. Taking one, Jack recognized the flowing script of Coca Cola's familiar logo molded into the cold glass.

Jack dropped onto the settee; the Captain, into his big chair.

"Well," the Captain said, raising his bottle in a toast. "Ye've settled in to Juneau life a good mite faster than our last visitor from the future. I hear you're a hard worker."

Jack felt himself blush at the compliment. Still, he had to wonder: "How'd you hear that?"

"Juneau's a small town, lad. Never forget that."

"Then you must know what that kerfuffle outside was all about."

"Kerfuffle?"

"Hullabaloo." Jack couldn't resist a smile.

"Ah, that." Jack thought he caught a glint of humour in the Captain's deep gray eyes. "The feller on the *Cetus* is Stanley Bayne. He's a biologist, he says. Trained in it at school, anyway. But he has more heart than brains sometimes. He claims the whales are running out, says we need to put an end to the fishery."

"But they *are* in danger. And they're *not* fish!" The heat in Jackson's tone surprised even himself.

"I know what the creatures are!" the Captain shot back. "I've peeled the fat from more than a few carcasses myself. But Stanley doesn't reckon with the town, what it would mean to the whole territory, for that matter. He's stirring up a lot of bad feeling."

"But Captain, he's right. I studied it for school. They hunted the whales almost to death, just like the buffalo and the..." He groped for an example. "... The dodo!"

"It's true the hunt's been spotty the last while," the Captain conceded. "But it puts a lot of money in pockets all 'round the coast. And with these new guns and fast boats, the ships are coming back full again. Men are protecting their livelihood. If Stanley's not careful, he'll find himself feeding whales instead of saving them."

Jack felt a distance grow between him and the old sailor. He was grateful for the Captain's help, but it revolted him to think he'd made friends with a *whaler.* He felt his temper rise. "It won't matter!" he blurted. "They *will* stop hunting them, because there won't hardly be any left to kill. It's *going to happen* ... right before the Second World War."

As soon as the words left his mouth Jack wished he hadn't said them. The Captain's face took on a bleak expression and his shoulders sagged. For a long time he looked down at the table. When he finally spoke, his words did not seem intended for Jack at all.

"Another war," he breathed. "So it will come to that." He sounded tired.

Gathering himself, the Captain stood and collected their empty bottles. "I wish I'd not heard that, Mr. Kyle," he said, turning to put the empties beside the sink. "I'm no lover of the hunt. The big fish are the most magnificent things God put in the sea. I'd sooner see them swimming free than butchered to put cream on the face of fancy women.

"But it's not right to know more about tomorrow than we're meant to. It tempts a man to try and change more things than he should — especially now, with feelings running high as a spring tide. I suggest you give that some thought before you let your tongue run loose again."

Jack could sense dismissal in the Captain's tone. He stood and reached for the little ladder that led off the boat.

"Thanks for the Coke," he said in a neutral voice.

"Aye, and by the way," the Captain said, his back turned. "Ye might want to drop by the Chinaman's. He'll boil those clothes of yours for a nickel. If you ask, he may sell you a change for not much more. Folks are forever leaving things there and forgetting them."

Climbing the ladder Jack noticed for the first time the ripe odor of sweat in the clothes he'd worked in for the past five days.

Eleven

STARTING FRESH

WHAT *a jerk!*

Jack cursed himself as he made his way back to shore. *I can't keep my mouth shut. I've ticked off the only guy here who knows what's up with me. And I stink. Like,* I really *stink.*

He turned a corner and aimed an angry kick at a rope that lay coiled on the dock. The coil rolled off into the water and began to sink into the green depths, unspooling as it went.

"Hey, kid," an angry voice called out behind him. Jack looked back to see a burly man climb from a boat and begin pulling the wet brown line onto the dock. "Whatcha do that for?"

Through a haze of self-directed anger Jack caught a blast of the colourful phrases he'd only recently learned directed his way.

By the time he reached the parking lot at the top of the gangway Jackson felt truly down for the first time since he'd crawled through the hole in the fence. Until this moment he'd been too pumped by where he found himself to question how he was handling it. Carried along by the impossible *magic* of what had happened to him and the excitement of living out an adventure even wilder than anything Al McMann had talked about, he'd felt like he was in the middle of the best role-playing, virtual-reality Nintendo game ever invented.

But somehow, he saw now, he'd also acted as though he could just log off any time he liked. He'd forgotten that until he figured out *why* he was here in 1935, he was also a prisoner in the past, and that for Captain Harper and Miranda and Rose and her mom, this was no game.

A bark echoed from between two battered trucks. Looking between them, Jackson spotted the little white dog.

You! "I don't know what kind of game you think you're playing, Patsy Ann," he said, glaring at the creature. "But I don't want to play any more. Go work your magic on someone else, you dumb mutt."

"Whatcher wasting your breath for?" a thick voice called out from one of the pickups. "Dog's deaf as a stump. Cain't hear a word you're saying." Whatever else the man said was lost in a throaty gurgle of mocking laughter. Only the words "fool kid" came out clear as a dirty word in a church parlour.

Patsy Ann turned her back and vanished toward the gangway.

It was no use. There weren't going to be any cheat codes or shortcuts out of this game. The Captain was right. He was going to have to find his own way out.

What was Al's line? First things first: just do what's in front of you. The Captain had told him where to buy a change of clothes — *and get these ones fumigated or whatever it takes.* Jack blew a long breath out through his mouth and set out along the road that led downtown.

HOW "POLITICALLY INCORRECT," Jackson couldn't help thinking twenty minutes later.

Above a tiny storefront window, hand-painted red letters read: "Huk-sing's Chinese Laundry." He opened the door and heard a bell tinkle overhead. He stepped inside and was enveloped in a wave of hot moist air that tingled in his nose with the strong chemical smell of no-nonsense soap.

If the sign was short on political correctness, the rail-thin figure that emerged from a curtain behind the counter was even more so. A round cap of bright yellow silk, embroidered in red and green thread, covered black hair pulled into single long pigtail that reached down to the man's tailbone. A jacket in the same style had a high collar and buttons like short sticks made out of white bone. The man's pants were black and baggy; his shoes were more like slippers.

If I dressed any Asian person like this for a social studies assignment in the twenty-first century, they'd throw me in detention, Jack smiled to himself.

A new idea came on the heels of the first. If today's facts could become unacceptable sometime in the future, maybe future ones could be unacceptable in the past. The Captain's anger with him took on a different light.

The thin man leaned over the narrow counter to run his eyes up and down the youth in front of him. His nostrils flared and Jack thought he detected a slight frown on the broad face. For a moment he feared he wasn't going to be served at all.

Then the laundryman spoke. "Yes? Can I help?"

"Mr. Huk-sing?"

Huk-sing nodded gravely.

"Captain Harper sent me." Jack was relieved to see a warm smile break out on Huk-sing's face as the laundryman gave another nod. "I need my clothes washed." This brought a much stronger nod, albeit still with a smile. "And he says you might have some clothes to sell?"

"Ah! Yes. Can do, can do." Huk-sing's head tilted and his eyes narrowed as once again they traveled the length and breadth of the tall teenager. Then he disappeared through the curtain into the back of the shop. Jack heard the metallic *scriiitch, scriiitch* of clothes hangers sliding on a rack.

A minute later Huk-sing returned. In his arms were two pair of jeans in different states of fadedness, assorted shirts and a clutch of socks and undershorts. He nodded toward another curtain that closed off a corner to one side of the counter. "Try on over there," he said.

The jeans weren't exactly low-riders — *more like "dungarees" than jeans* — but they were clean, mostly intact and fit fairly well. So did most everything else with the exception of a couple of the shirts, which were too small. After trying on everything and choosing jeans and a white T-shirt to wear immediately, Jackson emerged with his dirty clothes under one arm.

"Give me those, I wash. You pick up tomorrow."

Jack made three piles on the counter: clothes he wanted; the shirts that didn't fit; and the jeans, T-shirt, socks and jockeys he'd been wearing for the past five days.

With quick, practiced movements Huk-sing folded those Jack wanted. Whipping white string from a big spool suspended near the ceiling, he tied them into a neat bundle. He next scooped up the dirty clothes Jack had worn in the door. As he did, the tag inside the jeans caught his eye: MADE IN CHINA. His double take was comical.

With no better explanation to offer, Jack just smiled and shrugged. Huk-sing gave his head a sharp shake, then carried the armload of laundry from the future into the back of the shop.

When Huk-sing returned, Jack asked: "How much is all this going to cost?" He felt his stomach knot. *Is this how Mom feels every time we shop for clothes at Wal-Mart?* It wasn't a pleasant feeling.

Huk-sing did some quick figuring with a pad and pencil. He held out the paper. "Three dollar, twenty cent."

Jack's face must have betrayed his astonishment because in the next breath Huk-sing's own expression became worried and he added, "Too much?"

"Oh, no! No, sir, that's fine!" He reached into the pocket of his new old jeans and pulled out his small wad of cash.

FEELING MUCH better than when he had walked into Huk-sing's, Jack strode back out into the Juneau afternoon.

A fresh breeze carried a clean salt smell up from the sea, ruffling his hair. An unbroken blue sky overhead recalled Miranda's eyes. Along the street in front of him wooden storefronts painted in green and blue and yellow glowed in the clear northern light.

Buoyed by the change in his mood, when he passed a shop that advertised "everything for the camp and working man," he turned in the door.

He came out ten minutes later with the Captain's rubber boots tucked under his arm along with his new secondhand wardrobe. On his feet were a pair of spanking new leather work boots. They had cost five whole dollars but the firm stitching and proper fit made him feel that maybe, just maybe, he could stand on his own two feet in Juneau after all.

One thing still bothered him, and he made a mental note to clean take care of it as soon as possible. As it turned out, the opportunity came sooner than he expected.

As he followed the shoulder of the shore road back toward the Bakers', he could see an erect figure in a blue jacket and blue cap coming toward him in the distance. Beside the approaching figure, a flash of white seemed to be keeping pace.

As the distance between them diminished, he made out Patsy Ann trotting along beside Captain Harper. They met at the neat gate with its cloak of cream and pink flowering vines.

The Captain tipped his head politely to Jack.

But Jackson hesitated. He looked at Patsy Ann, who flashed him her toothy, wrinkled grin. Then he summoned his courage and said, "Captain, sir, I'm sorry I spoke without thinking earlier. I guess I didn't realize that there's ... I don't know, *rules*, sort of, for this kind of thing."

The Captain's expression didn't change and for a moment

he said nothing. Then he nodded and said: "Apology accepted. In fact, I reckon I owe an amend myself. I've not seen the things you have, Jackson Kyle. Nor am I likely to. How you're here at all is a mystery I don't begin to understand. I should know better than to draw a course on a sea I've never sailed." The Captain held out his hand. "Square?"

"Square." Jack reached out his own hand and they shook.

"Just have a caution, lad," the old man added with a serious look. "You're in deep waters. What you do, you may not be able to undo."

At their feet, Patsy Ann let go a bark.

"She's either agreeing with me or reminding us there's a meal awaiting." The Captain's serious face broke into a smile.

Together they walked up the path to the door. Gravel crunched beneath his new boots and Jack caught the sweet scent of flowers. He felt better for squaring things with the Captain. But that remark about *deep water ...* that sure was right on. *I'm swimming as hard as I can, dude.*

At the door Jack stood aside for the Captain to enter ahead of him. Then he followed.

The Bakers' front hall seemed smaller than usual. Jack quickly realized that it was just a lot more crowded. Rose, Miranda and Sylvia Baker stood in a tight semicircle facing a tall man whose back was to the door. Their upturned faces were intent with evident interest and Jack felt an unexpected stab of jealousy at the open admiration in the blonde girl's eyes.

Sylvia Baker looked past the tall man and smiled. "Why Ezra, Jack," she said, and put her hand on the big man's elbow, turning him gently to face the newcomers. Jack recognized the plaid bush shirt with its bright silver star over the pocket: it was the lawman he had seen earlier on the docks. "Jack," she carried on, "let me introduce Deputy Alan McMann, the district's new federal marshal."

A huge wave seemed to roar up around Jackson, picking him up and spinning him head over heels into new and even stranger depths.

Alan McMann?

Twelve

NEW OLD FRIENDS

FROM FAR AWAY, or maybe it was long ago, Jackson heard a voice speak his name.

"Jackson, is it? Good to know you." The voice was comfortingly familiar — and eerily not.

Very slowly, like a person floating to the surface from the bottom of a deep pool of water, Jack's consciousness returned to the present.

Now Sylvia's voice was also calling his name, "Jack? Jack, are you all right?"

Giving himself a little shake, Jack thrust out his hand and forced himself to focus on the tall young man in front of him. "I'm sorry, that was just, I don't know ... felt weird there for a moment. But I'm fine, really. Hi, deputy, nice to meet you."

They shook hands. Young Al McMann's grip was strong and firm. Jack's felt a little shaky, even to himself.

He looked his new old friend in the eye. *Oh ... my ... God, it* is *him. Only he's hardly any older than me ...* Way *younger than Mom.* The effect was almost creepy.

The deputy's head tilted to one side in a familiar gesture. He gave the teenager a searching look. Jack dropped his eyes. Al already had that unsettling ability to make him feel as though his most secret thoughts were an open book. He glanced at the Captain. The old man's sun-weathered face wore a thoughtful look.

"You here on a case?" Jack recognized the voice as his own. *Oh, jeez ... How paranoid is that going to sound?*

The tall man laughed, an easy, relaxed sound. "Not really. Juneau's part of my territory. I come through every couple of weeks."

"And when he does, he boards with us, I'm happy to say," Sylvia explained.

"So any outlaw better think twice about bothering *us!*" Rose said with spirit.

"That's right," Al said, a smile mocking the implied threat.

How about someone who's only breaking the laws of physics?

Jack was suddenly aware he still had a bundle of fresh used clothes and a pair of rubber boots under one arm. "Excuse me a sec," he said.

The marshal and the others stepped aside to let him pass. As she stepped aside Miranda caught Jack's eye and smiled. "Those look new," she said, dropping her eyes to his clean T-shirt, "and nice."

A small bubble of pleasure burst through Jack's state of confusion. He smiled his thanks and retreated to the room off the kitchen.

JACK HIP-CHECKED the door shut behind him, let the rubber boots fall to the floor, dropped Huk-sing's bundle on the dresser and sank down onto the bed. With relief, he let his thoughts spin off into the slipstream of this new turn in events.

Al — in Juneau!? Of course, he'd heard "old" Al talk about his time as a deputy U.S. Marshal in Alaska. But this was ... Well, it was *freaky* was what it was!

I don't think he recognizes me, though.

Well, duh! Of course he doesn't recognize you, moron. He can't. *He hasn't even* met *you yet. In the future, I mean.*

This was going to take some serious getting used to.

And surely this must have something to do with what the Captain had said, the reason why Patsy Ann had brought him back to 1935 in the first place. *But what?*

Then there was Miranda's smile. Maybe she didn't think he was such a total loser after all.

He gave his head a shake and swallowed hard. Then he stood and reached in his pocket for his jackknife. He opened the blade and slid the point under one of the strings securing the bundle of clothes.

With a jolt, Jack recalled that the knife was a gift from *old* Al. Once, it had been the ex-policeman's own. *Does he already have it?* Jack wondered.

But then there'd be two of them and then ...

Some things were just too impossible to even *try* to figure out.

He pulled out a drawer and began to put away his clothes. He thought of his closet full of clothes back home in Brampton — and how often he'd complained to Mom about them not being "right." These drawers looked pretty sparse but at least the clothes in them were clean, they were his and he'd paid for them all himself.

He couldn't help thinking he'd see things differently if he ever got home again. *When!* When *I get home.*

LATER, at the big dining table, Jackson again put *old* Al's tips on working undercover to use: *"Keep it simple. Forget everything and anything you know that's not part of your cover story."* He smiled inwardly as he imagined how old Al would chuckle over the idea that Jack was using them on his own younger self.

Of course, he had to "forget" rather a lot: that this cheerful young guy was going to join the Canadian army to fight Nazis in Europe; that he would come back and join the Royal Canadian Mounted Police; that he would very nearly die when his bush plane crashed in the tundra.

All I know about you, he reminded himself, *is that you're a deputy U.S. Marshal and you had a set-to with a guy on that boat with the funny name, the biologist, Stanley whatsisname.*

It helped that the Captain and the Marshal seemed to be on warm terms. The two were already deep in conversation, the seaman demanding news of places Jack had never heard of but which he figured must be settlements along the Alaska coast ... how things were in Ketchikan, and what the U.S. government was going to do about the Canadians and the fight over who owned some place called Dixon Entrance.

Rose and Miranda helped Mrs. Baker carry food to the table. Tonight it was a big tureen of chicken stew with lots of dumplings, fresh green beans and a steaming basket of her trademark fresh-baked bread.

"And did you read that Alfred Dreyfus died?" the Captain asked the Marshal.

"The actor?" Jack spoke out before he could bite his tongue.

"Who?" Rose screwed up her face.

Oops. And anyway, wasn't that actor a "Richard"? "Sorry, must be somebody else."

"A famous scandal," the Captain addressed himself to Rose. "A French soldier accused of treason. It wasn't true, but he spent years in prison for it. It broke him. Poor fellow finally passed on just the other day."

"A shameful thing. They railroaded that man," Al McMann said hotly, colour rising to his cheeks. "They taught the case in training. That's not a law officer's job — just to put somebody behind bars. We're supposed to serve justice, not prejudice."

Jack spread yellow butter on a piece of bread and bit off a melting bite, but for the first time at Sylvia Baker's table he barely tasted his food. Somehow tonight the overwhelming *weirdness* of everything hung around him like a secret fog, dulling the lively conversation around him. There was Al, *young* Al, right there across the table. Yet the voice wasn't the one he was used to, its edges softened with time. And he could just imagine what this straight-arrow young officer would think if Jack blurted out that they were in fact old friends — *seventy years from now*.

His thoughts drifted and he wondered what Mom was eating tonight. *Probably another takeout Denny's burger.*

A familiar name snapped him back to attention.

"I heard you butting heads with Stan Bayne again this morning," the seaman said.

"I did that," the Marshal replied, laying his fork down with a sigh. "I know he thinks he's doing the right thing. But Juneau's a whaling town and it won't stand to see its livelihood attacked. If he does what he's threatening to do, I'll have no choice but to arrest him."

"What's that?" Jack asked.

"Oh, it's his latest idea. Says he's going to run that boat of his right under the harpoon guns, put himself between the gunners and the whales."

"Some of those fellows, they'd be as happy to put a harpoon into Stanley as into a whale," Sylvia said from the end of the table.

"Then I'd have a manslaughter on my hands," said Al McMann. "I'd like to keep it from getting that far."

"He's already causing trouble, you know." The heat in Miranda's words startled Jack.

"How's that?" Sylvia wondered.

"Why, he's using the radio in that boat of his to send out all kinds of lies!" Miranda said, indignation firing up her blue eyes. "Wrong calls about where the whales are, sending the chasers out in all the wrong directions. Father says he's even tried to send the men onto the shoals."

"If it's true that's a damnable act," the Captain growled.

"And a criminal one."

"Hard one to prove," said the Marshal.

Jack could contain himself no longer. "But you said it yourself, your job isn't to put him in jail. It's to do justice!"

"Justice in service to the law," Al said mildly. "It's a legal hunt."

"But he's got to do *something*!" Jack warmed to his theme. "The whales will disappear if someone doesn't stop the slaughter."

"Oh, that's just him trying to scare people," Miranda scoffed. "There are thousands of whales in the ocean, maybe millions. And it's not a *slaughter*, it's just fishing."

"It's *not* fishing!" Jack protested for the second time that day. "They aren't *fish*. They're mammals: warm-blooded, like humans. They have lungs. They give birth to live babies and feed their children with mother's milk."

Miranda looked taken back but Sylvia cut him off. "That's enough of that kind of talk!" she interjected. "We don't need *biology* over dinner."

"I'm with you, Mrs. Baker," the young marshal agreed. "I'll leave biology to the biologist. And with all respect, Jackson, I don't see the argument at all. Whaling's a lawful activity and as long as it is, my job is to defend it against *un*lawful activities."

Jack subsided into silence but the same questions continued to trouble his mind. *How could* you *end up being the Al I know? Is* nothing *what it was? Or what it will be?*

"Girls, would you bring in the pie and coffee?" Sylvia was

saying now. "There's that 'Manhunter' program on the radio tonight. I'll bet Marshal McMann can give us a commentary."

"If it's like the rest of what's on the air," Al smiled, "I can tell you now it'll be a lot more sensational than anything in real life."

Okay, so maybe some things haven't changed.

ABOUT THE TIME tempers started running high around the boarding house table Patsy Ann made a discreet departure. One hard shove of her nose opened the screen door out of the kitchen.

Thirty minutes later one clear bark outside the Longshoremen's Hall brought Clancy to the door. "Hello, old girl," he said, standing aside to let her pass. "Where've you been keeping yourself?"

The white dog trotted past a group of men drinking from mugs around an upended wooden spool that still had the oily smell of sisal rope. To one side of the potbellied stove she nosed at a thick pile of burlap sacks. With a ladylike lift of her paws she stepped onto it and began scuffing at the rough-woven brown fabric. Her movements carried her in circles around the bed. It took three or four complete circuits before she had it exactly how she wanted it, but finally she dropped down with a thump and a soft sigh.

Clancy bent and put a blue bowl within easy reach. It smelled thick and dark and rich. The black nose snuffed the air.

"Bon appy-teet, madam," he said.

Patsy Ann tipped him a quick lick of approval before he straightened to his feet.

"See your three cents and raise you," a thin, weather-beaten fellow said, tossing four pennies into the center of the table. He wore a soft, shapeless shirt, a green eyeshade and a severe expression. He leveled a piercing look across the table. The big man sitting across from him had a heavy, black-brushed brow that overhung deep-set eyes and an overgrown jaw that gave him the look of some human ancestor. "You do understand, Petrov, that Bayne has as much legal right to spread his views as you have to whale. That's what makes us different from Russia. We call it freedom."

"That's fine, Judge," the big man answered, throwing in a penny of his own. "But he don't have a right to interfere with legal crews."

"If he goes beyond handing out his leaflets, you go find Marshal McMann. Take things into your own hands, and we'll find ourselves together under less agreeable circumstances."

"See you both and take it up another penny," Clancy spun a coin into the growing pile of coppers in the center. "There's right and there's smart. He's playing with fire. The hunt means too much to this town to let it go without a fight."

"The law's the law," a younger fellow, beefy and red-headed, said. "And the law says the hunt's as legal as Sunday service."

"True enough," said the man next to him, a dried-up little fellow. "But law's change, Mike. Wasn't so long ago that women weren't voting in this country."

"And maybe changing that law wasn't such a great idea, neither," Mike grumbled.

"I don't hear you saying so when the missus is around," the little man grinned, poking a sharp elbow into the beefy fellow's side.

A sour-looking fellow in a white shirt that was turning yellow at the cuffs and under the arms, looked for a long time at his cards. He threw them down in disgust. "Think I'll save what I've got left. I want to be able to take some of that payout cash off the boys. Coming in any day now, ain't it, Jerry?"

"Tomorrow or the day after," the huge man with the throwback physique said. His deep voice had a rough sound, as though it were traveling through a meat grinder. "Coming in by floatplane, special courier. Getting radio onto the boats, it's been a real good season." The full, heavy lips broke into a ferocious grin. "Pair of queens."

"Beats me," Clancy growled, showing a pair of fives.

A dry smile spread across the thin man's hatchet face as he turned up three jacks and two tens.

"If I didn't know you better, I'd say that was more than plain ordinary luck," the sour man said.

The Judge just smiled his grim smile and raked in his thirty-seven cents.

Thirteen

SCRAMBLED EGGS

AN EXPLOSION went off in the velvet darkness of sleep. Jack groped for the little button on the alarm clock and the fire-bell racket subsided into ear-ringing silence. He tried to blink sleep out of his eyes.

How can it be so light at four-thirty in the morning?

Still, he wasn't the first one up. As usual, Mrs. Baker was already in the kitchen pulling a pan of golden biscuits out of the oven. Brown nuggets of savory-smelling sausage meat swam in a big pot of creamy gravy on the stove.

Al McMann was up, too, pouring steaming dark liquid from an enamel pot into a thick white mug. He held the pot high and looked at Jack. "Coffee?"

"Uh, sure. Thanks." Mom discouraged coffee back home, but if he was going to be a working man here in the Thirties he might as well enjoy the perks. He pulled the bathroom door closed behind him and began to run cold water into the sink.

Five minutes later Jackson settled into a chair across the big dining table from the Marshal. On the plate in front of him a pair of biscuit islands swam in a sea of sausage gravy. For a moment it felt almost like old times. Well, not exactly *old* times, so much as *oh, seventy years from now.*

Then young Al spoke. "You're pretty young to be working the docks." He made it sound like a question and fixed Jack that *cop* look.

"I can do the work."

"I don't doubt that. You look strong enough. But where's your family?"

Jack swabbed a forkful of biscuit around in gravy. "My Mom's back east. I've never known my dad."

The Marshal nodded as though he understood.

"What about you? You seem pretty young to be a marshal."

Al laughed. "This is my first post. I've wanted to be a lawman ever since I was small. I got hooked on the North reading those Jack London books."

With a flicker of pleasure, Jack flashed on the well-worn volumes in old Al's den. "I've read that one about the dog," he said. *The one you're going to lend me some day.*

"*White Fang,*" the young man grinned. "Yeah. Pretty good, huh?"

By the time Jack slipped his plate and coffee mug into the kitchen sink he was thinking there might be a little more of *old* Al in the young version than he'd reckoned.

On his way to the front door he spotted a light blue sweater among the row of coats and jackets hanging in the hall. Miranda must have slept over again. *What* is *the deal with her?* Jack was growing more and more curious about the blonde girl who spent so much time at the Bakers' house. He thought he might be getting a little crush on her.

Bad idea, dude. He shook his head as he stepped out into the morning. Mist hid the channel from view and muffled sounds. The air smelled of dampness and the forest beyond the fence. *No point getting to like someone from the wrong time zone … the* really *wrong time zone.*

FROM A DISTANCE, Jackson saw Clancy step out of the Longshoremen's Hall. He sprinted the last fifty yards, pulling up just in time to hear his name among the first the stocky crew boss called out.

The chill morning mist had beaded his denim jacket with drops of water and he was grateful to step inside. The corner of the warehouse that served as a combination office and lunch room smelled of wood fire and damp work clothes. For the first time, Jack noticed the bed of burlap sacking tucked between the wall and the potbellied stove.

He noticed it now because it was occupied: Patsy Ann lay fully stretched out on her side, her legs sticking stiffly out in front of her. She whuffled in her sleep, four grimy feet making small kicking movements.

"Rats," smiled Nils. "Chasing 'em in her dreams."

At Clancy's call they followed the rest of the crew out to the wharf.

A ship called the *Imo* was tied up alongside. Stubby masts and a high deckhouse were lost in the white mist. The ship was smaller than the *Tyee King*, but once again he and Nils had to rush to stay ahead of the crew boss' constant cries to "Hurry it up, there." Once again, many of the crates and boxes were destined for "Eric Ericson & Sons."

The mist burned off while they worked. Soon Jack was sweating in the sun's slanting rays. He was grateful when, after several hours of rolling and pushing and lifting and hurrying, Clancy's whistle signaled a late break.

For once, the Benevolent Association's bottomless stew pot was cold. Instead, the crew made off as a group toward town. Roused from her dreams, Patsy Ann trotted at Clancy's heels. Jack joined the rest.

It was a short walk to a place called the Gold Dust Café, one of those eating spots that's friendly rather than fancy. A long counter with stools ran down one side. Booths lined the other. Clancy and some of the older crew settled into the biggest booth in the middle. Jack joined Nils and two more of the younger workers in a smaller booth closer to the door. A few stragglers took places along the counter.

Patsy Ann parked herself in the middle of the floor near one end of the counter. She sat with both back legs off to one side. Her thick white head and upright ears moved restlessly this way and that, small black eyes keeping a close watch on the diners.

Nils ordered coffee and something called a Klondike. "Best in the house," he advised Jack.

Taking his word for it, Jackson ordered the same thing.

A few minutes later a sallow fellow with a narrow chest and a small paunch under a stained apron dropped two oval plates onto the table. On each was a massive sandwich piled thick with ham, cheese and sliced beef. Jack smelled mustard and the distinct sharp scent of sourdough bread.

"Watch this," Nils said with a conspirator's wink. He ripped a corner from his sandwich and waved it idly over his plate.

Jack heard the scrabble of toe nails on the plank floor and turned to look. Patsy Ann was standing now, her back end scooted around so that she faced their booth. Her black nose twitched; her eyes locked intently on the morsel in Nils' hand. The boy smiled a sly smile and kept on waving his piece of sandwich back and forth over the plate, as though he were trying to cool it down.

The dog's dark eyes never left the food, but her plump little body begin to quiver with excitement. Suddenly she gave a sharp bark and the light caught a shower of unladylike saliva as the dog shot across the floor. Now several more diners in adjoining booths and at the counter were surreptitiously cutting the ends off sausages or pushing chunks of fried potato to the sides of their plates with their knives.

An even sharper bark warned that Patsy Ann was losing patience.

Breaking, Nils tossed the piece of sandwich in her direction. It rose like a high fly ball into the air of the diner, the dog's intent, dark eyes never leaving it. With a lunge that lifted her front feet off the floor, Patsy Ann snatched the sandwich out of the air. Her white teeth snapped down with a small grunt and a solid sound like a car door closing.

For the next few minutes she fielded a steady stream of incoming morsels, never missing a one. *I'm beginning to see how come she's so well-fed for a stray dog,* Jack thought.

And why she's so good at fielding fly balls!

Jack had just bitten into the second half of his sandwich when the bell over the café door tinkled. A moment later the buzz of conversation in the café fell silent as completely as though someone had hit a cosmic "mute."

Turning, Jack recognized the sunburned biologist from the confrontation on the docks. In his hand, Stanley Bayne held a sheaf of leaflets.

The biologist seemed to have no interest in a Klondike, or indeed anything else on the Gold Dust's menu. Instead, he began to make his way down the length of the café, dropping a leaflet in front of each person at the counter and one or two more at each booth.

As he moved down the room, the voices picked up again. Only now they carried an angry undercurrent.

When the biologist dropped a sheet of paper between Jack and Nils, Jack was quick to pick up. Bold print across the top declared: "Stop the Whale Hunt Before It's Too Late!" Beneath that several more paragraphs described how biologists like Bayne had searched the Pacific and counted fewer and fewer whales each year. On the back were drawings of several species of whale: the great humpback, the even bigger blue and right whales, and the barrel-nosed sperm whale. Tables beside each one showed how every year, fewer of the big sea mammals were to be found — and predicted that they might soon disappear entirely.

To Jack, it all looked pretty familiar. He'd discovered much the same information online and in the encyclopedia for his essay last term. But as the men in the other booths and along the café counter read the information, their anger grew.

Finally a broad-shouldered fellow slid out from the booth where he'd been sitting with Clancy. In his hand was one of Bayne's leaflets. Planting himself in front of the biologist, he made a show of tearing it into strips. Glaring, he flung the shreds of paper in the biologist's face. "That's what I think of your bull-crap," he snarled.

A hot buzz made it clear that the rest of the café agreed.

"Now get lost," the same man said. "You're not welcome here."

Jack could no longer help himself. "But it's true!" he burst out. "What's in here is right, every word." He got to his own feet, the leaflet held up like a flag in his hand. "It's the whaling that's going to destroy the town, not telling the truth about it."

The longshoreman spun around to face the teenager. "Who's side you on, punk?" he demanded.

A new silence descended. Jack could feel the heat in the room directed at him. But it was too late; his blood was pumping now. "Besides, isn't this 'the land of the free'? He's got a right to say anything he wants and the only one who can ask him to leave is whoever owns this place."

"Then I'm not askin', I'm *telling*!" It was the waiter in the stained apron, his voice from behind the counter almost as belligerent as the longshoreman's. "And you can go with him."

"I don't need you to defend me," Stanley Bayne snapped. "As long as you're working Ericson's cargo you've got as much blood on your hands as anyone."

Eh? Jack took a step backward. *What's that supposed to mean? I'm on* your *side.*

The biologist turned and stalked out of the café, leaving behind a shocked silence in which the little bell over the door tinkled like a badly timed joke.

"And that'll be forty cents before you go," said the man in the apron, stepping between Jack and the door.

Ears and neck burning up, Jackson reached into his jeans. Counting out a quarter, a dime and a nickel, he put the coins into the outstretched hand of the unsmiling café owner and followed the biologist outside.

The strong afternoon sun made him blink. Stanley Bayne was nowhere to be seen. Jack felt his gut knot up. *Ericson's a whaler, too? I've been offloading whaling supplies? Can this get any worse?*

Apparently it could. He heard the door of the Gold Dust slap behind him and then Clancy was there. The crew boss seemed to be channeling his inner pit bull even more than normal.

"Nice going, kid."

"What's he mean, Ericson's a whaler?"

"He's a lot of things," Clancy's voice was dense with barely contained temper. "Manages the Bering and Pacific, has his own company, too. Ericson brings in supplies for all the ships on the coast. But kid, this is a whaling town, and you'd better learn that right quick."

"But Clancy, what if Stanley's *right*? If there's no more whales to kill it won't matter what the town thinks, will it?"

The bullet head cocked and seemed to measure Jack for size. Finally it gave a tight shake. "Son, I'll give you guts, but you'd better start learnin' some smarts, too. The way feelings are in there, I don't want to see you back on the dock today."

Jack felt like someone had just taken a log and driven the end of it into his stomach.

Maybe the sick feeling showed on his face, because when Clancy spoke again, some of the heat had drained from his voice. "Look, kid, you're young. You're new here. You ain't had time to get things square. And you're a good worker. I'd hate to lose you over this." The stocky man seemed lost in thought a moment, then went on. "Change your attitude and I'll give you another chance ... *tomorrow*."

He turned back to the café. As he went inside, he nearly tripped over Patsy Ann coming out.

The dog came up to the boy.

"Not doing so great, am I?" Jack said. "You sure you didn't bring back the wrong guy?"

The black nose nuzzled him high on the leg. Jackson's spirits lifted a little. He reached down to scratch the grimy white neck.

So what now? Clancy's words weighed on his mind. He'd have to decide before tomorrow morning whether to take up his offer to go back to work. Meanwhile, he had the rest of the day ahead of him.

Another "Al-ism" — an *old* Al-ism — came to his rescue: "Do what you *can*. Don't spin your tires over what you *can't*."

"So hey, Patsy Ann, want to take a walk?"

THE SMELL of soap and steam hit him the moment he opened the laundry door. Huk-sing was nowhere to be seen. From somewhere behind the curtain came the strains of music, a sad sounding melody in a style he vaguely associated with old-fashioned movies.

Jackson called out, "Hello?" and the music stopped in mid-bar.

Huk-sing emerged a moment later. In one hand he carried a musical instrument. It was long and black and flared at one end into a horn. Silver keys went up and down its length. The laundryman's face lit up with recognition. "Ah, yes. Made in China!" He seemed to find this very amusing.

Jack collected his washed clothes and paid his bill. It was thirty-five cents. Thanking Huk-sing, he stepped back out onto the street with Patsy Ann at his heels.

The sun had disappeared again behind a blanket of low cloud. Damp veils of cold white fog drifted up from the channel. Jack put his head down and set out for the warmth of the Bakers' house.

He crossed a narrow street and stepped up onto a raised boardwalk. Suddenly the way ahead was barred by three young men, all of them a few years older than himself and rough looking. Two he recognized. They'd been at the Gold Dust earlier.

"Hey, whale-lover," the tallest one taunted.

"You a friend of Stanley's?" the one beside him asked. "Maybe you're looking for trouble, just like him."

"Hey, you know anything about crabs, whale-boy?"

the third wanted to know.

This had Jack puzzled. It must have shown, because the grin on the tall one in the middle got a little wider.

"Thing about crabs," he said, "is crabs'll eat anything. *Anything*, if you get my drift."

"Even whale-lovers," said the second.

"Yeah, they got no discrim'nation at all," drawled the third.

Jack stepped to one side to walk around them. They moved over to block his way. He stepped back in the other direction and they moved again.

If this was going to end in a fight it wouldn't help Jack to have one arm around Huk-sing's neatly tied parcel. He transferred the bundle to his left arm, leaving his right hand free just in case.

"Whuddaya say, you another radical like Stan the *fish-man?*" This time the tall one put out a hand and shoved Jack hard on the shoulder, making him stagger for balance.

A deep growl made all four looked down. The fur along Patsy Ann's neck and back stood up in a stiff ruff. The sound that came from her was one Jack had never heard before, menacing and hungry, like something out of the darkness beyond the firelight of a prehistoric cave. Her ragged pink lips were pulled back, baring sharp teeth. She barked, a ferocious sound that brought the hair up on the back of Jack's own neck.

If it came to a fight, it looked like he wasn't going to stand alone.

The three toughs seemed to rethink their odds. As one, they stepped aside.

"Go on, whale-lover," the tall one said, smirking. "Have a good day ... *today.*"

Patsy Ann was still growling as Jack stepped past them.

"Just remember," he heard from behind him, "you won't always have your little friend with you." Jeering laughter followed them down the street.

JACK FOLLOWED the shore road past the hills of black gravel. Since that first day he'd learned that the stuff was actually coal; the ships they loaded and unloaded used it for fuel, just like old-fashioned steam locomotives. Right now Jack's mood felt as black as the sooty mineral.

I've barely got a job any more. And, if I do, I'm helping to hunt down the whales. Whatever I do, half the town thinks I'm the enemy — and so does that Bayne guy.

"Hi, there!"

The greeting was so bright and cheerful that for a moment Jack thought it must be meant for someone else. But then the same voice called his name: "Jack! Jackson Kyle!"

Turning, he watched Miranda cross the street. In her arms she carried a pair of brown paper sacks.

"Hi," he said. "Whassup?"

"Just fetching some things from the store for Mrs. Baker," she said, giving him a smile from under her pale bangs.

"Can I carry some of that for you?" he asked, extending his free arm.

She tipped her head sideways before saying, "I guess you can." She handed over one of the bags. Together they set out again.

His curiosity was now stronger than ever. "Can I ask you something, Miranda?"

"Sure."

"How come you spend so much time at Rose's?"

She was silent for a long time, so long that Jack began to wonder if he'd bitten down on shoe leather once more. Finally she said: "Well, mostly so I'm not alone all the time. It was Father's idea, because I don't have a mother. At least, she died when I was born. And he's so busy all the time. Father, that is. He has a very important job, so he's not home much."

"I'm sorry about your mom. I know what it's like, having only one parent. With me it's my Mom. Just her and me, I mean, no Dad."

Miranda smiled and for a moment Jack felt less like a klutz.

"What does your dad do?" he asked.

"Oh, he just runs things at his big company," Miranda said, her light tone betrayed by an undercurrent of resentment. "Pays bills, mostly, from what he's always complaining about."

They turned in at the gate, with its climbing vines and cream and pink flowers, and started up the gravel path to the Bakers' front door.

I guess we all get our own problems to live with. Mom pays too much attention to me. Miranda's dad doesn't pay enough attention to her. It's a weird world.

He was juggling the paper sack of groceries so that he could open the door, when something else occurred to him.

"Hey, you know I don't even know your last name."

"It's Ericson," she said softly. "I'm Miranda Ericson."

Jack's right hand jerked. He managed to grab the door in time to let Miranda slip by into the house, but lost his grip on the paper sack. It struck the ground with a crunch.

The door swung shut and Jack just stood there looking down, watching a wet yellow stain soak through torn brown paper.

Fourteen

SUNSHINE & SHADOW

THE TABLE that night was set for four. Marshal McMann was off on his circuit of Alaska Panhandle settlements. Captain Harper was eating aboard.

"Just as well we're a couple of mouths short tonight," Sylvia said, lifting the lid from a platter of scrambled eggs and boiled potatoes.

Rose and Miranda settled themselves in their usual places across from Jack. "Maybe your father hasn't even heard about it," Rose was saying reassuringly, as though carrying on a conversation they had been having.

There was a commotion under the table. Rose flinched and Miranda's eyebrows shot up under her bangs in a warning look.

Everyone, it seemed, had something on his or her mind.

Jackson's thoughts weighed on him. He had offered to pay Sylvia for the broken eggs. She wouldn't hear of it, but he wouldn't be able to pay his board much longer if Clancy fired him for good. On the other hand, if he *did* work, it seemed he'd be helping the whale hunt.

He didn't need to close his eyes to remember the poster hanging at the foot of his bed — *my* real *bed, back in Brampton* — and the fluid, majestic shapes dappled in green and blue light.

There was a chance that Miranda might be beginning to like him, but her dad turned out to be the head whaler. Things were so screwed up that the only person actually fighting to *save* the whales thought he, Jack, was another one of the bad guys.

He wished he could go for a cup of sweet camp "coffee" and talk it over with Al. But his best friend in the world — his *old* world — was barely older than himself and thought it was his job to stand up for the same bad guys slaughtering whales.

And, oh yeah, did I mention that a deaf dog brought me back seventy years to do some job she can't tell me about?

Maybe it *was* only a really, *really*, bad dream after all. He bit down on the inside of his mouth until his eyes watered, but nothing changed.

NOT EVEN a bread pudding, its crust bubbled to a caramel gloss and smelling of toasted sugar, entirely relieved the mood.

When the dishes were cleared, Miranda said that it was probably time for her to head to her own home. She said it without much enthusiasm, brightening just a little when she added: "Patsy Ann can walk me."

The white dog danced eagerly around her knees.

"I can walk with you," Jack volunteered.

"Oh, no!"

Well, you could at least think about it a second.

She must have seen his look. "I mean, thanks anyway, but that ... wouldn't be such a good idea."

"Why not?"

Miranda took a moment to answer, her blue eyes troubled. "If Father's home, you'll be in trouble. And me, too. He doesn't like me spending time with boys."

Especially anti-whaling boys, I bet. He wanted to ask about her father's business, and how she felt about it. But this didn't seem to be the moment to underscore their differences. "Yeah, sure, whatever's cool."

She smiled uncertainly.

"I mean ... Goodnight, then," he tried again.

"Goodnight, then," Miranda smiled back as she shrugged into her light blue cardigan. She followed Patsy Ann out into the late Alaska dusk.

DARKNESS comes very late to Juneau in mid-summer. The sky was a faded blue-gray, bruised with purple. It glowed, casting a soft light that drew the colour out of everything. Still, the light was enough for Miranda and the white dog to see by, as they followed the shore road toward town.

Shreds of mist clung to the mountainside on their left and there was an ashen smell of wood smoke in the still air. Miranda could hear the machinery working in the Empire Gold Mine south of the boat docks.

They passed the long row of sheds belonging to the Bering and Pacific Company, then the glistening black hills of the coal yard. They carried on past dark windows of silent stores and the noisy, bright doors of Juneau's several saloons. They passed the Gastineau and Alaska hotels, whose chefs, otherwise implacable rivals, both kept bowls of leftovers tucked out of the way for Patsy Ann, not that she stopped at either tonight. They skirted a big square building of plain red brick, where the mayor, the police, straitlaced old Judge Burns and the town's lawyers all had offices.

The blonde girl walked quickly in strong, steady strides. Patsy Ann paused here and there to accept a pat and a little something from the hand of a passerby.

As they left downtown behind, the sidewalk began to climb. It soon stopped being a sidewalk at all and turned into a series of steps interrupted by steep ramps. Houses on both sides of the street stood on stilts in front and had back doors that opened onto narrow yards carved out of the hillside.

At one of these, Miranda turned in. Larger than its neighbours, it stood three storeys high on the downhill side. A broad porch gave a sweeping view of the rest of Juneau and far down Gastineau Channel toward Canada and the distant Pacific, both lost in the fading blue light. But its grand windows were dark and the place had a sad and neglected look.

One light burned on the first floor. Miranda's pale face grew pinched. She stepped quietly up stone steps to the broad porch, then almost tiptoed across it to double doors with elegant insets of frosted glass. The big brass doorknob felt cold in her hand as she turned it.

Inside, the wood-paneled hall was dim. A square patch of light glowed on red and gold patterned carpet from a room off to the left. Miranda moved to the right, where the wide hall was in shadow.

Patsy Ann followed close at her heels.

"Girl!"

Miranda froze. Her shoulders slumped. She wondered, sometimes, if her father even remembered her real name, he used it so seldom. Still, the rage in the deep voice tonight startled her.

"In here!"

She turned toward the lit door.

A tall, standing lamp cast a cone of warm yellow light over a man sitting in a deep red leather chair. Eric Ericson's broad shoulders and trim waist gave a powerful impression that made most people overlook the fact that he came up only to the chins of most other men. His shirt collar was open. The light brought up golden notes in his sculpted hair and clipped beard. A book lay in his lap.

He offered no welcome, not even a hello. "What do you know about what happened today at the Gold Dust?"

"Nothing." Miranda had long ago learned how to keep her voice carefully neutral.

"I hear the Baker woman is harboring that young radical."

"Who?"

"Young fellow. Hothead. Working the docks, they tell me, but going around stirring up the same trouble as that quack biologist."

"Lots of people come and go at the Bakers. It's a *boarding* house."

"Don't you smart talk me, girl! The powerful man leaned forward. His eyes were the milky blue of glacier water. They bore into the girl standing before him. "I'd better not find you mixed up in this. We have enough trouble *finding* whales these days without these fanatics trying to turn the town against the fishery."

Miranda's head lifted and she met her father's eyes with a suspicious look. "I thought you said there were lots of whales. Thousands, you said. 'Thick as flies,' you said."

"Don't you contradict me."

And they aren't fish anyway. They're mammals, just like us. Did you know that?"

"Who's filling your head with this rubbish?" Eric Ericson's rumbling voice was approaching a bellow. His handsome face, haloed with golden hair and beard, glowed with anger. "Are you picking this up at the Bakers'?"

"At least they *talk* at suppertime."

His face darkened another tone of red. "Are you stepping around with this troublemaker? I warn you, girl, if that's it I'll have him taken care of in a way he won't soon forget!"

"I don't *know* any *radical*," Miranda cried. "I just know you've been telling me lies. And you don't care anything about me!"

Turning on her heel, Miranda ran from the room. Footsteps drummed on hardwood and a door slammed somewhere upstairs. For the first time Ericson noticed the white dog watching from near the door.

"You!" He leapt to his feet and slammed his book onto the desk. "You mangy, scrounging, waste of a good dog skin, get your stinking flea-bitten hide out of my house!"

The dog turned and ran to the front door. Still raging, Eric Ericson followed her and wrenched the heavy glass-and-wood panel open. "Get out of here!" He aimed a boot to her back end. "Out!"

At the foot of the stone steps the white dog stopped. For a long time, she shook her entire body, from the tip of her black nose to the point of her tail, as though she were trying to shake off the sour, fearful smell that clung to the darkened house.

AFTER MIRANDA left the Bakers' boarding house, the other three drifted into the living room. Sylvia Baker settled into an armchair and picked up a book. Jack dropped onto an overstuffed sofa and began shuffling through the collection of magazines on a low table, looking for something to read.

Rose took a seat in a straight-backed chair that faced a table against the wall. A small wooden cabinet sat there, about the size of an electric toaster placed on end. It had straight sides and a pointed top like an old-fashioned church window. But instead of stained glass, its front surface sported the silhouette of a boy blowing a horn, cut out of the wood and filled in with a cloth screen. Three black knobs and a glass dial no bigger than the knobs were set in a row at the bottom.

Rose reached over and turned one of the knobs. A click sounded and a light came on in the small window but at first nothing else happened.

Then, slowly, several points of orange light began to glow behind the cloth screen. The hiss and crackle of electric static filled the room. Rose twiddled another knob and Jack saw numbers move inside the tiny dial. In a moment, the static faded.

"Calling all adventure fans!" said an announcer. Then: "Here comes Dick Tracy now." The melodramatic voice was lost in the whine of a siren.

Holy cow ... it's TV on the radio! A moment later the announcer returned with a commercial for Puffed Wheat.

There may not have been the dozens of channels he often flicked through at home without finding anything on, but Jack was soon lost in the adventures of someone named "Junior." Junior, it seemed, had been trapped since the last episode in a Yukon cabin by gangsters working for a villain named Vernon Barrow — until a masked rider happened along and snared the bad guys with a lasso. Stretching himself out sideways in the worn comfort of the sofa, Jack closed his eyes but had no trouble following the action.

The episode ended with an invitation to "girls and boys everywhere" to send in cereal box tops to join "Dick Tracy's Secret Service Patrol." Jack thought that was pretty lame but said nothing. Then the program switched to ballroom music.

Jack's thoughts drifted back to the morning.

"Ms. Baker?" he said.

"Mmm?" Sylvia answered, looking up from her book.

"What's Mr. Ericson's connection to the whaling? I thought Ericson and Sons was some kind of store. We're forever unloading rope and clothes and food for them."

"They're outfitters," Sylvia said. "They bring in things that people need for the bush or for working on ships."

"When it's for boats they call it 'chandling' and they're 'chandlers'," Rose revealed.

"There's others, but Ericson's is the biggest because he supplies all the whalers," Sylvia said.

"Co-in-ci-dentally," Rose's sarcasm and raised eyebrows made it clear she didn't think it was such a coincidence at all.

"What? He owns Bering and Pacific, too?" Jack asked.

"Technically, I think he's only a managing partner of the B&P," Sylvia murmured from behind her book.

"Doesn't matter, he's rich enough," Rose said, her indignation plain.

"If that's such a wonderful thing," her mother said in a mild voice, "why do you suppose Miranda would rather spend her days here with us?"

Rose looked like she might say something to that, but then she shut her mouth, picked up a book and began reading.

Jack was left with his thoughts.

Stanley Bayne had accused him of being no better than the whalers. But not everything that came in to the wharf was destined for Ericson and Sons, and it seemed that not everything Ericson received went to hunt whales either. He was beginning to enjoy working as part of the longshore crew. A part of him, he had to say, took pride in the new muscles he was developing. Then there was the definite fact that by tomorrow Mrs. Baker was going to expect another five dollars. He had enough money left for that, but only barely.

Then what?

The announcer brought an imaginary curtain down on the "Starlight Ballroom." Another announcer introduced, "The new adventures of Rin Tin Tin." Instead of a siren, this was accompanied by the sound of a dog barking.

"Rin Tin Tin's all right," Rose spoke up. "But he's nothing like Patsy Ann. He's just a show dog, an actor. Patsy Ann's the real thing."

The real thing.

Jack thought he wasn't sure *what* the stray bull terrier was, exactly, except that for sure she had snatched him from near-death-by-boredom back in Brampton and answered his prayers for more independence and a little adventure. *In spades!* Patsy Ann had brought him here — *here,* to Juneau, to the Bakers, to Captain Harper. She had introduced him to young Al ... *It must all tie together somehow.*

He remembered how one peremptory bark had brought Clancy back from the door of the Longshoremen's Hall that first morning — how her presence had convinced the human pit bull to give Jackson a chance.

A clock struck, a sharp, clear note. Eight more chimes followed. Jackson thought about the harsh ring of the alarm clock and opened his eyes with an effort.

"You'll have to excuse me," he said, suppressing a yawn. "But I've got to get up early in the morning."

Fifteen

MONEY & EXPERIENCE

YESTERDAY'S overcast had gone inland, over the mountains to Canada. Today the early morning sky was piercing blue. As he walked, Jack could smell salt blowing in off the whitecaps out on Gastineau Channel and mud drying in the shoulders of the road.

At the sight of the Longshoremen's Hall in the distance, that old school-test-day knot began to form in his stomach. At the door, one or two of the men waiting there turned their backs toward him. Nils gave him a vague nod and went back to talking to someone else.

Clancy stepped out the door and ran his eye over the men and youths waiting there, hoping to be included in his call. If he noticed Jackson's presence, his manner gave no hint of it. He pulled out his list and began reading names.

"... Tyler, Kirov ..."

Kyle?

"Young, Larsen ..." Nils stepped forward and through the door.

Jackson could feel hope leaking out with each new name Clancy called.

"... Dosantos, Hepler ..." The crew boss stuffed the sheet

of paper into his back pocket and turned away. Only then, almost as an afterthought tossed over his shoulder, did he add, "... And Kyle."

Jack blew out a lungful of relief and stepped through the door before it swung closed.

That day he threw himself into his effort, determined to show that his opinions had nothing to do with his value to the crew. As it turned out, he didn't find his scruples tested anyway. The ship alongside the wharf was the largest he'd yet seen, but most of the crates, barrels and sacks that swung down onto their handcart were on their way to various mining outfits or Juneau's hotels and saloons. Few were addressed to Ericson.

As the day lengthened, his start-of-the-day tension dissolved in sweat and the lingering sting of rough brown rope in his palms. Any doubts about his reception were drowned out by the groan of pulleys, the rattle and shriek of cranes, salty leg-pulling from the other stevedores and the tireless chorus of "Let's move it in there, boys ... Keep it moving now" from Clancy.

That afternoon, when Jackson lined up for seven dollars and fifty cents to be placed in his hand, the crew boss seemed almost friendly.

"Play cards, kid?" he asked, counting out the bills and adding two quarters.

"Cards?"

"Poker. There anything else?"

Poker!?

As it happened, Jackson *had* picked up a little about the game. He and Al often played it, for peanuts — actual peanuts. It was yet another reason Mom didn't like his hanging around with the old northern lawman.

"Some," he answered cautiously.

Clancy chuckled. "Well, if you fancy getting rid of any of that, come on back any time after eight. There's a few of us getting together for a hand or two."

"Thanks," Jack nodded. "I'll think about it."

Before he reached the coal yard, black mineral hills casting cool shadows over the street, he'd thought about it enough.

I think old pit bull just invited me into the club!

SUPPER THAT NIGHT was an even quieter affair than the night before. Rose was there alone. Mr. Ericson had ordered Miranda to spend more of her evenings at home, Rose said; but she refused to say anything more on the subject. Marshal McMann was still away on his circuit. And Captain Harper liked to dine "with the boys at the Red Dog," Sylvia said, before he indulged in a night of cards.

"At the Longshoremen's?" Jack asked casually.

"I believe so," Sylvia gave him a sharp look.

Cool! "I'll see him there, then," Jackson said, spooning a liberal helping of ground beef and mushroom casserole onto his plate.

Sylvia frowned. "Have you ever played poker before?"

"Sure. Al and I play all the time."

Oh, damn. Jack almost bit his tongue for letting the name slip out. *Of course, there are other Als in the world.* "Mostly for peanuts, or matchsticks or whatever." In fact, *only* for that, but he wasn't going to admit it, not with Rose's eyes on him.

"Matchsticks don't count," Sylvia was saying. "This is a real card game with real money and experienced card sharps."

"I'll be careful, Mrs. Baker. And here," Jack said, reaching into his jeans and pulling out the five dollar bills he'd set aside for this purpose. "Here's my rent for another week."

Sylvia took the bills and tucked them into a pocket. "That's smart, Mr. Kyle," she said with a nod. "It's always wise to secure lodging *before* a poker game."

But Jack could have sworn a smile was fighting for face-time beneath her severe look.

She fixed him with a look. "You know what they say about experience and money."

Jack shook his head.

"When a man with experience meets a man with money ... the man with the experience gets the money and the man with the money gets the experience."

Rose giggled.

WHEN JACK ARRIVED at the Longshoreman's Hall, five or six people were settled in chairs around the big upended wooden spool. A black metal teapot hissed on the potbellied stove. The vat that usually sat beside it, sending up mouthwatering aromas of stew or chili, stood bottom-up in a big sink. Between the stove and the rough plank wall,

Patsy Ann snored gently on her bed of sacks.

Clancy was shuffling a deck of cards. He looked up to give Jack a nod. Captain Harper greeted him with a pleased look and pointed to an open chair beside him.

Jack recognized Nils and a beefy, red-faced young man named Mike, but other faces were unfamiliar. Beside Nils sat a sour-faced, middle-aged guy whose name was Clarky. Next to him, a much older fellow wore a soft buckskin shirt and green eyeshade; the Captain introduced him as "Judge Burns." He gave the newcomer a hard look, as though he disapproved of youngsters, or maybe just amateurs, at the table.

Jackson dropped into an empty chair between *DogStar*'s master and the crew boss. *"These are experienced card sharps,"* he heard Sylvia saying, feeling a momentary doubt for the first time.

Clancy handed the shuffled cards to the man in the eyeshade.

"High card deals," the judge said in a voice that sounded like it had been left to dry in the desert for a long, long time. He flipped a card face up in front of everyone at the table: a three, a seven, a five, a black queen, a red jack, a ten and, in front of Jack, the king of hearts. With a dubious look, the judge handed the deck to the boy. "The game is dealer's choice."

Let this be a sign of things to come, Jackson thought, sweeping the dealt cards off the table and riffling the deck another time.

Everyone put a penny in the center of the table.

"Seven card stud," Jack called, in his best poker voice. He dealt two cards face down to each player then one turned up for all to see. "High card bets," he added to the Captain, who gazed reflectively at the jack of spades lying face up before him.

"One cent," the old seaman said, and pushed a copper coin to the center.

Mike added his own cent to the pot and the play moved on to Nils, who raised the stakes by a penny. The sour-looking Clarky made a face and tossed in two coppers.

"Two cents to you, Judge," he said.

"Call," the judge said, tossing in his coins.

Clancy and Jack both did the same to close that round of betting.

Jack dealt each player another card face up. The two of diamonds fell in front of the judge, making a pair with the two of clubs already there. "Deuces high. Your bet, Judge," Jack said.

The Judge shot him another gallows look and threw two pennies into the center. "Two cents to stay," he said to Clancy, sitting to his right.

The crew boss snorted and pitched his hand face down into the center of the table. "No use sending good money after bad," he said.

Jack slid two pennies across the battered wood to the middle of the table. The Captain, Mike, Nils and the sour guy each did the same.

"All stay but one," said Jack, feeling pleased with himself and his art of the deal so far. He skiffed another card across the table to each player still in the game. Now each of them held two cards close to their chest, visible only to themselves, and three more on the table, visible to everyone.

"The Judge is still high man with a pair of twos showing," Jack called out. "Nils is working on a possible flush."

Once again the judge bet two cents.

Jack considered his own hand. The cards on the table in front of him were a queen, a three and an eight, each a different suit; that added up to nothing at all in the way of a poker hand. But his "hole" cards, the ones only he could see, were another queen and a king. With two queens — one hidden, the other face-up — he was still in the game. He matched the judge's two-cent bet and raised him a penny.

The Captain folded and Mike did the same. Nils put three cents into the pot, Clarky threw down his cards with a grimace and the judge tossed another penny onto the table to stay in the hand.

Jack picked up the deck to deal a fourth open card to the remaining players.

As he did, the door of the Longshoremen's Hall banged opened. A man stepped into the room. He was below average height but the shoulders inside his pin-striped suit were broad and powerful-looking. The light glinted on blond strands in his carefully brushed hair and golden beard.

Mike, Nils and the sour-faced Clarky exchanged raised eyebrows. It took Clancy startled moment to gather his wits and greet the new arrival. When he did, he spoke respectfully: "Mr. Ericson, what brings you down here?"

Jackson's hands stopped in the middle of his deal and he

looked again at the new arrival. *Mr. Ericson? Miranda's father?*

Ericson pulled over an empty chair and sat down between the Judge and Clancy. "I'm here to play poker, what else?" he said, spreading a confident smile around the table.

"Deal the cards," the Judge's dry voice spoke. "You can gape all you want when the hand's over."

Reddening, Jack finished the deal, scanned the table and called out: "New high man. Nils bets with two fours."

The young longshoreman bet three cents and the sour man called him, sliding across three pennies of his own.

Jack studied his cards for a while, but his thoughts kept straying to Miranda's father.

"You reading or playing poker?" the dry voice of the Judge asked.

Jack tossed a nickel into the pot and took back two cents. He forced himself to focus. "Last card. Down and dirty," he said, using old Al's favorite closing line for luck.

The deal went around and the four players still in the hand each got a card, face down.

Jack turned up the card he'd dealt himself and struggled to keep his face blank. The card was a queen — making three in his hand altogether. He breathed calmly, the way he'd practiced in Al's kitchen.

"Nils is still high man with two fours," Jack announced, reflecting the cards on the table.

Nils slid two more cents over the table and the judge matched the bet. Jack did the same then bumped the betting up to four cents. One by one the rest of the players at the table matched Jack's wager.

Jackson placed the two queens from his hand beside the one already on the table. "Three ladies," he announced in a smug voice. "Read 'em and weep."

Nils's face wore a disgusted look as he threw his cards down. The man they called the judge leveled a long, thoughtful look at the young dealer from under his eyeshade.

Woohoo! Jack raked the pot into a pile in front of him. *If I can keep this up, I might not have to unload ships anymore.* Did they have still riverboat gamblers in 1935? He restrained an urge to count his winnings. What was that song old Al would sing at moments like this? *"Never count your money when you're sitting at the table, there'll be time enough for counting when the dealing's done."* Yeah, that was it.

"Captain's deal. Ante up, Eric, if you want in," the judge growled.

Ericson reached into his pocket then spilled a fistful of copper and silver onto the table.

"Five card stud," Captain Harper said and began to deal. "One three-card draw."

Miranda's father slid a penny into the middle of the table, ice-blue eyes flicking over to look at Jack. "I heard there was some ruckus at the Gold Dust yesterday," he said.

"Nothin' much to it," Clancy muttered. "Just that Bayne fella peddlin' his flyers. Nobody paid much attention."

Still floating on his winning hand, Jackson didn't even try

to bite back his words. "Maybe they should. Facts are facts. And he's got a right to talk about them, doesn't he, Judge?" *C'mon, give me a little support here.*

Clancy glowered, but Jack detected a difference in the Judge's sharp look this time. *Maybe some respect?*

"It's legal. Doesn't always make it smart." The judge picked up his cards and began to sort them. The backs of his hands looked a lot like old Al's, Jack noticed, darkened by time and weather except where they were sickled with pink scars. "But this is supposed to be a card game not a town meeting," the dry voice added.

The blond man leaned back in his chair and considered the teenager a moment. A knowing smile spread over his face. "You must be that 'Jack' I've heard talk about. I didn't make you to be so young." He glanced briefly at his cards and flicked a nickel into the center of the table. "Trust me, sonny, give it a little time and you'll grow out of these lady-like sensibilities for brute animals."

Jack felt his cheeks redden and was about to say something. Then he caught gray eyes watching him from under the green eyeshade and bit his tongue.

The betting went around. Once again, Erickson threw in a nickel. When his turn came Jack stayed in, more from stubbornness than out of any realistic hope that his lonely ten of clubs might somehow grow into a hand. His reward was a knowing smirk from Eric Ericson when the businessman raked in the pot.

For a guy who didn't play poker much, Miranda's father was either very good or very lucky. He soon owned a sizeable mound of copper and silver that until recently had belonged to other players at the table.

The deal had come back around to Jack when Ericson looked at his wristwatch then pushed back his chair. Not bothering to gather up his winnings, he rose to his feet. "If you'll excuse me just a few minutes gentlemen," he drawled, "I need to go and check on my daughter. Don't lose all your money before I get back." He winked heavily and slipped out the door.

"Take your time, boss," Clancy murmured.

"Do we have to let him play?" Mike asked of no one in particular. "He bets a little rich for my taste."

"Nothing says you have to stay in the game if your wallet's not up it," the judge sniffed. "But he's got too much of my money," he added, a fierce light burning in his gray eyes. "I want a chance to get some of it back. Deal the cards."

Five or six deals went by without a lot of money changing hands before Ericson returned. He dropped back into the empty chair and waited for the others to finish their round. From the pocket of his suit jacket he produced a handful of peanuts and began cracking the shells.

The fire in the pot-bellied stove shifted with a dry crunch and a fresh waft of pungent wood-smoke filled the room.

"Your daughter okay?" Jack asked, hoping the question sounded like ordinary small talk.

The blond man shot him a sharp look. "What? Oh, she's fine. Fine." His attention went back to his cards.

AN HOUR LATER Jack had fresh reason to remember Al's mantra of "never count your money 'til the dealing's done." Worse, only now was he recalling another piece of poker wisdom from his old friend: "Never bet more than you can afford to lose."

"Fold!" he threw down another worthless hand. Reluctantly he picked up the seven pennies still in front of him and slipped them into his pocket. They felt pretty lonely in there.

Eric Ericson cracked another peanut and smirked across a substantial pile of coins. The only other player doing as well as the businessman was the Judge, his eyes impossible to read under his green visor.

Jackson pushed his chair back from the table. He nodded good night and turned toward the door.

"Looks like you'll want to make call tomorrow," Clancy said behind him.

Looks like I don't have much of a choice, Jack thought.

Bright stars burned in a dark sky as he made his way back to the Bakers'.

Sylvia had been right: he'd just traded money for experience. Now if he could only parlay some of that experience back into a winning hand.

Sixteen

BIG BAD NEWS

THE EARLY northern dawn smelled sweet, like honey on pine needles. The sky overhead was baby blue and light yellow, too bright to look at where the sun still hovered behind the black mountain.

Too beautiful a day to waste being bummed. He'd have to remember to put aside a little more than just his board money before accepting another invitation to the Longshoremen's Hall poker club. His fingers found the seven remaining cents in his pocket. *But hey, what a club!* The guy with the eyeshade was an actual *judge*. At least, Jackson was pretty sure he was. And Miranda's dad was a big wheel in Juneau.

In fact, Eric Ericson hadn't seemed at all the person Jack had begun to imagine. Pretty full of himself all right, he sure liked to flaunt his success, sort of like a pint-size Donald Trump. *Yeah, with better hair. Now, there's a joke no one within a million miles, or seventy years, will get!* Jack laughed out loud. But Eric Ericson did seem to care about his daughter: he'd at least bothered to go check on her last night.

With a jolt Jack found himself thinking about Mom. What she thinking right now? How long had he been "missing" back in 2005? ... *Whatever I mean by "now" — then ...* Were people searching for him? Was Mom on TV asking his "abductors" to send him home? Or did everyone just figure he'd run away? "Lured" by one of those Internet creepos. He felt a sudden twinge of guilt for the trouble he must be causing, then gave his head a shake.

Nothing I can do about it now. "Do what you can ..." said old Al's voice.

The boardwalk rang under the heels of his new boots. He drew in a deep breath. The honey and pine scented air flowing down the mountain was mixed here with the sour-bread breath of the saloons. *Ueeeew* ... and real strong barnyard reek.

A sudden whuffle inside a larger creaky, jingling noise drew his attention up the street. A wagon loaded with sacks and boxes was starting to move into the street from in front of Amory's Outfitters. He watched as the man seated in the wagon twitched a whip over two horses straining into their harness. As the wagon pulled out, the reason for the barnyard smell was plain.

Guess 'poop'n'scoop's still got some way to go in 1935. Jackson was still smiling at this thought when Clancy called his name.

Working improved his mood further. The set-to at the Gold Dust seemed to be forgotten and the stew pot was back and bubbling on the Hall stove. (*Thank you, God,* Jack whispered silently when he noticed this. He somehow doubted that even in 1935 just seven cents was going to buy him much of a lunch.)

They were loading today — cube-shaped pallets of "Alaska

King Kanned Salmon" moving in a steady stream from warehouse to waterside. He and Nils barely spoke. They had their moves down to a steady rhythm now, and neither had breath or energy to spare.

Jack could feel the new strength developing in his arms and legs. During his first days at the wharf he had felt worn out by mid-afternoon, aching and gritting his teeth to keep going. Today he was comfortably putting his back into the last load of canned salmon when Clancy came up.

"You two're looking strong today," Clancy said. His bullet head came forward on its thick neck. "Like to earn back some of what you lost last night?"

Nils and Jack exchanged a shrug. "Sure." "I guess."

"Good, we have a second ship." Clancy gave his quick little nod. The pit-bull features broke into an even briefer grin. "Overtime, boys." The smile vanished and he turned down the wharf.

They followed him.

Clancy led them along the wharf past the bow of the ship they had been loading to an unoccupied stretch of dock. A few hundred yards out in the channel, a ship called *Ketchikan Spirit* glided toward them. It was smaller than the freighter they'd been working on earlier, but still several times bigger than *DogStar* or any of the fishing boats down at the marina.

A flash of white drew Jack's eye. Patsy Ann stood under the eave of the warehouse, watching the ship approach.

Clancy stationed himself in the middle of the space the

ship was heading for. He sent Jack and his partner in opposite directions to stand by the edge of the wharf and wait. "Nils on bow line, Jackson on stern."

A moment later a light rope snaked out from the side of the ship and landed in front of Clancy. The crew boss grabbed it up and pulled it in until he had his hands on a much heavier line that ended in a loop. He dropped this over a heavy iron post flared at the top to keep the loop from slipping off again.

Now water boiled beneath the *Ketchikan Spirit*'s stern rail. With the ship's forward movement checked by the rope Clancy had looped over the iron post, the propeller slowly pushed its stern in toward the pier. A moment later another light line flew through the air past Jack. He grabbed it and copied Clancy's actions, hauling it in to retrieve a rope loop thicker than his own wrist. He dropped it over the flared post nearest him.

A narrow wooden bridge, like a giant see-saw built on wheels and with handropes, stood along the wall of the warehouse. They heaved this into line with an opening in the ship's rail and shoved it forward. In moments, sailors had secured the ship end of the gangplank. They stood back to make way for someone in a white officer's cap.

His first words surprised everyone.

"Hey Clancy, d'you have a telephone? We need the Marshal here double quick!"

The *Spirit*'s captain started down the gangplank. Behind him came two men who didn't look anything like sailors.

One wore a flyer's leather jacket and a peaked cap. The other wore a bush jacket and a deeply worried look. Both of them looked like they'd spent the night in the shower and only partly dried out.

They huddled for a moment with the longshoremen's boss, then all four hurried off in the direction of the warehouse and its old crank-handle telephone.

Jack caught only fragments of a tense exchange as they passed him.

"... said a boom broke," leather jacket said. "Told me to drop her down way out in Barlow Cove ..."

"... took it all ... the whole eight hundred thousand ..." the other fellow said. His voice shook.

"... sank the damn plane..." leather-jacket sounded indignant.

IT WAS NOT until much later, after the *Ketchikan Spirit* had been both emptied and reloaded and they were collecting their pay, that Jack got something like the full story out of Clancy.

It seemed that a small floatplane had set out from Fairbanks for Juneau yesterday with only one passenger on board: a courier bringing cash to pay the whaling crews for their season's work. Such planes normally landed in Gastineau Channel near the waterfront. But as this plane neared Juneau last evening, its pilot had received a radio call: this usual landing area was closed.

A log boom had broken free, the caller said. Now logs were floating loose all over the water. It would take days to corral them again. Meanwhile it wasn't safe to land. The pilot would need to put down instead in a quiet bay outside the harbour. B&P would send a boat out to meet the plane and collect the payroll.

But when the plane landed no agent of the Bering and Pacific Fishery Company was in sight. Instead, a masked man in a speedboat leveled a rifle at the pilot and demanded the cash. Before roaring off, the gunman had put bullets through both the plane's floats. The pilot and his passenger had barely time to don lifejackets before the plane went to the bottom.

The pair had spent a night on the water. It was mostly luck that the *Ketchikan Spirit* had come by this morning and spotted them.

It was the biggest news to hit Juneau in ages. But Jack had trouble understanding the account. Beyond Gastineau Channel — the broad stretch of water between Juneau and the mountain out to the west — he had no real idea of the local landscape. This 'Barlow Bay' where the plane was supposed to have set down was a mystery.

Captain Harper surely had a map on board *DogStar* — and probably a thought or two on the whole affair, as well.

Jackson headed for the boat basin.

From the graveled parking lot overlooking the docks he could see *DogStar*'s twin masts, dipping gracefully on the restless water. Next to her was the fast, aggressive profile of Stanley Baynes' boat, the one with the funny name. *Cletis? Seatiss?*

As he started down the gangway toward the docks, he saw someone step off the powerful craft. *Has Stanley heard yet?* The biologist might think it served the whalers right, he reflected.

Once at the bottom, Jack forgot about the biologist as he struggled to stay upright; the floats bobbed and rocked as unpredictably as ever. The only person he passed on his zigzag route to the outermost dock was a very big, heavily built man with an unusual face. His prominent forehead overhung deep-set eyes; his jaw seemed similarly oversized and his hair was dark and coarse. *Looks kind of like a caveman,* Jack thought, trying not to stare as they passed each other on the narrow float.

Jack had his hand on *DogStar*'s railing before he remembered his manners. "Permission to come aboard," he called loudly.

Movement sounded down below and a moment later a face popped out the cabin door.

"Ahoy there, Diamond Jim," Captain Harper said, a smile playing over his grizzled features. "Step aboard then."

Jack winced inwardly but managed a "been there" grin. He gripped the rail and pulled himself up to the deck.

Down in *DogStar*'s cozy saloon the Captain nodded Jack to the settee and put a kettle on the small stove. Settling into his own deep chair he looked over at the boy expectantly. "Well, let's have it then. You're clearly bubbling over with some kind of story."

Jack filled him in on the day's dramatic developments.

"So what do you think," he finished. "You said yourself that everybody knows everybody else's business in Juneau. Who'd do something like this?"

The Captain shook his head and ran a weathered hand over white stubble on his chin. "That's a good question without a good answer. Aye, we have our rough lots, but nothing like a professional criminal class. And a crime like this, it takes some planning, someone with brains."

"It sure couldn't happen to a more deserving guy though," Jack said lightly.

The Captain frowned. "How's that?"

"Maybe the universe is paying Mr. Ericson back for killing whales."

"I doubt the universe takes things quite that personally," the Captain said dryly. "In any case, Eric's money is safe enough in a bank somewhere. That payroll belonged to the people who work for him. There will be a lot of families eating out of empty cupboards now. It's a bad thing for the whole town of Juneau."

Jack remembered his reason for seeking out the *DogStar*'s skipper. "Captain, have you got a map of this Barlow Bay place?"

"You mean a *chart*, lad," the Captain said, getting to his feet. "Aye, of course."

A few minutes later the two of them bent over the table to examine a map — *a chart*, Jack mentally smacked himself — that overflowed the tabletop. Juneau was a cluster of streets beside a needle of blue water in the middle of the chart. Shading and expanses of white indicated that behind the town's dramatic mountain backdrop were still more mountains, cut by deep valleys and capped with massive glaciers. Opposite the town, the mountain that formed the far side of Gastineau Channel turned out to be an island with the shape of a T-bone steak. Beyond that was a maze of blue water — channels leading eventually out to the Pacific Ocean — and more islands in all sizes and shapes, and numbers beyond count. A deep gash in one of the biggest of these was marked Barlow Bay.

"It was a smart choice for dirty work," the Captain was saying. "No one lives there and there's precious little reason for anyone to go there. Not much chance of being caught in the act. Deep, too. They'll never bring that plane back up." He stood a moment lost in reflection. "They're damn lucky the *Spirit* happened along. Could have been just another floatplane lost and never heard from again."

"Like the Bermuda Triangle," Jack mused. "Or Amelia Earhart."

The Captain shot him a sharp look.

A hubbub from outside broke into their thoughts. Heavy footsteps sounded on the wooden float and a loud, familiar voice said, "Keep everyone off this dock. I want this boat secured."

Exchanging a startled look, man and boy put down their mugs as one and headed for the companionway. Jack followed the Captain out onto the deck.

Off to the right a small crowd was gathering at the corner where the *DogStar*'s dock met a wider one leading back toward shore. A large man in a blue police uniform kept the gawking onlookers back.

Two more police officers stood in front of them, their backs turned to *DogStar*. Their attention was focused instead on the sleek powerboat that shared the float with *DogStar* — Stanley Bayne's boat.

A fourth man, wearing bush clothes, bent over the lockers that lined the other boat's open cockpit. Marshal McMann looked up from the locker and for a moment, his eyes met the teenager's. Jack recoiled. The look on his friend's face was like none that he had ever seen before — on either old *or* young Al. It was an expression of absolute concentration and cold calculation — and no sympathy whatsoever.

The marshal turned and ducked inside the powerboat's small cabin. Less than a minute later he came back out. His face was flushed with excitement.

"We got him," Al McMann announced to the police on the dock. "See here." In his fingers he held a slip of paper by one corner. "That's a cash wrapper from the Territorial Bank in Fairbanks. Where was that payroll coming from?"

"The Territorial Bank of Fairbanks," replied the police officer with three gold sergeant's stripes on his uniform.

Satisfaction showed in Al McMann's face. "Right," he said, as if speaking to himself. He took a notebook from his shirt pocket and slipped the torn paper between its pages. Then he slipped the notebook back in his pocket.

The marshal ducked back into the tiny cabin. He was gone longer this time but when he emerged, one hand held a red handkerchief carefully wrapped around the stock of a rifle. He held the gun's breech to his nose and sniffed.

"Yup," he addressed the police officers. "It's been fired recently."

Al handed the rifle up to the sergeant and stepped out onto the dock. "Don't let anyone go aboard," he instructed the junior officer. Then he nodded to the sergeant. "Let's go pick him up."

Together, they strode off toward shore.

Seventeen

STARS, TRUE & FALSE

IT HAD BEEN a long, full day.

The sun had disappeared behind the mountain across the Channel — Douglas Island, according to the Captain's chart — some time ago. It had taken much of the day's warmth with it, although the clear northern sky continued to glow brightly. A moldy smell of dampness was rising through the salt and dead fish stench that always clung to the docks.

The looky-loos on the float had followed Marshal McMann back to shore. There didn't seem much more to see or do here.

"Dinner will be waiting," the Captain said, pulling the door to *DogStar*'s cabin closed.

They dropped to the dock and turned for shore. Looking back Jack saw the remaining police guard plant his wide behind on the narrow deck that ran along the side of Stanley's boat. Scrolled across the back of the boat in gold letters was its name. *Cetus* ... that was it.

It didn't mean anything to Jackson. "What is that, Captain, a 'Cetus'?"

"It's a word in Latin," the Captain said. "It means 'whale'."

"Good name for Stanley's boat then."

"Aye, it is that. But to a seaman or an astronomer, Cetus is more than that."

Jack thought a moment. "A star?" he asked at last.

"A whole constellation, one of the largest. The ancient Greeks thought it was a sea monster. Later on, people claimed it was the whale that swallowed the prophet Jonah from the Bible."

"And spat him back out?"

"Aye, that's the fella. But it's a mysterious constellation, too. It has a star that's sometimes there ... and sometimes not. At least, you can't always see it. It's called Mira."

Jack shot him a look. "Sounds like 'Miranda.' Do you suppose she's named after it?"

The Captain considered this. "Maybe," he said at length. "Eric Ericson wasn't always such a narrow, grasping man — not when his wife was alive. When she died, it seemed as though she'd taken away everything he cared about in life."

Whatever the truth about her name, Miranda was certainly present and visible when they got to the Bakers'. She and Rose had watched the chattering crowd follow the Marshal past the house minutes earlier. Now, they were eager for a firsthand account of the search.

"I heard the Marshal found the gun Stanley used!" Rose burst out.

"And the money," added Miranda.

"Not exactly," Jack protested. "They found *a* rifle. And one of those wrappers the bank puts on bundles of money. But they didn't find any money."

"But why would that Mr. Bayne do such a thing?" Sylvia Baker wondered. "He certainly seemed strong in his views, but I wouldn't have said he was the *criminal* type."

"Looks may deceive, my dear," the Captain said.

"This could be just another way to mess up the whalers," Jack suggested. "Maybe Al ... I mean Marshal McMann, has an idea. Is he here?"

"No, and I don't expect he'll be in 'til late," Sylvia answered. "So let's sit down before dinner gets cold."

Tonight was beef stew with huge carrots, crumbly potatoes and more of Mrs. Baker's killer biscuits. *I'm going to gain a million pounds before I get home,* Jack thought, ladling aromatic gravy in a generous lake over the pillowy islands of hot biscuit.

"If the money wasn't on his boat," Miranda wondered aloud, "then where is it?"

"At his camp maybe," the Captain suggested.

"His camp?" Jack asked.

"On Stephen Channel, out on the far side of Douglas Island," the Captain explained. "His wife stays there most of the time with that new baby of theirs, while he's out chasing after whales."

"And whalers!" Miranda put in.

"I can't think that's much fun for her," Sylvia said with feeling.

"I bet she comes back into town now," said Rose.

"This certainly takes the wind out of his campaign against the hunt," the Captain said. "It won't get far from inside a jail cell."

Jack shot him a sharp look at that. Not even a healthy wedge of rhubarb pie entirely dispelled the sense of disappointment souring his stomach. He had started to hope that Patsy Ann's reason for bringing him here to Juneau had something to do with helping Stanley save the whales. Now it looked like his admiration for the biologist had been misplaced.

The out-of-sorts feeling stayed with Jackson to bedtime. He couldn't even look forward to losing himself in work tomorrow. No ships were due in. The wharf was idle. He wished Patsy Ann were there, if only for the comfort of her solid little body pressed against him through the covers.

The long northern dusk had finally given way to full darkness before Jackson finally fell asleep.

JACK ROSE LATE the next day — although after his early calls of the last few days, that only meant shortly after six o'clock.

Al McMann was already up and at the table. But the young deputy's former friendliness had turned decidedly frosty. Al gave Jack a cool nod and turned his attention back to a bowl of cereal.

Jack spooned brown sugar over his own bowl. The silence ragged on his nerves. He took a deep draft of hot, milky coffee, swallowed hard and spoke up. "So, did you get him? Stanley, I mean?"

Al's face gave nothing away. "Mr. Bayne is in federal custody," he said after a moment.

"You're sure he did it?"

"All the evidence points his way."

"You mean that bank wrapper."

"And the rifle, recently fired," Al ticked points off on his fingers. "His boat fits the pilot's description of the hold-up vessel. It's got a radio transmitter — pretty much the only boat in Juneau that does. And the man doesn't have an alibi."

"But what about motive? Why'd he do it?"

"Eight hundred thousand dollars is a pretty good start."

Jack whistled. That was *still* a ton of money, even in 2005. "But he's a scientist. Isn't he more interested in whales than money?"

"Money buys a lot of pamphlets — or gas for his boat. Plus, this is a hell of a blow to Bering and Pacific. Mr. Ericson's not sure they'll be able to fish at all next season."

"They're *not ...*" Jack began. "... Very good reasons to break the law," he finished.

"Bayne's already broken the law," Al McMann said, his voice hard. "He did that when he started interfering with legal whaling. Sometimes people think they're doing right, but it comes out wrong."

A charge went up Jack's spine. *Where have I heard that before?*

But the deputy only leveled his "cop" look at the teenager across the table. "Maybe you need to give that some thought yourself," he said. Then he picked up his dishes, took them back to the kitchen and left the house.

Jackson finished breakfast in solitude. It was *possible,* he supposed, that Stanley Bayne had let his feelings about the whale hunt go too far. Or that he'd come to believe he could use the whalers' own money against them. It was even possible the biologist was just plain greedy.

But somehow none of that seemed to fit the little he'd seen of the guy. Stanley might want to stop the killing of whales, but if anything he seemed a little *too* stuck on principle. Would he really put *human* lives in danger to save *animal* lives?

And then, what was it Al had just said? "Sometimes people think they're doing right, but it comes out wrong"? Jackson had heard Al say something like that before.

Then he had it.

Hastily he gathered up his dishes and hurried back to the kitchen. He rinsed them fast and left them drying beside the sink. In his room he pulled on his new boots, then headed for the front door.

In the hall he nearly ran straight into Rose and Miranda. The two girls were still rubbing sleep from their eyes.

"Did you see Marshal McMann?" Rose yawned.

"And find anything out?" Miranda asked.

"Yes ... no ... sorry, gotta run," he shouted over his shoulder as he tore out the door.

Grabbing the cream-and-pink flowered gate-post he made a speed turn at the end of the lane, almost colliding again — this time with Patsy Ann. "Hey girl," he burst out. "I think I've got it. I think I know why you came and got me."

The white dog gave him a bark then fell in step as Jackson set off for the boat basin on the double.

Ten minutes later he turned onto the last float, the one

the *DogStar* shared with Stanley Bayne's *Cetus*. A different police officer stood sentry this morning. He stepped out to block Jack's way.

"Get lost kid, this here boat's sealed off," he warned.

"I'm not here for that," Jack said, breathing hard. "I'm here to see Captain Harper."

The police officer eyed the teenager suspiciously, but let him proceed.

"Permission to board," Jackson called, rapping hard on the sailboat's low cabin door.

Eighteen
ON THE CASE

SEATED ONCE AGAIN in the small saloon, Patsy Ann tucked in beside him and his hands wrapped around a mug of sweet, milky tea, Jackson got down to it.

"Captain, I think I know why I'm here."

"Aye?" The gray eyes opened wide with expectation.

"I don't think Stanley did it. I think he's innocent."

"You're sure you're not letting your sympathies run away with you?" It sounded like the Captain was more than ready to believe Stanley Bayne was guilty.

"I'm sure — and what's more, I think I'm here to prove it."

"And what's made you think all this?"

Just something Al's going to say in, oh, seventy years. "Captain," Jack hedged, "you told me yourself I need to be careful how much I talk about my own time. Let's just call it a strong hunch."

The Captain shook his head doubtfully. "It'll take more than a hunch to change the Marshal's mind — and undo the evidence."

"But if he *didn't* do it," Jack insisted, "then there's an innocent explanation for that 'evidence.' And whoever *did* do it, they must have left some evidence too."

"Aye, fair enough. But how are you going to prove it?"

"Old-fashioned detective work," Jack grinned. *Hey, I've seen* Law & Order *and* CSI, *I know how this goes.* "I'll start by talking to anyone who could give Stanley an alibi. Check out the marshal's theory of the crime. Look for alternate suspects."

"That's a tall order."

"I know, but ... There was something Al ... I mean Marshal McMann, said ... it reminded me of something he ... that is, something I've heard before, at home. Captain, if I don't figure out what really happened out there, the wrong man is going to jail."

Captain Harper looked at him long and searchingly. Then the steady gray eyes dropped to the white dog curled beside the boy. Patsy Ann's head lay in Jackson's lap but her small dark eyes were fixed on the old man.

"What do you say, old girl." The Captain tilted his head at the dog. "Is this why you've brought young Jackson all this way?"

It may have been true that Patsy Ann was deaf. But it is also true that after locking eyes with Captain Harper for a long moment, she scrambled to her feet there on *DogStar*'s settee and gave out a solid bark. She barked again, her skimpy tail whipping hard against Jack's shoulder.

The mariner's face cleared. "Well, I'll risk being an old fool but her word's good enough for me. So, what next?"

Jack had to think about this.

"Well," he started slowly, "I guess we need to know more

about the Marshal's theory of the crime. That'll give us an idea where to look for holes in the case against Stanley. That's a start to finding out what *really* happened."

The Captain nodded. "We'll need some cooperation to get to the bottom of this. Folks can guess where you stand. It might be best if they didn't know where I stand, not right away."

Jack ducked his head in agreement. "Besides, if you act as though the case is closed who knows, the guilty party might slip up right in front of you." Didn't that work all the time on those old *Columbo* reruns?

The old man leaned back in his chair, craning to look out a brass porthole. "And maybe I'll start with Officer Mills out there. See if he doesn't warm up to a mug of coffee and a plate of eggs," he grinned, and got to his feet with a heavy wink.

Jack gently pushed Patsy Ann out of his way. "Meanwhile, I'm going to find a newspaper. No point turning down free footwork." That was yet another Al-ism. More than once the old lawman had shared his belief that some reporters were the best detectives he'd ever met.

FIFTEEN MINUTES later Jack strode past the gate with the cream and pink flowers.

The Bakers' door flew open so hard it slapped back against the wall and two figures in skirts shot out of the house and down the gravel path.

"Hey!" Miranda yelled, "Wait up!"

Jack slowed his pace for them to catch up.

"Where've you been?" Rose demanded. "And where're you going?"

"And why the big hurry?" Miranda wanted to know.

Jack hesitated. "Knowledge is power," old Al used to say. "Don't waste it."

Just then a solid body check below the knees made him stagger. "Hey!" he protested, looking down in time to catch Patsy Ann, her head cocked, eyeing him closely. *Was that a nudge?* He reminded himself that the white dog had brought him not just to Juneau, after all, but to Rose's backyard. *Gotta be a reason for that.*

"Okay, I'll tell you," he said. "But for now, you have to keep it to yourselves, got that?"

Both girls nodded fiercely. Rose emphasized her promise by drawing her finger in a cross over her heart.

"Alright then, I've been down at the *DogStar* and," he took a deep breath, "I don't think Stanley did it. I think he's the wrong guy."

Miranda's eyebrows shot up. "Who d'you think *did* do it?"

"That's the trouble," Jack answered shortly. "It doesn't matter *who* anyone *thinks* did it. There's a little thing called evidence."

"What do you call the rifle?" Rose fired back.

"I don't suppose it's the only rifle in Juneau."

"Well then, what about the money wrapper?" Miranda objected. "That's sure not something you see every day and they found it right on his boat!"

"Isn't it pretty strange that he'd hide the money, but leave *one* wrapper on his boat!"

"Okay then, so what are you going to do?" Rose asked.

"Some due diligence," Jackson said, making his voice heavy with implication.

"Some what?"

"I'm going to investigate. Ask questions. Let the evidence tell the story. Like the dudes on CSI."

"On what?"

Whoops.

"It's a show ... a *program* ... back in Canada," he scrambled for cover. "Sort of like Dick Tracy."

"Like Dick Tracy?" Rose piped up. "Swell! Can we help?"

Again Jack hesitated. These two knew Juneau way better than he did. Miranda's dad must have known the plans for bringing the payroll in — and might know who else had the same information. "Yeah," he drawled, "I expect you can. Just let me think about *how*."

They had continued to walk as they talked and now they were getting close to downtown. Jack looked around for the store he'd spotted on his second day, when he'd still been looking for work.

There ... Treadwell's Pharmacy.

He sprinted across the street. The rack near the door still had a few copies of the *Alaska Daily Empire.* He pulled one out and stepped inside to drop a nickel on the counter.

"I see your buddy finally showed his real colours," the man behind the counter smirked.

Jeeesh! I don't even know *this guy!*

"He's not my buddy," Jack said hotly. "But as far as I know he's innocent until someone proves him guilty."

"Yeah, sure," the man guffawed. "Maybe Dutch Shultz did it."

The laughter followed him out of the store.

THE SMELL of food frying drifted out from one of the restaurants and mingled with the iodine-and-salt wind blowing off the channel. They found a bench in the sun near the waterfront and settled on it. Miranda and Rose sat on either side of Jack and leaned in to read.

Big black letters across the top of the front page shouted: "RADIO HEIST!" Other headlines, nearly as bold, read: "RADICAL ARRESTED IN FUTURISTIC ROBBERY" and "MONEY STILL MISSING."

There was a large photograph of Stanley, scowling in handcuffs. There was a statement from Marshal McMann and another from Miranda's father; both were happy that the crime had been quickly solved. A map showed Barlow Bay and the outline of Douglas Island. An "X" marked the "Suspect's Camp." Police had searched there for the stolen payroll but come up empty-handed.

One story described the biologist's anti-whaling activities, with pictures of the pamphlet he had been passing around town. Another offered a lot of inventive ideas about where he might have hidden the money. But even after reading every article twice, Jack couldn't find much upon which to begin building a case for Stanley's innocence.

The pilot and bank courier had identified *Cetus* as the boat the robber had used. A search of Stanley's boat — only the stories mostly called it "the radical scientist's" boat — had turned up proof the money had been on the boat along with a rifle matching the one the robber had used.

Stanley's alibi was thin as air. He claimed he'd been out on his boat two evenings ago, "monitoring the whale hunt" in Lynn Canal. But the biologist admitted he was alone, and Lynn Canal was right at the end of Barlow Bay. In any case, both places were miles west of Juneau. Dozens of witnesses swore they'd seen the B&P's whaling ship tie up in Juneau that very same afternoon.

"See," Miranda pointed out, "he couldn't have been watching the whaling, 'cause there wasn't any whaling to watch!"

"Still think he didn't do it?" Rose asked.

"Nothing here proves it *was* him," Jack insisted. "Only that it *could* have been."

Motor noise interrupted him.

A boat was coming in to the wharf. It was about the size of *Cetus* but was closer in style to a fishing boat, built more for sturdy utility than speed. While they watched, its skipper tucked it neatly under the tarred timbers. A boy jumped ashore with a rope in his hand and a moment later the boat bobbed gently alongside.

A woman in trousers and bush jacket clambered awkwardly onto the wharf. When she straightened, they could see that the bundle she held close with both arms sheltered a small baby. She looked up and down the wharf distractedly while the man in the boat heaved suitcases, bundles, baskets and small cases with handles on them up to the boy.

When the last bundle was on the dock, the boy undid the ropes and jumped back into the boat. A moment later, it was away across the channel, its wake slapping against the timber wharf. Caught by the wind, a cold shower of sea water surprised the woman from behind. She clutched the baby tighter to her chest.

"Hey," Rose burst out. "That's Vera Bayne — Mrs. Stanley! She must have come in from the camp."

"Really?" Jack said with sudden interest. "You know," he added after a beat, "it looks to me like the lady could use a hand."

Leaving the newspaper on the bench he stepped across the wharf towards the woman. Rose and Miranda followed.

"Hi there, my name's Jackson," he said. "I'm a big fan of your husband's work."

Vera Bayne was thin and pale. Her brown eyes were rimmed in red and her tawny hair needed a wash. She met Jack's enthusiasm uncertainly, but pulled one arm free from the bundle of blankets to shake hands with the boy.

"Can we help you with your things?"

Vera Bayne looked over his shoulder at the two girls, then back at Jack, then over at the pile of boxes and suitcases and bags.

"Why, yes, thank you," she said. "That would be very nice." Her voice sounded even more worn out than the rest of her looked. "I need to get all this over to the Alaska."

Eh? We're already in Alaska.

"The hotel?" Rose rescued him.

Vera nodded.

"Right," Jack said firmly, and reached for the two biggest suitcases.

Between them the other two managed to gather up everything else except for a basket of baby things. Vera freed one arm long enough to hook it through the wicker handle, and they set off.

"This is all such a shock," she said as they walked. "They say Stanley took all that money, but I don't think we even have enough to pay his bail."

"They're saying Stanley was out in Lynn Canal yesterday," Jack prompted.

"I suppose. I know he heard something on the radio about lunchtime and went off in the boat. I'm not sure when he got home. It was just the baby and me and we go to bed early." She gave him a wan smile. "I'm not getting much sleep through the nights."

Jack thought a moment. Then he asked, "Do you know if he'd used his rifle lately?"

"A few days ago. There was a bear. He fired a couple of shots just to scare it away. He'd never actually shoot one unless he had to. He says they're next to go, after the whales."

Up ahead, two pairs of deep bay windows jutted out over the street. A sign hanging over the boardwalk read "Alaska Hotel."

They had almost reached the door when they heard running footsteps. Two men in hats and suit jackets appeared. One carried a square object the size of a breadbox with a lens and a silver bowl stuck on top, rim forward.

"Mrs. Bayne! Mrs. Bayne," the other one called out, pulling a notebook free. "Allen Willoughby, the *Daily Empire*. Why'd your husband do it, ma'am? Can you tell us what he was thinking?"

For a moment Vera Bayne looked just like the proverbial deer in the headlights. Suddenly there was a brilliant flash that left Jack blinking.

"But he didn't," Vera was saying. "He didn't do anything at all."

"Oh, c'mon Mrs. Bayne," the other one persisted. "What about the rifle?"

A piercing wail erupted from the bundle of blankets.

"Please," Vera Bayne pleaded. "You'll have to excuse me, it's his feeding time." She ducked into the small hotel lobby.

Jack and the girls followed with her luggage.

Nineteen

STATIC INTERFERENCE

BY THE TIME Rose, Miranda and Jack came back out to the street, the newspapermen had vanished. Jack called a quick huddle.

"The way I see it," he said in a low voice, "two things are key. One is that radio call to the plane. We know Stanley *could* have made it. But if he *didn't*, then someone else *did*. The other is what the pilot and courier are saying about the boat: that it was *Cetus* for sure. We need to find those two and talk to them."

"They were working for Father," Miranda spoke up. "He'll know where they are. Let me see what I can find out."

"Be careful," Rose cautioned her friend. "You know what he's like."

Miranda flashed an off-kilter smile, then headed off.

"What about us?" Rose flashed a bring-it-on grin.

"I think I'm going to have a chat with the only radio man I know in Juneau," he answered. "Want to come along?"

They headed off along the shore road.

As they neared the first of the warehouses that housed the Bering and Pacific Company, a powerful figure stepped around the corner of the nearest building. With a start, Jack recognized the caveman he'd seen the day before on the boat docks.

To his surprise, Rose greeted the man by name: "Hi, Captain Petrov."

"Miss Baker." The man raised his hand to touch the peak of his cap.

Wow, it's true then. Everyone here does *know everyone else.*

"Who's that?" Jackson asked as soon as the big man was out of earshot.

"Jerry Petrov? He's captain of the *Bering Harvester,*" Rose said. "That's B&P's biggest ship."

Jack nearly tripped over his own feet at that. *What was the captain of the whalers doing down on the boat docks yesterday?*

"Rose," he had a sudden inspiration, "you know pretty much everyone in Juneau."

"Not *every*one."

"Well, near enough. Do you think you could find a way to talk to Stanley himself?"

Rose screwed up her face in thought a moment. Then she said, "Mayyybe. Sometimes Ma sends a pie down to the jail, when the hotel doesn't want all she's baked."

"How much does a pie cost?" Jack dug into his pocket.

"Forty cents."

Jack counted out a quarter, nickel and a dime from yesterday's pay. "Here, let me buy one from her. Take it to the jail. See what you can do. Here's what I want to know ..."

FIVE MINUTES LATER, Jack knocked lightly on the door of Pontch's radio shack.

"C'min der," a deep voice rumbled from within.

The large man swung around in his chair. His face broke into a broad grin at the sight of Jack.

"Why, how you doing, you? You find work? Look like you keepin' fed." A huge laugh filled the small room.

"Yeah, that's for sure," Jack said, patting himself on his stomach. "And hey, thanks for your help. I'm working on the docks, like you suggested." He dropped into the only other chair in the place.

"Dat's good." The dark eyes twinkled. "But mebbe you still got room for some of ol' Pontch's special Cajun treats, you t'ink?" He popped the lid from his tin can and held it out.

"Don't mind if I do," said Jack. "Thanks." He pulled a generous fistful of nuts from the tin and cracked one open. A rich, mysterious smell of wood smoke and fiery spices filled the small room. The aroma tugged obscurely at Jack's memory. *I've smelled these somewhere else,* he thought, *but where?*

No connection came to him. Instead, he cleared the peanut crumbs from his throat with a cough and got to the reason for his visit. "Actually, I was hoping I could ask you a few questions?"

"Mais b'en sur. You doan' need no permission to ax ol' Pontch no question. You better ax 'em fast, though. I got to be down to the Red Dog pretty quick." He glanced up at a large clock on the shack wall.

Jack leaned forward in his chair. "Pontch, all this stuff here," he nodded at the panels of dials and knobs, "it's a radio transmitter, right?"

"Dat's right."

"You said before there's not much work for a radio man in Juneau. Aren't there any other transmitters in town?"

"Well, 'course there's a few." The big Cajun thought a moment. "The army base up north of town, and the airfield, they got one or two. We got the station on the *'Arvester*. Dat's the one I mos'ly talk wit'."

"The *Bering Harvester*? Captain Petrov's ship?"

"Oui. And of course d'ere's d'new radio station, dat KINY. It's got one."

Jack cracked another nut and thought about this. "Do they all work on the same frequency?"

"Mais non! The radio station, she only works where she be set. Otherwise no one in town know where to look for it, they want to catch that Jack Benny fella," he chuckled. "He some funny fella that Jack Benny!

"Now me and the *'Arvester*, we can use a bunch o' diff'rent wavelengt'. It just depend what we decide. Sometime we moves around, jus' so 'dem other ships *doan'* know where to find us." He gave a conspiratorial wink. "It d'same wit' the airport. Dey can use a bunch'a wavelengt' too, same as us."

"The same ones?" Jack leaned forward. *This could be important.*

"No, no. D'ey got dere's, we got ours."

Damn.

"Equipment, she pretty much d'same. But d'law give us all our own wavelengt'. I use someone else's airwave, I break d'law."

Jack's pulse raced. This sounded like a lead. "So let me get this straight, if you *wanted* to send a signal on the airplane frequency, you *could*?"

"Why sho'," the big man nodded. "Only like I say, I doan'. Doan' want to lose my license, me." He looked up at the big clock again. "You got mo' you want to know? I got to be goin' soon. Tony and Huk-sing be waitin'."

Huk-sing?

"Just this," Jack tried to get this out right. "Were you working a couple nights ago, about nine, nine-thirty?"

The big man laughed his deep laugh. "B'en oui, I be workin' mon ami. But not 'ere."

Eh?

"I be where I s'posed to be right now, down d'*Chien rouge*." Pontch heaved his bulk out of his chair and reached into a corner. When he turned back he had a battered leather case in his hand. It was round at one end and flared out at the other like the mouthpiece of a horn.

Pontch laughed again at Jack's evident confusion. "Dat be d'Red Dog to you, mebbe. Tony, Huk-sing and me be dere playin' dat good ol' Dixieland. Two night ago, las' night. Ever' night dis week."

Jack followed him out in stunned silence. *Huk-sing plays Dixie music? Go figure.*

He waited while Pontch pulled a ring of keys from his pocket and inserted one into the radio shack's door.

"Do you always lock up when you leave?" Jack asked.

"Tighter dan a drum," Pontch answered solemnly.

"And you're *sure* you locked up two nights ago?"

Pontch looked insulted. "I'm goan' preten' you din't ask me dat question."

"Sorry," Jack said quickly. "I just need to check, that's all. Can you tell me, who else has keys to this place?"

Pontch thought a moment. "Only other key I know 'bout be in d'office. But it be in d'safe, all lock' up safe an' soun'." The moon face had darkened into suspicion. "But why you be askin' me all dese questions? You t'ink somebody come in here when Pontch not be on d'job?"

"I don't know. Yet."

Jackson thanked the big man for his help and watched him set off toward town, instrument case at his side.

FIFTEEN MINUTES later Jack settled himself on the bench by the wharf once more, a new notebook on one knee. He used his knife to put a point on an equally new pencil and began making notes. "Record everything," Al — *old* Al — always said. "You never know what's going to mean something later on."

He was still there when Miranda found him, adding the last few things he'd learned from the Cajun radio operator to his notes.

"Where have you been?" she asked. "I've been looking all over town for you!" Her face was flushed and she looked excited.

"What's up?" Jack asked. "Got a lead?"

"I found the pilot and the bank courier. They're at the Gastineau Hotel and they'll talk to you!"

"Way to go!" Jack raised his hand to give her a high five.

He was startled when Miranda stepped away from him in fright. *Ohmigosh, she thinks I'm going to hit her!* With a sickening adjustment he wondered if Miranda's father did just that.

"Hey, I wasn't going to hurt you," he said quickly. "I just wanted to high-five."

"High *what*?" She moved cautiously closer again. "Is that some Canadian thing?"

Not hardly, he almost laughed. *But maybe they don't do it yet.* "Right, exactly. Here, I'll show you. Put your hand up ..." He clapped his palm on hers. "It means 'good going'!" he explained.

"That's swell!" For a brief moment the pale face lit up with pleasure. "But come on, I'll take you to the Gastineau."

The hotel was clearly a step up from the Alaska. Its lobby was floored with marble and the art on the walls looked like real paintings.

I wonder how these guys can afford to stay here?

Miranda must have read his mind, or maybe his face. "Father's paying for them to stay here until they can testify," she said as they stepped into an elevator.

Now why on earth would he do that? The brass cage rattled and began to glide upward.

The bush pilot and bank courier had rooms next to each other on the third floor. They found the men together, drinking coffee and playing cribbage in the pilot's room. Once Miranda explained that Jack was "helping Father sort things out," they willingly answered his questions.

Unfortunately, little they had to say helped Stanley Bayne.

The small floatplane had been flying only a few hundred feet in the air, following landmarks along the coast toward Juneau. "No problem for him to see us coming," the pilot said.

The decoy call was clearly meant for them. The voice on the radio had said it was the "Bering and Pacific base," calling the "Bering and Pacific charter flight, shortly after nine p.m." No mention of money, just the phony story about the harbour being covered in loose logs.

They couldn't say much about the man behind the gun. He was tall, dressed in the same khaki trousers and flannel shirt that most men wore for the bush and had a knit cap pulled down over his face, with holes cut out for his eyes.

"Son'uv'a B was pretty serious though," the courier said, colour rising in his face and his voice angry. "I thought we were goners for sure when he fired at us. Didn't realize right away that he was shooting out the floats."

"We could have been goners, too," the pilot added with feeling. "Just lucky that ship came along."

But they were positive about the boat. "The Marshal took us down to see that, whatsitsname? *Cetus*?" the pilot said. "It's the boat that robbed us. I'd swear to it on my mother's grave."

"You saw its name?" Jack asked.

Both men shook their heads. "Nope, he had it covered over," the courier said. "But that was her alright."

"Or her spittin' twin," agreed the pilot.

"Thanks for your help," Jack said at last, rising to leave. "If I have any more questions, can I find you here?"

"Here," the pilot grinned. "Or downstairs. Working on your dad's expense account, miss." He gave Miranda a sly smile.

ON THE WAY back down in the elevator Jack searched for cracks in the two men's accounts. There wasn't much.

It was funny though: Why *did* the man with the rifle leave the pilot and the courier alive to describe the robbery?

"Think, Miranda, think hard," he said. "Are there any other boats anywhere on this coast that look anything like *Cetus*?"

"I don't need to think hard at all," she answered lightly. "There used to be lots of chase boats just like that one. They're just not used anymore."

"Chase boats? What are chase boats?"

Miranda gave him a "duh" look. "For chasing whales, silly."

The elevator banged to a stop at the lobby. Jack's stomach felt a different kind of jolt.

Twenty
SHELL GAMES

JACK AND MIRANDA stepped out into the street and blinked in the sudden rays of the late afternoon sun. The far side of the street was bathed in shadow. The smells of warm tar and food frying drifted in the still air.

A pang in Jackson's gut reminded him that he'd eaten nothing since breakfast apart from a handful of spiced peanuts. "You coming back to the Bakers' for supper?" he asked the blonde girl.

She made a face. "I better go home. Father thinks I'm spending too much time there. Especially now."

Now that there's a radical, whale-loving boy *there, I bet.*

But he only nodded. "Right." He looked up and down the street, avoiding eyes that were the same colour as the pale sky over the street. "Listen ... I'm working tomorrow. Maybe I'll see you later?"

"Sure," the blue eyes lit up over a quick smile and Miranda turned away.

Jackson watched for a moment as she walked away, her back straight and step confident. Then he turned in the other direction and began walking.

As he walked he turned over what he'd learned so far.

It wasn't much. Vera Bayne could give her husband no alibi. There were several places where the phony radio warning could have been sent. And the pilot and courier were sure they had seen the biologist's powerboat.

No matter how he rearranged the pieced, they still added up to "means, motive and opportunity" for Stanley Bayne. *No wonder Al thinks it's him.*

He heard his name and turned. Rose was running to catch up to him, red pigtails whipping back and forth, her face flushed.

"Hey!" he greeted her.

"They let me in," she grinned.

It took him a moment. He had been deep in his thoughts. *Oh yeah ... the jail.* "Cool! You get anything?"

"I had to give Billy a slice to make sure there wasn't a file in it."

"Say what? Billy?"

Rose rolled her lively green eyes. "The guard! Slice of *the pie*, silly. It was *your* idea. Anyway, after he ate it he let me talk to Stanley."

But Stanley's story added nothing new. The day of the robbery he had been listening to the whalers' radio frequency. He did this often: if he overheard where they were hunting whales, he explained, he could go out in his boat to observe them at work and maybe disrupt them before any whales died. A little after noon, the *Bering Harvester* radioed that a lookout had spied whales in Lynn Canal. Stanley insisted that he had spent the whole day looking up and down Lynn

Canal in vain for the whalers. He hadn't gotten back to the campsite on Douglas Island until nearly dark, after ten that evening.

"I don't know," Rose concluded with a heavy shrug. "Maybe it *was* him, after all."

"Then where's the money?"

"He went home to the camp from Barlow Bay, then he came here to Juneau ... he had to go right around Douglas Island. It could be hidden anywhere — it's a big island. Maybe he *sank* it!"

But now Jack remembered the one question he'd asked Rose to ask Stanley. "So what time, exactly, did he get to Juneau, the day after the robbery?"

"First thing in the morning, he says, about nine o'clock. He says he went to the library and then to the Post Office to send some kind of report to ..." Rose groped for the name, "the ... Inter-something Whale something-or-other."

"The International Whaling Commission?"

"Yeah, that," Rose said, surprised. "Are you *sure* you're not another activist?"

"Promise. I just studied it for school, that's all."

"Hmmmph," Rose accepted this with a skeptical look. "All we get is long division and who won the Battle of Gettysburg."

They were nearly to the Bakers' gate now. Ahead of them a trim figure in a blue nautical cap approached from the direction of the boat basin. The Captain came up to them as they waited in the balloon of fragrance exhaled by the cream and pink flowers.

Captain Harper confirmed at least one part of Stanley's account. "Aye, *Cetus* came in just after nine. I stepped out to take a line. Stanley rushed right off, said he had to go use the public typewriter at the library."

"Did he come back?" Jack asked.

"To the dock? Not that I saw."

The Captain waved Rose ahead of him up the gravel path to the door. Jack followed them, deep in thought. It had been well past four o'clock by the time he'd carried the news of the robbery to *DogStar*'s skipper. *If Stanley was at the library all that time ... who was it I saw getting off* Cetus*? And why was he* on *the boat to begin with?*

SYLVIA BAKER had prepared a deep-dish pie for dinner. When everyone was settled — the Marshal seated beside Rose across the table from Jack and the Captain — she pierced the buttery pastry crust. A creamy, peppery aroma filled the room. Jack's empty stomach grumbled loudly.

"Since it sounds like you need it the most," Sylvia said with a smile and a wink, handing Jackson the first bowl of flaky pink salmon swimming among fresh green peas in thick white gravy.

But with only one subject on everyone's mind, conversation was oddly subdued.

Jack did manage to slip one question in.

"Marshal ..." he began cautiously. It felt odd to call Al that, especially now he was hardly much older than Jack himself. But that was how everyone here seemed to address him and, as *old* Al said, "When in Rome, don't talk like a Newfie." "Marshal, where'd you find Stanley Bayne yesterday? I mean, when you arrested him."

Al seemed to measure his words. "He was coming out of the Post Office. That's all I should say. The investigation's still under way."

Later that night Jack set the alarm for four-thirty and tried to fall asleep quickly. Sleep resisted him for a long time, however. Instead, he lay staring at the ceiling in the strangely bright mid-summer Alaskan night and tried to "listen to the evidence."

No matter how hard he listened, though, everything he knew so far about Stanley and the circumstances of the crime kept saying "guilty."

ONCE AGAIN the young marshal was up first. Jack carried a plate of scrambled eggs and hotcakes into the dining room to find Al already there, a mug half-full of coffee and an empty plate in front of him.

As it turned out, Al was up and waiting for Jackson. "I wanted a couple minutes with you."

"Oh yeah?" Jack swigged some hot, milky coffee. *Wake up, brain!*

"You say you're from Canada?" For the first time, Jack noticed a notebook lying beside the deputy marshal's plate.

"Yeah. Brampton, near Toronto in Ontario." He watched as Al made a note.

"You have any involvement there in the anti-whaling cause? Or any other political movements?"

This was a tricky one. He raised his eyes and caught *that* look, the one it was almost impossible to lie to. Jackson *had* signed petitions against whaling. He'd even sent some allowance money to Greenpeace once. *But that's "then" ... No way can he ever know that.* "No ... Not 'til now anyway. No."

Al's eyes narrowed a little. He made another note. "How long have you known Stanley Bayne?"

"I *don't* know him. I never saw him before ..." Jack counted back the days in his head, "... Monday! The day you were down at the docks. I was visiting *DogStar* and you were arguing."

"*He* was arguing," Al said. "I was doing my job." He wrote in his book. "And you've never been involved in any way with his movement?"

"What do you mean, 'involved'? I think he's right, that's all. About the whales, at least. Is that a crime?" *Oh jeez. Coffee must be kicking in.*

The Marshal leveled a stony look at him. "And can you tell me where you were two evenings ago, between eight and, say, about nine-thirty?"

Howzat? "Me? You think I ..."

"I think Bayne had help. He's got a pretty short list of friends in this town."

"Playing cards. With Captain Harper. And a judge!" Jack hoped this was true. The guy in the eyeshade sure hadn't looked much like any judge he'd ever seen on TV.

Another note went into Al's book. "You can be sure I'll check that out." The deputy marshal put away his notebook, stood up and collected his breakfast dishes. "In the meantime, don't try slipping back into Canada." With a shock, Jackson registered for the first time how much taller and broader-shouldered *young* Al was than his older self.

He cut a piece of hotcake and brought it to his mouth. *Like I know how to get back home.*

THE WARNING still rang in Jack's blood forty minutes later as he joined the other youths and older men waiting outside the Longshoremen's Hall. It stung to have Al, even *young* Al, think he might be thief. He was grateful to hear his name called.

The morning was cool and the wide, scarred timbers of the wharf were damp with dew. It took Jack a moment to register that the timbers rising up from the far side of the wharf belonged to a ship. He was more startled to see, rising above the ship's wooden sides, four tall wooden masts. Angled against each were wooden poles bundled in dirty gray canvas. *Holy cow, it's a sailing ship. And whew ...* A strong smell of earth and decay and captive water, like the breath of a closed cellar, blew from the ship's open holds onto the wharf.

"Heads up there!" Clancy barked from down the dock. Chains rattled and wooden booms creaked aboard the old ship. A rope tightened and a moment later a rope net the size of a

Volkswagen Beetle and bulging with brown sacks lifted into view. When the load rested on the wharf the net was released, spilling sacks in an untidy heap.

The coarse fabric sacks were heavy — each one hundred pounds, with red-stenciled letters that said, "Finest State of Idaho Potatoes." It took both Jack and Nils, each grabbing an end, to move one. Jack lost count of how many they slung between them into a stack on their dolly, rolled into the warehouse and added to a growing potato-sack mountain before racing back for more. All to Clancy's tireless encouragement to "Get it on in there! Keep it moving now!"

By the time the crew boss called a break Jack had pushed the morning's conversation well to the back of his mind. Gratefully, he dropped onto a chair and spooned deeply into a bowl of what he'd come to think of as "longshore stew."

Not until a good half of the stew was inside him did Jackson notice much else. Then it was a persistent, almost frantic, scrabbling from somewhere down near his feet. He looked down and burst into laughter.

Patsy Ann's head and shoulders were pushed through the wooden rungs of a chair as she strove to reach something underneath the lower rim of the big spool table. It sat like a yoke across her wide withers as she pushed forward with single-minded focus. Pawing at the table rim, she barked with mounting annoyance.

As he looked on, Patsy Ann turned her head sideways and gave another push. With a crash the chair fell on its side, taking the dog with it. Barking madly, Patsy Ann wriggled and pawed the air in an unsuccessful effort to get back to her feet. The chair banged and thrashed wildly over the floor. Even Clancy was laughing now.

Jack's eyes were streaming as he put down his bowl. "Hey, Patsy Ann, let me help you," he said, gently pulling the chair free from the writhing dog. With a skattle of claws on the plank floor, Patsy Ann gave herself a thorough nose-to-tail shake, as though that might restore her dignity.

Jack knelt down and lowered his head almost to the floor. "You goof," he laughed at the white head butting impatiently at his shoulder. Stuck between the floor and bottom of the spool were four or five peanut shells. "It's only shells."

He stuck a finger under the table and pulled one out. Or maybe not so *only*. The shell was an unusual colour. A few grains of reddish dust clung to it. He held it to his nose: it had a strong smoky, spicy smell.

He pulled out two or three more empty husks and examined them in his hand.

"Does Pontch play poker with you guys much?" he asked Clancy.

"Old Pontchartain? The radio man over at B&P?" the crew boss said. "Nope. Never. Won't. Says he likes it 'too much,' whatever that means."

Really! Well, *someone* had been in Pontch's radio room and here at this table. Jack tried to replay the night of the poker game. *Someone* there, he felt sure, had been popping peanuts into his mouth. But who?

The door opened and a newspaper hit the floor. Clancy

picked it up, pulled off the front section and tossed the rest on the table.

Jack found a page of grocery ads and pulled it free. He wrapped the shells in the newspaper and shoved them in his pocket. Save everything, old Al always said. "If it turns out later you don't need it, you can always throw it out. But you can't do it the other way around."

He looked up and met Clancy's eyes studying him coldly over the top of the newspaper. Clancy was no longer laughing. The crew boss cracked the paper in his hands. "Says the law don't think Stanley could of did it himself," he said. "They're lookin' for a second man." He turned the front page toward Jack.

Oh ... my ... God! There, right under the words *"Alaska Daily Empire,"* was a big picture of Vera Bayne. Right beside her, arms loaded with suitcases, was Jackson. Next to the picture large capital letters shouted: "POLICE SEEK SECOND SUSPECT." The excellent stew seemed to turn to ice and stone in Jackson's stomach.

"I'm thinking maybe you better take a few more days off," Clancy growled.

"But I didn't do anything!" Jack felt his temperature rising. "How could I? I was right here ... playing cards ... with *you!*"

But Clancy's mind was made up. "Always got some answer, don't you? A little too cocksure of y'rself, you ask me. You're a strong kid and you're steady enough. But there's somethin' not square about you. I seen it that first day."

"But that's so not fair!" Jack could feel his face burning. *Fired!* For something he didn't ... *couldn't have* done.

Clancy was on his feet now. So were one or two more longshoremen. One of them was the huge guy who'd confronted him at the café.

Jack threw up his hands and got to his feet. "Believe me, guys, you're making a mistake here. But ... whatever." He began to walk to the door.

"Hold on." It was Clancy. Jack turned to see the pit bull count two dollars and seventy-five cents out into his left hand. He held it out. "Your morning."

Jack swallowed the smart remark that was on his tongue. He took the money with a curt nod.

"Marshal McMann gets this thing cleared up, you come back and talk to me," Clancy said evenly.

"If you're still walkin' the streets," the big guy added in a sarcastic tone.

Jack turned back to the door. He could feel his neck burning up. Patsy Ann was at his side. "Thanks for nothing, Patsy Ann," he muttered.

"Moron," he heard behind him as the door swung closed. "Damn dog's deaf."

THE WHITE DOG kept up with him as Jackson half-walked, half-ran along the Juneau boardwalk. His thoughts boiled with anger and shame.

At Treadwell's Pharmacy he couldn't keep from glancing over at the newspaper rack. There he was ... right on the front page ... "SUSPECT." Was it just his imagination, or was he getting dark looks from the people they passed?

Sunlight sparkled off the low hills of shiny black coal, briefly dazzling him when he looked that way. In the swimming, bruise-coloured darkness afterward, something caught his toe and he almost fell. He spun hard and struggled to regain his balance but suddenly he was falling backward, his footing lost as his weight tumbled him over something low, heavy, solid and ... *furry*!

With a painful blow to his tailbone Jack came down on gravel — and exploded. "You!" he yelled. "Stop that!" Angrily he shoved the white muzzle out of his face before Patsy Ann could land a lick. "And what're you so happy about anyway? I'll never figure anything out if I'm inside a jail cell." He glared at the dog.

"She can't hear you, you know," a woman said with a laugh and walked on.

The dog just looked at him, eyes as bright and black as coal, her pink tongue lolling from a wide grin and skimpy tail beating the air back and forth.

Jack got to his feet, dusted his bum and set off once more. He walked fast, putting the shore road behind him in long, angry strides. Patsy Ann stuck to him like a radio jingle he couldn't push out of his mind.

When they reached the boardinghouse she followed him right down the hall, across the kitchen and into his room. He turned to close the door but found her thick head in the way. He opened it slightly to push her out, but instead she pushed the rest of herself inside.

Jack slammed the door in defeat and disgust and threw himself on the bed.

It was all, *all* of it, so ... *unfair!* He hadn't *asked* to come back to this *hick* town and its *ignorant* people without even *TV!* Whatever he was supposed to be doing here, he obviously wasn't any good at it. His detecting was going nowhere. Now he'd been fired *again* ... and this time it was probably for good. He had no clue ... no hope ... and pretty soon he'd have no *money*.

JACKSON WAS just getting good and going along these lines when a sharp rap sounded on the door.

"Jack?" Sylvia Baker's voice came through the thin wood.

"Yeah?" he said loudly, not bothering to get up or even put much politeness into his voice.

"Can you give me a hand?"

He got to his feet and opened the door. Sylvia Baker stood there holding a wicker basket by its round handle.

She smiled. "Since you're home a little early, could I ask you to pick us some raspberries for dessert?"

"Home" ... not exactly. Still, he didn't have anything better to do. And it was a pretty sure thing that the dessert that resulted would be worth the effort. "Yeah," he said again, this time a little more pleasantly. "Sure."

He took the basket from her and stepped out into the backyard.

Sunlight filled the quiet space. It glowed warmly through

blades of overgrown grass and saw-toothed leaves on tall canes that filled the far end of the garden. The green brightness was so strong it made him squint. Insects buzzed and the air was sticky and tart with the smell of ripe berries.

A breeze caught some of the raspberry leaves, turning them up to reveal their silvery bottoms. The sigh and rustle of tree branches moving carried his gaze up. Through the tallest of the canes he could just see the top of the fence. Behind that was a thick, restless confusion of green foliage, cool brown shadows and bare rock where the mountain rose up toward the sky.

The canes rose over Jack's head, as big around as his thumb and spiked with lethal thorns. But they bent low with heavy fruit. It wasn't long before bright red and black berries covered the bottom of the basket and began to creep up its sides, even allowing for the considerable number that ended up in his mouth (not to mention Patsy Ann's).

By now he had, without really noticing it, penetrated deep into the thicket of copper-coloured canes and saw-toothed leaves. It was there a bee, interrupted at a late-blooming flower, buzzed unexpectedly past Jackson's face.

With a yelp, he batted it away. The sudden movement upended the light basket. Red and black berries exploded out of it and scattered like sweet-smelling confetti into the shadows of the canes.

"Fritzin blatten GRORF!" Jack swore, biting down hard on some riper phrases he'd picked up recently. He dropped to his knees and began a search-and-rescue effort. *For cryin'*

out loud! Can't you even pick berries right?

Most of the large, fresh fruits had survived their fall quite well, barely picking up a stain from their soft landing on the mossy dirt beneath the canes. But Jack's efforts quickly turned into a race with Patsy Ann. Flopped down on her belly, fat little back legs stuck out behind her, she proved to be very good at *finding* berries, but could not be counted on to release them back into the basket.

The last of the fruit had landed deep in the canes. Crawling on his elbows now to reach them, Jackson could see the fence up ahead between the canes. Light filtering through leaves dappled its pale planks in shades of green. He sniffed with pleasure at the rich fragrance of berries, damp earth and ... *eh?*

His nose wrinkled. Something, some scent in the air didn't ... *fit,* somehow. He snuffed deeply. Berries, *yeah ...* dirt, *yeah ...* cut grass ... *yeah ... Wait a minute, hang on.* Jack took another deep nose-full. *Yeah, that is it ...* Hot sun on new-mown grass! Nothing like it.

And nothing like it at the Baker's either. Their yard was lush but uncut. There had been no one mowing lawns at the neighbours' houses either. Only weeds and brush grew along the narrow footpath beyond the fence.

As he listened, the sound of a lawnmower started up ahead of him. For a moment he thought he could smell the acrid odour of exhaust. Squirming to avoid well-armed thickets on either side, he spotted the hole in the planks. At once the hot grass and exhaust smells grew stronger and the lawnmower buzzed loudly in his ears. Now he noticed that the light through the broken gap in the fence was brighter, *yellower*, than it should be in the blue shadow of the mountain beyond it.

He could hear voices beyond the fence. Kids ... children, playing and laughing. A radio. A familiar jingle ...

Ohmigosh. It's right there ... home! Brampton. 2005. Color TV. The Web! The earth seemed to give way under him. The fiercely tall raspberry canes swam and wavered in his vision. He looked around for something solid.

With an almost physical jolt he found Patsy Ann. The white dog stood in the green chapel of the canes looking intently back at him. A breath of wind moved the canes and a shaft of sunlight broke through the green roof, striking stars alight in the black eyes.

As Jackson gazed into their depths he felt as though he had plunged into some green and tropical sea. The swaying canes bent into the current of time and he was drawn down into still deeper pools of dark water and distant starlight.

Then he began to see something else.

It was Captain Harper's face, that first day in Juneau. "There *is* a reason you're here," Jack read on the thin old lips. Then Vera Bayne swam to the surface, pale and exhausted and eyes red from crying, with that deer-in-the-headlights look and her baby wailing in his blankets. She faded and Al — *old* Al — appeared, his face clouded with misgiving the last time they'd been together. "Sometimes people make mistakes," he could see Al saying. "They think they're doing right, but it comes out wrong. And there's no going back."

A waft of wood-smoke and soap blew up Jack's nose, an impression so strong he looked around for Al himself.

Then he was seeing Patsy Ann again, her dark eyes holding his in their steady gaze.

"Stanley's why I'm here, isn't he?" he asked the deaf bull terrier. "If I go home, he stays in jail and it all comes out wrong again, doesn't it?"

Powerful jaws opened wide. The long pink tongue lapped out and across Jack's nose. It was accompanied by a most un-dream-like puff of bad dog breath.

But that's what you're showing me, isn't it? There is *a way back, when it's time.*

Patsy Ann barked.

Jackson laughed despite himself. "Okay, okay! I get the picture." He took the basket back in his hand and scrambled to his feet. "But you are too weird, dog."

Standing up, Jackson breathed in the fresh, sticky perfume of ripe berries in the thin northern sun. The air buzzed with insects and the riffle of distant surf. The chatter of a radio and the young laughter were gone, along with the sound of mowers.

Looking past the boy's legs, Patsy Ann could see that the ragged hole in the planks led only into dark shadow now. The air that drifted through it smelled of moss and ferns, cedars and small, busy creatures.

Twenty-One

THE PEANUT FACTOR

DINNER THAT NIGHT was another tense affair. The marshal and Captain Harper discussed "the Ethiopian Crisis" and some "New Deal" that was supposed to fight the Great Depression. Al said barely a word to Jack except to ask him to pass the salt and pepper.

Jack decided he was best off keeping his mouth shut.

He almost managed it. But when Rose and Sylvia started talking about the new movie showing in town, *Mutiny on the Bounty*, Jack thought he was on solid ground. He'd seen it once on TV.

"Yeah, Brando's great in that," he offered. For answer he got back a bemused silence and a round of "what planet are *you* from?" looks. He lapsed back into silence for the rest of the meal.

Yet somehow not even the strained mood could shake his newfound confidence. *If I'm really here to break the case against Stanley,* he reminded himself, *then it's going to happen — one way or the other.*

That night he slept easily and well. Next morning he was spared another awkward meeting with young Al; the deputy marshal was up and gone by the time Jack rose late. Only

Rose still dawdled over a bowl of raspberries and cold cereal. Jack squared off with a plate of sausage and eggs and they ate in companionable silence.

He was just wiping up the last streaks of yolk with the end of a sausage when a pungent aroma of tart sweetness and buttery hot pastry wafted in from the kitchen. *Dessert for breakfast,* Jack thought. *Awright!* He pushed his plate aside to make room for another course.

But when Sylvia appeared a moment later it was clear his appetite would have to wait. "I have a rhubarb special to spare," she announced. "That's Ezra's favorite. Would one of you mind taking it down to the boat?"

"I will," Rose and Jack said as one.

They set off as soon as they'd rinsed their breakfast dishes. Jack cradled the warm pie in his arms.

A strong wind gusted up Gastineau Channel. It brought a wild smell of the distant ocean and kicked the blue-black water into advancing lines of whitecaps. Leaning into the wind, Jack nearly missed the distant sound of a bark at their backs. Turning, he saw a stocky white dog and a slight girl with a pennant of blonde hair blowing in the wind.

They stopped to wait for Miranda and Patsy Ann. When the pair caught up with Jack and Rose, Miranda's eyes were rimmed in red, her face pulled tight. Jack thought it might just be the wind, but her greeting seemed half-hearted.

They made their way together down the slanting gangplank and across the rocking maze of floats to where *DogStar* dipped to the wind on her lines. Captain Harper stood on the foredeck, doing something to the end of a rope. His feet were planted wide and his body rocked effortlessly to stay upright against the roll of the deck and the gusts of the wind.

"Permission to board?" Jack sang out.

The Captain turned. A grin broke out on the weathered face, surrounded by a wind-blown halo of silvery hair and gray beard. Sizing up the situation quickly, *DogStar*'s skipper invited everyone aboard to "try out" the pie. "Make sure your mother's not losing her touch, Miss Rose."

There was just room for the two girls on the galley settee. Captain Harper found a bucket and upended it to make a seat for Jack at one end of the table where the cabin narrowed into a hallway. The white dog took up station at their feet and they went to work. When everyone had finished "testing" they had to agree that Mrs. Baker had not lost her touch. After tasting a little saved from every serving, Patsy Ann made it unanimous before setting off on her rounds.

By now everyone had a mug of sweet, strong, milky tea and Jack had his notebook out. He gave them the highlights of what he'd found out yesterday. It didn't seem to lead anywhere — except to more questions.

"What about the boat?" Jack wondered aloud. "Miranda says there used to be others like *Cetus* around Juneau."

"Aye," said the Captain. "Bering and Pacific had 'em, but they wanted bigger guns and those wooden frames wouldn't take them. How Bayne got one, I don't know."

"He lied," Miranda said, her expression sour.

"Eh?"

"When he first came here. Said he was going to help the men find the whales, help the fishery. That's why Father sold him a boat, why he says he can't be trusted."

"What happened to the rest?" Jack asked.

Miranda just shook her head and shrugged.

"Probably tied up somewhere," Captain Harper speculated, "or hauled ashore."

"We need to know."

"I can ask around," the Captain said.

That left who had made the radio call to the plane.

"Did the other boats have radios?" Jack asked.

Miranda shook her head again. "No, he must have put that one in."

"There's only a few other places it could have come from," Jack consulted his notebook. "The only other radio transmitters in Juneau belong to the army, the airport and the whaling company."

"It wasn't the fellows at the airfield," the Captain said. "I talked with Clive Harding up there. The tower was closed. They weren't expecting any more planes."

"What about the army?" Jack asked.

"My influence doesn't run to interrogating the army. But," he tipped his head to the side where a policeman stood sentry over the impounded *Cetus*, "I did winkle out of Officer Mills there that Marshal McMann had a talk with them. They insist it wasn't them."

"There's KINY," Rose suggested.

"They couldn't have," Jack said. "They use a different frequency."

"A different what?" she asked.

"*Amos 'n' Andy,*" Miranda said softly.

"A what?" Now it was Jack's turn to be confused.

"KINY," Miranda said, eyes downcast and hidden behind her bangs. "They were broadcasting *Amos 'n' Andy*. I was listening."

There was silence for an uncomfortably long time. Patsy Ann had been napping at their feet. Now she stood, gave herself a shake and scrambled up the short ladder to the wheelhouse. A moment later she barked. The Captain rose to let her out.

When he returned, Jack tried another tack. "Well," he began, quoting from his library of Al-isms, "this sounds like one of those a situations where, when you've ruled out everything else, whatever is left, however unlikely, must be the truth."

"Meaning?" asked Rose.

"Meaning that if the signal didn't come from the airfield, or the army ... and if it didn't come from Stanley, it had to come from Bering and Pacific — either the whalers' ship or their base."

"But that doesn't make any sense," Rose objected. "They're the ones who got robbed!"

"*However unlikely,*" Jack repeated. Although really, why *would* anyone steal their own money?

Then again, didn't "inside jobs" turn up all the time on TV? And now, he considered the idea ...

Jackson reached into his pocket and pulled out the twist of newspaper. Carefully he unwrapped it and placed the three peanut shells it contained gently on the table. "Look what I found under the table in the Longshoremen's Hall," he said.

His three co-detectives looked at this "evidence" blankly.

"Well?" Miranda drawled the word out, blue eyes wide with sarcasm.

"They're peanut shells," Jack began. "But not just any peanut shells. Notice the red powder on them? And the smell?"

Each of the others picked up a shell and sniffed it. Even from his place at the end of the table, Jack could smell the smoky spice of the big radioman's "special family recipe."

"I think these are some of Pontch's Cajun peanuts," Jack said. "They are available nowhere else in Juneau except his radio shack at the B&P."

They still weren't getting it.

"I found these shells under the poker table at the Longshoremen's Hall. That is, Patsy Ann found them. I just pulled them out. But the thing is, Pontch *never* plays poker. Someone else was in the radio room — *and at that table.*"

"You were there," Rose said, her green eyes bright with amusement. "Who could it have been?"

Jackson looked up and his eyes met the Captain's. As Jack watched, the expression on the leathery face changed. In the gray eyes there was something like shock. *"If you'll excuse me a few minutes, gentlemen,"* the player had said, *"I need to go and check on my daughter. Don't lose all your money before I get back."*

Now both girls were leaning forward with excitement. "Come on," Miranda prodded. "You know, I can see you do!"

The Captain raised his eyebrows, leaving it to Jack to speak.

"Tell us," Rose begged. "We're supposed to be your fellow detectives after all!"

Jack tried to choose the right words. "Well," he began. "One player did leave the table for about twenty minutes. After he came back, he kept snacking on peanuts from his pocket."

Across the table the Captain nodded.

"But ..." *How to do this?* "Miranda ... That evening, the evening of the robbery, you were at home watching ... I mean listening to radio?"

Miranda looked puzzled. "Sure. But what's that got to do with anything?"

"Your father was out?"

Miranda nodded. "Yes, but not to play poker. He had a meeting with Captain Petric, something about the ship."

Jack and the Captain exchanged looks.

"And did he come home partway through the evening to look in on you?"

"No. His meeting went really late. I didn't see him 'til next morning." She looked from Jack to the Captain and back. "What's wrong? Why are you looking like that?"

"My dear," Captain Harper said very gently, "I'm afraid your father *was* at the poker game. He left the table about quarter to nine. He said he was going to check up on you."

"That's a lie!" Miranda's face reddened. "He doesn't even *play* poker. If he came home to check on me, I would have seen him. I was awake until it got dark, after ten o'clock."

"That's what I'm saying," Jack replied. "It *was* a lie, what he told you. Seven people saw him there that night. They saw him leave and they saw him come back. And they saw him eat these peanuts."

"It's not possible!"

"He knew the plane was coming — that's opportunity. He had keys to the radio room — that's means. And he had a motive — $800,000, plus he gets rid of Stanley."

"No!" Miranda screamed. "*You're* lying!" She leapt away from the table and ran up the steps to the wheelhouse. She leaned back long enough to shout, "And I don't want to play your *stupid* detective game anymore."

Jack could see tears starting down her face.

DogStar rocked and they heard her feet hit the dock, then the sound of fleeing footsteps.

Rose got up. "She tries so hard to love that awful man. Now this." She shook her head, pigtails whipping. "I'd better go talk to her." She followed her friend off the boat.

Great, Miranda's going to hate me for the rest of her life, Jack thought as he watched her go. "Well," he looked at the Captain. "That went well!"

The gray brows frowned and Captain Harper tipped him a quizzical look.

"Now what?" Jack asked after a moment.

The old seaman's brows lifted and he gave a little jerk of his bristly chin. "Now you need something a little harder than peanut shells before you go around Juneau accusing Eric Ericson of robbing his own company. Eric draws a lot of water in the Territory."

"But *you* see it, don't you? It has to be him!"

"You and I remember that he was eating peanuts. Does anyone else?"

They lapsed back into silence. Jackson's thoughts seemed to stall out as he looked down into the gray puddle of tea cooling in the bottom of his mug.

DogStar dipped ever so slightly and a scrambling noise came from overhead. A moment later Patsy Ann tumbled down the steps and a potent stench filled the small cabin.

"Hey! Yuck!" Jack yelped and shoved twenty kilos of wet dog off his lap.

Patsy Ann's short white hair was plastered to her pink and gray skin. Juneau's town dog was noticeably cleaner than usual — but also much, much smellier. She pressed her cold wet flank self against the dry, warm boy.

"Been for a swim, have you old girl?" the Captain asked mildly.

Jack tried to move away. The dripping dog just pressed closer to him. A salty, sticky chill began soaking through Jack's jeans.

And suddenly an idea began to form.

"Captain," he asked, "Patsy Ann is Juneau's official boat greeter, right?"

"Aye."

"And when she goes down to meet a ship, pretty much everyone in town goes along too, right?"

For the important boats, the mail boat, passenger ships, aye, they do."

"Mr. Ericson too?"

"Aye, usually."

This just might work. A grin began to take over Jack's face.

Twenty-Two

A COLD PLUNGE

JACK PRESSED the *Alaska Daily Empire* flat against the bedspread to read it for the umpteenth time. The heavy-handed suggestions that "at least one other militant young conservationist" remained at large in Juneau's "crime of the century" no longer bothered him. Instead, he checked and double-checked the listing under "Shipping News": due today, Monday, July 22nd, 1935. It hadn't changed since the last time he looked: the *Excelsior*, cruise liner and mail ship, was due this morning.

Please, please, please let this work!

Breakfast was sausage and eggs. *Too perfect!* It was no trouble at all to slip a couple of extra links of sausage into a scroll of newspaper and slide them into his pocket.

And when Rose came down, he asked about the other items he would need.

"I think so," she said. "Let me go see."

Rose was back in a couple of minutes. The purse hanging at her side wasn't her usual look. But she grinned as she patted the leather bag and threw him a wink.

An hour later, they were again parked on the bench by the waterfront. "On stakeout," Jack said.

The day was clear. The remnants of yesterday's cool breeze

pushed puffy white clouds in front of it. Scents of salt and dead fish mixed with the waterfront's usual smells of saloon-smoke and tarred timbers.

It wasn't long before Patsy Ann trotted by at the head of a small parade of men, women and young folk. The crowd was chattering gaily, casting looks down the channel.

"There she is!" a little boy about five years old yelled from the very edge of the wharf, pointing down the channel.

Patsy Ann plunked her white self down beside him. Her back was straight and her black nose and deaf ears pointed alertly in the same direction.

Jack scanned the crowd anxiously.

Soon the proud profile of the *Excelsior* came in view, gliding slowly toward the wharf. With a new professional interest, Jackson noticed Clancy and three other long-shoremen take up positions, waiting for the ship's lines to come ashore.

An elbow dug sharply into Jack's side. "There he is!" Rose hissed, pointing rudely with her other hand.

A short, broad and strongly built figure strolled idly along the edge of the crowd. The sun glowed on his golden-red hair and trim beard. *And still wearing the same suit — perfect!*

"I wonder if Miranda's here, too?" Rose said, craning to look around. But there was no sign of her blonde friend.

Just at the moment Jack was much more interested in her father. "Okay Rose, remember, you're my backup. When Mr. Ericson leaves the dock, we can't lose him!"

Rose nodded, and Jack got to his feet. *This better work,*

he thought. There wouldn't be any second chance; that was for sure.

Hands in his pockets and trying to keep a casual expression on his face, Jack made his way through the crowd. It was easy to remain unnoticed; all eyes were on the approaching ship. In a moment he stood beside Patsy Ann. From his pocket he pulled the greasy twist of newspaper.

Patsy Ann's nose twitched and her head turned. Her interest in the approaching ship had temporarily dissolved and her bright eyes were on him now. Keeping his back to Mr. Ericson, he removed a plump sausage end from the paper twist.

A rope snaked through the air and landed lightly in front of Clancy. The crowd followed the longshoreman's movements as he hauled the line in, hand over hand, until he had retrieved a loop of heavy rope and dropped it over an iron post.

Jack held the aromatic plug of meat just in front of Patsy Ann's nose. "Sorry, girl," he whispered, even though he knew she couldn't hear him.

Then, with one hard shove of his knee, he sent her flying off the dock.

Patsy Ann yelped once on the way down. There was a loud splash and Jack peered anxiously over the wharf. But Patsy Ann's white head was already in sight. She puffed and snorted mightily as she paddled for shore, her ears back in annoyance. Around him, there was laughter and people were pointing and leaning out to enjoy the spectacle.

So far, so good. Now for phase two.

Trying to keep the casual look going, Jack moved through the crowd once more, stopping now and again to pretend an interest in the passengers crowding the *Excelsior*'s rail. In a few moments he was where he wanted to be — behind Mr. Ericson's broad pin-striped back.

A minute passed ... then another. Jack felt his stomach begin to knot. *Where is she?* Ericson began to stroll down the wharf. *No! Don't leave yet.* Jack followed him, trying to stay inconspicuous.

Then he heard it: small claws clicking on scuffed wooden timbers. Jack's hand came out of his pocket. He let it dangle idly at his side, the sausage end held like a stubby cigar between his fingers. Then he closed in on Mr. Ericson.

Suddenly Patsy Ann was there. And ... *YESSS!!!* ... shaking herself vigorously.

Red muck and salt water sprayed in all directions. Jack stepped out of the way so that the full force of the smelly geyser could catch the broad back in front of him. As he did, he gave Patsy Ann her greasy, meaty reward.

Ericson spun around on the dripping dog. "You again!" he raged. "You scrawny, rotten, mangy beast. You flea-bitten excuse for a dog. Town greeter? You're a town menace!"

Around him the crowd — or at least everyone who hadn't been dowsed in mud and seawater themselves — was laughing heartily. The open enjoyment of his predicament only inflamed Ericson's temper. "Blast you!" he fumed, twisting and turning to examine his soiled suit. "I had at least another week out of this jacket! You ought to be put down, not put on a postcard."

Still muttering, he stormed away from the wharf.

Jack and Rose fell in behind him at a discreet distance. "Remember," he whispered, leaning over to catch her ear. "Watch everything and remember everything. You may have to testify about this in court some day."

"You think so?" she asked, eyes alight.

They followed Ericson through the center of town. As they left the main streets of Juneau and headed uphill, Jack's confidence in his scheme began to falter. At a three-storey mansion, Ericson turned and stamped up the stone steps.

Half a block down the hill Jack and Rose heard the glass in Ericson's expensive front door rattle as he slammed it shut.

"Now what?" Rose asked.

"Now we wait," he growled.

Rose rolled her eyes.

"That's what a stakeout *is*," Jack said, trying to sound like he did this all the time. "It's waiting."

They made themselves as inconspicuous as possible behind a holly hedge and settled in. But in fact, they didn't have to wait long. In less than five minutes Eric Ericson reappeared in fresh clothes — a sharp blue blazer and gray slacks. In one hand he carried a bulging brown paper sack. Dark wet stains were already soaking through the paper.

They gave Ericson a head start then fell in behind him.

This time he led them straight to Huk-sing's door.

The businessman was inside less than two minutes. He came

back out empty-handed and turned toward the waterfront. From where they stood in the shade of an alley Jack could see a furious anger aflame in his flushed cheeks.

As soon as Ericson was out of sight, the two teenagers crossed the street to Huk-sing's. On the counter was a rumpled bundle of navy blue woolen pinstripe, smelling strongly of seawater and dotted with spatters of red mud and wet stains.

"Ah, Miss Rose, Master Made-in-China," Huk-sing greeted them cheerfully. "How can I help today? You need more clothes?"

"Not today, Huk-sing," Jack replied. "Just a favor." Huk-sing's smile vanished. "A small one, really. I need to look at the clothes Mr. Ericson just dropped off, only for a minute."

Huk-sing's expression darkened. "Why you want Mr. Ericson's clothes? They not for sale. He come back Wednesday to pick them up."

"I know that," Jack said. "And I won't hurt them, I promise. I just need to look at the pockets."

Huk-sing was still doubtful.

"Mr. Huk-sing, this really *is* important," Rose pleaded. "Someone might be about to go to jail for something he didn't do. This could help prove he's innocent."

Huk-sing seemed to be wavering.

"It'll just take a minute. You can watch everything I do and I *promise* it won't hurt anything," Jack said again.

The laundryman shook his head as though already regretting his weakness, but he pushed the soiled pile of fabric across the counter. Then he stepped quickly to the front door and turned the key in the lock. Turning back to face them he said: "One minute. That's all. One minute. No damage. One minute."

Jack swiftly separated the trousers from the suit jacket and began pulling out the pockets, examining each lining closely and holding it up to his nose. At this, Huk-sing's own nose wrinkled in distaste. But it took only seconds to rule out the trousers. He turned to the jacket next — the pocket on the left, then the one on the right. He pressed the lining to his nose and breathed in. *Yes!*

He spread Ericson's jacket out on the counter, the lining of the right-hand pocket pulled out. "I need the sticky tape and paper now," he said.

Rose snapped open her purse and removed a roll of cellophane tape and several sheets of letter paper. The look on Huk-sing's face was becoming anxious again.

"Don't worry," Jack assured him. "This won't hurt the clothes." He pulled off several pieces of tape, each a few inches long. "Rose, watch this. You need to be able to back me up on what I've done."

"What for?"

"In case this ever goes to court."

Huk-sing's brows lowered at the mention of "court."

"To court?" Rose asked. "Gee, do you think I'll wind up with *my* picture in the *Empire*?"

"You never know." Carefully, Jack pressed each piece of the tape, sticky side down, against the pocket lining, paying special attention to the seam, where a line of red dust showed amid the lint. When he pulled the tape away, pieces of fluff and red powder came with it. He pressed several lengths of the tape onto one sheet of letter paper, then stuck the last on a separate sheet.

"What you doing?" Huk-sing asked suspiciously.

"I'm collecting evidence that's going to show us what Mr. Ericson had in his pockets," Jack said. "Then I'm going to compare it to Pontch's peanuts. It's a trick I learned from CSI."

"CSI?" said Huk-sing.

"It's a radio program," Rose spoke up. "Like *Dick Tracy*."

"Okay, now I need two envelopes," Jack said.

Rose reached into her purse and brought out two envelopes.

Jack placed the two pieces of paper on the counter. Pulling out his pencil he wrote the date on each one. Then he did the same on the outside of both envelopes. Finally, he held the pencil out to the laundryman. "Huk-sing, would you please put your initials beside each of these pieces of tape for me?"

"Why?" Huk-sing asked, suspicion now clearly deepening into alarm.

"To prove I collected these samples in your presence, on this date. Then I'm going to ask you to do the same on the envelope."

For a moment, he thought Huk-sing might refuse. But then the laundryman took the pencil and drew an elegant Chinese character on each sheet of paper. When Jack put the sheet containing several strips of tape into an envelope and sealed it, Huk-sing wrote his name where Jack pointed, across the sealed flap.

Jack slipped the other sheet of paper, with its solitary strip of cello-tape, into its own envelope and handed it to Rose. He tucked the linings of Erickson's jacket pockets right side in and gave everything back to Huk-sing.

"There," he said. "Good as new."

"Thank you, Huk-sing," Rose said.

"You may have just changed history," Jack couldn't resist.

Huk-sing shook his head doubtfully. "You unlock door on way out," he said. "And no mention this to Mr. Ericson."

"Don't worry," Jack promised him. "We won't."

Outside the laundry Jack turned to Rose. He held out the sealed envelope with Huk-sing's signature. "Here, you take this. It's evidence. I don't want anyone to think I tampered with it. Whatever you do, *do not open it.*"

Rose nodded and put the envelope in her purse. "What's next?" she asked.

"We need two more things," Jack's mind was racing now. "I need you to go see Pontch and get him to give you some of his Cajun peanuts. Shouldn't be too hard. Put them in another envelope then head down to *DogStar*."

"Where are you going?"

"I'm going to see Vera Bayne."

Rose shot him a troubled look but all she said was, "What if he asks me why I want peanuts?"

"Tell him you heard they were the only thing in Juneau

as good as your mother's pie," Jack said with a smile. "Just don't tell him the truth. We don't want this getting back to Miranda's father. Not when we're getting so close."

THE LOBBY of the Alaska Hotel was dark and smelled of furniture polish and stale disinfectant. The front desk was nothing more than a cramped space tucked under stairs that led to the upper floors. A gray-haired woman in a cardigan sat behind the narrow counter reading a newspaper.

Jack stepped to the counter. "Can you tell me what room Mrs. Bayne is in?"

The woman looked up from her newspaper with unfriendly eyes. "You another reporter?"

"No ma'am. I'm a ... friend." *Or as close to a friend as she's got in Juneau.*

"Hmmph." The woman's dark eyes narrowed and her doubtful expression deepened. Turning back to the newspaper she flipped through until she had the front page. She peered at it, then at Jack, then back at the page.

"Hmmph," she said again. Then, with something like disgust in her voice, she grunted, "Second floor. Room 213." With a harrumph she returned her attention to the paper.

"Thanks," said Jack under his breath and headed for the stairs.

Please let her be there. And please let Stanley have what I need.

Behind the door of room 213 a baby was crying lustily. A good sign. He rapped hard on the door.

"Who is it?" a tired voice sounded from inside the room.

"Jack Kyle. We met at the wharf the other day."

After a moment the door opened. Vera Bayne stood in the opening, pale and looking even more drawn and hopeless than she had earlier. "Yes?" she sighed, jouncing a bundle in her arms.

"Mrs. Bayne, I'm sorry to bother you. But does Stanley have a microscope?"

She looked at him as though he'd asked whether her husband walked on his hands or juggled jellyfish in his spare time. "I'm sorry, a what?"

"A microscope. He's a biologist. Doesn't he need a microscope to look at samples and stuff?"

Vera looked vaguely behind her. Piled haphazardly in the corner behind her were the boxes and baskets they had carried up from the wharf. A fresh wail went up from the bundle of blankets. "Yes, he does. I brought it along with everything else from camp. But why?"

"I need to borrow it."

Vera hesitated, doubt drawing lines around her thin mouth and pale eyes. "I don't know." Her renewed jouncing seemed only to make the wailing worse. "It's not his. It's the university's. I really shouldn't."

"Ma'am," Jack lowered his voice and held her eyes. "It's important. I think I can prove someone else sent that radio message and stole the B&P payroll. But you need to help me."

"But what's that got to do with Stan's microscope?"

"I need to examine some evidence, *microscopic* evidence.

I only need it for a few hours, but what it shows me could set Stanley free."

"You'll bring it back?"

"Of course!"

"Alright then," Vera sighed. "If it might help I guess it's alright." She turned back into the room and sank down on the narrow bed. "It's there, at the back." She stretched a toe toward a small suitcase like a shoebox turned on end, with a handle on top.

Yes! "Thank you, ma'am." The small case was heavy but his new muscles could manage it easily. "I'll take care of it, don't worry."

The thin woman just nodded and buried her face in the bundle of blankets in her arms.

She looks so tired, Jack thought with a pang. *Did Mom have times like this?* "Mrs. Bayne ... Ma'am?" She looked up. "I think it's going to be okay."

Tears welled in red-rimmed eyes.

"Really."

"I hope so," she said in a voice without much hope left in it.

Twenty-Three

PROOF UNDER GLASS

"PERMISSION TO BOARD?" Jack sang out.

A moment later Captain Harper appeared at *DogStar*'s door. Jackson handed him the brown case and stepped aboard.

Down below the Captain placed the case on the galley table then stepped away to put the tea-kettle on the small galley stove. Jack filled him in on the events of the morning while he unpacked Stanley Bayne's microscope.

"That explains it, then," the old seaman chuckled. "Patsy Ann turned up a while back none too pleased about something and smelling like a beached fish. I had to send her to the foredeck to air out."

Stanley's microscope was not very much different from ones Jackson had used in science class. It had a mirror to reflect sunlight through whatever was under the lens, instead of an electric lamp, but Jack easily found a ray of sun beaming through one of *DogStar*'s portholes. He positioned the instrument so that the warm beam fell on its small mirror.

From outside came a muffled call: "Permission to come aboard?" It was a girl's voice.

But instead of Rose it was Miranda who a moment later

stepped down the short ladder from the wheelhouse. Blonde bangs fell over her pale face and she avoided meeting their eyes. Taking a deep breath, she said: "I have some information ... for your investigation."

There was a silence. "And ...?" Jack pressed.

She looked up. For the second time that day Jackson saw tears overtake a troubled face. "I asked around some of Father's workers ... and I know where they are."

"Where what are?"

"The other chase boats." She lapsed back into silence.

Jack raised his eyebrows and threw open his hands. *So ...? Get* on *with it girl.*

Miranda's pretty face was twisted in anguish. "They're in one of the sheds at the Bering and Pacific docks." She let out a long breath. All her energy seemed to empty from her, like a balloon when the air is let out.

"Miranda! That's great!" Jack enthused, until he caught the look on the Captain's face ... and the hurt in Miranda's. *Oh you flippin' idiot!* "I mean ..."

Another request for "permission to board" saved him more embarrassment. This time it *was* Rose. She tripped eagerly down the stairs waving a bulging envelope in front of her.

"Got them!" she sang out. Then catching sight of the other girl, her expression changed. "Mira!" Rose cried, tossing the envelope onto the galley table and throwing her arms around her friend.

Jack opened the envelope Rose had dropped on the table just enough to see that it contained half a dozen dusty red peanuts. A scent of smoky spice filled the small saloon. "Rose," he said, "can you swear that you received those peanuts from Pontch in his radio shack?"

She nodded vigorously. "Sure. And you're right, they *are* about the only things in Juneau as good as Momma's cooking."

"Okay, now give me the other two envelopes — the ones from Huk-sing's."

Rose produced these from her purse. Jack set to one side the envelope sealed with Huk-sing's elegant Chinese characters. From the other he removed the sheet of paper with the single strip of cello tape stuck to it.

"This is dust from the inside of Mr. Ericson's pocket," he explained. "Now I need the tape," he added to Rose.

Next, he removed one of Pontch's peanuts from the envelope Rose had brought. Carefully, he pressed a length of cello tape against the peanut and then placed it on the paper next to the tape from the laundry . "Here," he slid the paper over to Captain Harper and pulled out his pencil. "Put your initials beside this second tape, so it's clear which is which."

The Captain did as he was asked and handed the sheet back to Jackson.

"Rose, you seal that envelope with the peanuts, and sign the flap. We need to make this case air-tight."

While she did that, Jack used his knife to cut away the paper around the two strips of cello tape. Then he placed the trimmed paper with its taped samples onto the little platform at the bottom of the microscope.

This had better work. He breathed out a deep lungful of air.

Rose, Miranda and Captain Harper watched with rapt fascination. Jack felt a cold emptiness in his gut. *If this turns out wrong, I am sooo done.*

Jackson bent over and peered into the microscope. At first there was nothing but blur. He twiddled the knob that adjusted the lens. Suddenly the view leapt into focus.

In the bright circle at the end of the microscope he clearly saw the two pieces of tape. Stuck to each were dozens of identical little boulders coloured deep red, smoky yellow, milky white and dark brown and black.

"Gotcha!" he breathed.

He heard a muffled cry and looked up in time to see Miranda's heels disappearing up the steps to the wheelhouse.

"Miranda! Wait!"

He scrambled up the short ladder and was across the wheelhouse in two steps. But as he ducked his head to go out *DogStar*'s low door someone else was ahead of him. Patsy Ann barreled down the narrow deck, pushed past the boy and dropped heavily to the dock. With only the briefest of shakes, she set off after the fleeing girl at a gallop.

Jack felt a strong hand restrain his shoulder.

"Let her go," the Captain said. "She'll not want to face you right now. Besides, you've got other work to do." He turned to Rose. "But perhaps you'd best get home. We've no idea how this will turn out. There could be trouble."

Rose's eyes widened and she shook her head with an impish grin. "No sir! You tried to leave me behind once before and it didn't work, now did it?"

The Captain looked nonplussed. Recovering, he tried again. "Well, this is no time to be arguing. We need to find Marshal McMann."

"You guys do that," Jack said. "Show him the specimens in the microscope and give him the envelopes. He'll believe you ahead of me anyway. I'm going to find those other boats."

"Wait for the Marshal," cautioned the Captain.

"No, Captain. They're the last piece of the puzzle. We need them to make the case."

"Aye, well ... Be careful. These are dangerous men."

Jack dropped off the boat onto the dock. One hand still on *DogStar*'s rail he turned back to them. "Hey, something else. I don't know how it fits. But tell Al ... I mean the Marshal, I saw Captain Petric on the docks the day after the robbery. I think he could have planted that bank wrapper on *Cetus*."

Jack spun to leave and almost ran straight into the policeman still standing guard over the biologist's boat.

"Hey there, Officer Mills!" He grinned, then tore away down the float.

The other two only gave him a smile, shrugged, and set off the same way at a more sedate pace.

Twenty-Four

NEW BOATS FOR OLD

PATSY ANN caught up with Miranda at the foot of the gangway that led up from the docks. Once they reached the road along the shore the girl slowed her pace. The white dog matched her step and stayed with her through the centre of town. They started up the hill.

She seemed glad of the company. "Why, Patsy Ann? Why would he do it?" Tears streamed down her cheeks and occasionally a deep sob escaped her chest. "And what am I going to do now?"

Miranda scaled the stone steps reluctantly and crossed the wide porch. She pushed open the broad doors with their elegant frosted glass. After the freshness of the day, the air indoors smelled trapped and stale. She ran for the stairs at the far end of the hall, steps ringing loudly on the polished floor.

Miranda was halfway to the safety of the stairs when something caught her by the arm. Propelled by her own on-rushing momentum she swung around, losing her balance until her captor pulled her upright and close to his own body.

Miranda looked up into her father's face.

Ericson pulled his daughter into his lighted study. "You've been crying! Why?"

Miranda hung her head, avoiding his gaze.

"And get that dog out of here." He aimed a kick at Patsy Ann, but she easily dodged his blow.

"Where have you been? Down at the docks again with that young thief?"

Miranda's head shot up. Her blue eyes blazed. "Which thief, *father*?" she spat out the word.

His eyes bored into her face. When he spoke, it was with a deadly calm. "What do you mean by that?"

"You know exactly what I mean." Her voice had an acid sweetness. "It was you all along, wasn't it? You robbed your own company! It wasn't ever Stanley Bayne."

The arrogant face gave nothing away but the flushed cheeks were puffed and sallow. Ericson's grip tightened on his daughter's arm. "Who have you talked to?" he hissed.

Miranda saw something in her father's face she had never seen before and started to scream.

Ericson clamped a hand over her mouth. "Shut up!" He released her mouth just long enough to snatch a handkerchief from one tailored pocket. He forced the cloth roughly between the girl's teeth.

Miranda's wrists trapped in one powerful hand, her father reached with the other for the telephone. Beside it on the desk was a framed photograph of a woman. In the picture, the woman's eyes were laughing, her hair a short, tousled helmet of blonde.

Ericson saw where his daughter was looking and snarled. "It should have been you, not her."

Something let go in Miranda's chest.

Patsy Ann turned from the scene and bolted out through the open front door. This time she didn't stop for even the briefest shake at the foot of the stone steps. Without a pause she galloped straight out to the street and turned downhill.

No bull terrier is designed with running in mind and Patsy Ann looked like an oversized jackrabbit as she raced down the sidewalk. Her tail stuck straight out behind her and her back legs almost overtook her front ones in their impatience.

But she ran like the wind.

JACKSON TRIED to work out which of the sprawling Bering and Pacific buildings might be hiding boats. *Boats live in water,* he reasoned.

When the whaling station came into sight he left the road, cutting toward the shore across an empty lot strewn with rusted bits of machinery. Beyond it, a steep bank led down to blue-green water. If he stayed down near the waterline, the bank would hide him from anyone who glanced from the company's offices or work yards toward Gastineau Channel.

There were small whitecaps out in the channel. Waves broke and washed around boulders shaggy with lumpy, olive-green seaweed. Purple starfish clung wetly to the rocks and the air smelled strongly of salt and iodine and sea life.

It was difficult to walk without slipping. By the time Jack neared the first warehouse painted with "B&P" in big, fading letters, his palms stung and his jeans were stiff with greasy, green and black stains from where he had fallen.

The first building ran to within a few meters of the water. He passed it and saw another just like it. Beyond it, the bank curved away out of sight.

Jack reached the spot where the shoreline turned. Around the bend was a shallow cove in the bank — and a building he had never seen before. Looking past it, Jack realized it must be hidden from the street by newer additions. Gray wooden sides that sagged on mossy stilts hung far out over the cove into the channel.

He scrambled up the bank, grateful to leave the slippery seaweed behind. He followed the weathered walls to the side that faced inland. It was blank except for a plain wooden door and a small window heavily dusted with grime. Someone had recently rubbed a small clean patch in the soiled window glass. The someone had been a little shorter than Jackson. He put his eye to the spot.

Green light glowing up from the water dappled the inside of the shed. A thin band of sunlight sparkled under the broad door that closed off the opposite wall, the side that faced the channel. In the rippling light he made out three long, sleek, powerful shapes rocking gently from a float in their ropes and fenders.

Yes!

He grabbed the door and shook it hard. It rattled but didn't open. A shiny new brass padlock secured it firmly to the weathered gray wood of its frame.

"Okay, now *go get the Marshal!"* Jackson could almost hear the sensible whisper.

Not a chance! "When you get this close you can *taste* it," Al used to say. Now Jackson understood. His whole body seemed to be ringing with adrenalin.

He went back around the side of the boathouse and looked down the bank. The rotting planks ran right down to the water. Mud and rock lay bare, seaweed and starfish drying where they had been abandoned by the tide. Only a few yards of wall still extended out over the water. Jack could see the ends of the planks not far beneath the surface.

He yanked off his new leather boots and put them out of sight behind a wooden barrel. Picking his way carefully in his socks, he crept down the bank. At the bottom, he braced himself, then slipped into the water.

Yeow! Cold!

He gulped in a lungful of air and ducked beneath the surface. Salt water stung the cuts on his palms as he groped blindly for the bottom of the rotting planks. Then he was under and coming back up. A moment later he burst back through the surface. He gasped in air, feeling for a moment in the rippling yellow and green light as though he were still underwater. Flicking wet hair from his forehead, he hauled himself up onto a float.

In the stillness the only sounds were the light creak of ropes, the soft slap of water moving under the floats and the deafening pounding of his heart.

The bank under the boathouse had been dug away so that deep water ran almost to the back wall. Floats ran around three of the sides, with a gangplank like the one at the docks up to a landing just inside the door. On the fourth side, tall panels hung from a rusty track up near the roof.

Three boats were tied to each other side-by-side, their bows pointed toward the door, the last one moored to the float on the far side of the boathouse. Apart from one thing, they were each the "spittin' twin" of Stanley Bayne's *Cetus*.

Two of the boats could never have been mistaken for the biologist's. At the point of their bows, those boats both had what looked like big rifles mounted on post. Instead of open barrels, the vicious points of rusting harpoons stuck from the weapons' business ends.

The third boat, however, the one nearest to Jack, was missing its gun.

Jack got to his feet and squelched around the floats. From the float that ran across the back of the boathouse he could see the sterns of the boats. The two boats with guns were *Hunter I* and *Hunter III*. The third boat's name was hidden behind a square of thick cardboard held in place by gray tape.

Jackson walked onto the third float and climbed into the first boat. Dust covered the decks and cockpit. There were the smells of mould and stale gasoline.

The second boat looked as forgotten as the first. He smelled the must of old canvas. Untidy gray folds were piled in one corner of its neglected cockpit.

The deck of the third boat dipped as he swung his weight onto it. Compared to its sisters, this boat appeared to be cared for. Its brass gleamed and its dark woodwork glowed as brightly as *Cetus*'s own. Still, a dusting of white spots and blotches speckled the polished surface. They were thickest over the front deck and windshield.

Bending to look more closely, Jack could see that each spot was actually a small cluster of fine white crystals. He leaned over and licked one.

Salt!

The boat had been to sea at least once since it was cleaned up. Wherever sea-water had splashed and dried, it had left behind these salt spots.

Stepping forward, Jack peered into the cramped cabin. A polished wooden steering wheel was set off to the right — opposite where it would be in a car. On the dashboard were several dials and two levers topped with round knobs. His stomach knotted as he recognized the long barrel of a rifle lying on the settee seat.

He turned and examined the cockpit. Just as on *Cetus*, both sides were lined with benches. The seats were designed to lift up and reveal lockers underneath. One by one, he began to lift the lids.

He found what he was looking for in the third locker he opened.

In the dark space under the seat were three square canvas satchels. Heavy leather belts and buckles held each satchel closed.

He reached for the one closest to him, then pulled back. He looked quickly around the cockpit, but it was bare. Standing on one foot, he wrenched off his left sock and quickly squeezed it more or less dry. His hands shook as he worked the stiff buckle, the damp sock slipping between his fingers and the metal.

Finally he had it loose. Still using the sock, he pulled the belt free from the buckle and carefully pulled the edges of the canvas apart.

Oh ... my ... God! He'd been certain. But somehow, the actual sight of neatly wrapped and stacked bundles of money put his stomach into freefall anyway.

Jack stepped away from the locker. *Don't contaminate the evidence. But, oh jeez, just wait 'til Al sees this!*

He scrambled back over to the middle boat. Halfway across the cockpit he froze. Against the soft lap and rhythmic creak of the disused boathouse, the sound of metal scraping against metal cut like a rusty blade.

Jackson looked up.

The door flew open. Captain Petric stepped inside. Behind him came Eric Ericson, struggling with something behind him — or with some*one*.

Twenty-Five

OVERPOWERED

MIRANDA!

Ericson and Petric stood framed in the light from the door. There was only one way out. *Dive, now!*

But he couldn't. Not while Ericson had Miranda. Nor was there time to plan. On instinct, Jack slipped a hand into his jeans and pulled out his knife. In a quick motion he tucked it beneath the mouldy canvas heaped in the disused cockpit. Then he rose and stood away, backing up against the low roof of the speedboat's cabin.

"There's the boy!" Ericson shouted.

Petric pounded down the ramp and vaulted over the transom of the first boat. He landed hard and all three craft rocked violently. Then the whaler with the caveman build was in front of Jackson. In the confined cockpit he looked even bigger, wider and more powerful. His heavy features were contorted in a black scowl.

Jack held out his hands, empty palms facing the whaling captain in a gesture of surrender.

"Turn around," Petric growled.

Jack did as he was told. A moment later rough hands

grabbed his wrists and pulled them together behind his back. Petric jerked him backward and he heard the man lift the seat over the boat's lockers.

Please — just stay away from the canvas!

But Petric had what he needed. Jack felt a coarse line encircle his wrists once, twice ... and then Petric was pulling a knot tight.

"On your knees," the coarser voice growled. The big man pushed Jack forward.

His knees came down on the hard deck with a painful crack. A moment later he felt the same thick rope wrap around his ankles and pull tight. Petric shoved him again and this time he fell onto his side.

Petric busied himself for another moment, then rose and dusted his hands.

Jack struggled but his wrists were bound tightly to his ankles, the knot somewhere out of reach. He felt the boat rock, then Miranda was standing above him. With a shock, he saw her hands already tied in front of her. A cloth gag covered her mouth.

Hot fury rushed through him. *You're sick! To tie up your own daughter!* He lunged and writhed but succeeded only in flopping over the deck like a fish out of water. "Let her go, you twisted ..." he yelled.

But Petric was there to cut off the sound, shoving a filthy handkerchief into Jack's mouth. He could taste things on it he didn't want to think about.

He tried to force it out of his mouth, but Petric had a knife out. Jack froze. He watched Petric step to the heap of old canvas.

Jack's heart stopped. *Please,* please, *don't search that pile.* He fought to keep his face poker-still.

But the whaling captain only lifted the top piece of mouldy cloth. With three quick flicks of his knife he slashed out a long strip.

Jack's heart started again.

Stepping back to Jack, the giant knelt. In a quick movement he wrapped the canvas strip around the boy's head and tied it roughly. When he was done, there was no more hope of spitting the crusty handkerchief out.

Petric stood up. "So, what do we do with him now? Take him with us and feed him to the crabs in the channel?"

An icy sensation tingled from Jack's stomach to the back of his neck. *Oh ... my ...*

"And what about that one?" Petric tipped his head at Miranda.

... God! You couldn't! She's your daughter!

Ericson's eyes narrowed. He seemed to think about this, looking from Jack to his daughter. In the green light his golden hair and beard looked dull, almost gray.

What's to think about, you bearded freak? Once more Jack lunged in vain, pulling the ropes painfully tighter around his wrists and ankles.

"Nah," Ericson grunted at last. "I don't want the law on us for murder. Just tie the brats and leave them."

Miranda's eyes closed and she sagged in her father's grip. Petric pushed her sideways and she sank onto the cockpit seat. He rummaged for another rope, which he tied around her ankles.

When he was done Petric stepped back and eyed his handiwork with satisfaction. "They're not going anywhere, either one of them."

Deep sobs wracked Miranda's thin body.

"You've got nothing to bleat about, girl," her father growled. "Someone will find you, sooner or later. They just won't find us. And by the time they do we'll be in Canada."

Without another word he stepped away and onto the outside boat of the three, *Cetus*'s stand-in. Ericson flipped up one of the seats and looked into the locker below. It was the one filled with square canvas bags. Jack watched the tension on the man's handsome face melt and a smile form there.

"Get the lines," he ordered Petric. A moment later the shiny powerboat swung free from its neglected sisters.

But the two did not drive off immediately. Instead they pushed the boat sideways, letting it drift free across the boathouse. Moments later, they tied it up again to the float on the far side.

Jack wriggled into a sitting position. From here he could just see over the edge of the boat's grimy cockpit. *Why aren't they getting away?*

The answer quickly became clear. Petric lifted a black hose from a bracket and snaked it onto the boat. A moment later, Jack heard a liquid rush and caught the oily, gagging smell of gasoline. *Of course! They're filling up for the run to the border.*

Ericson climbed out of the boat and stepped to the far end of the float, the end nearest the tall doors. A loop of chain hung over the water. He reached for it and began pulling. A moment later a rusty creak sounded overhead and one of the panels lurched sideways. A broad shaft of sunlight shone into the dark cave of the boathouse.

Petric put the hose back in its bracket and bent to untie the boat. He stepped aboard and into the low, swept-back cabin. A starter motor whined and then the thick burbling sound of a powerful boat engine filled the shed.

Jack heard a low k'thunk. Water boiled briefly under the powerboat's stern and it began to glide along the float toward the sunlight. As it came past, Ericson stepped smoothly into it.

He released the chain in one hand.

The boat disappeared from Jack's sight into the bright sunlight pouring through the open door. The boat did not immediately pull away. Its engine note raised its voice once and then fell back to a mumble. There was a bump and the door panels swung and gently clapped against each other. The big engine spoke again.

Then the tall doors began to creak and move again, now taking back the narrow band of sunlight like a curtain being drawn. They were alone, bathed in the emerald light of their echoing prison.

There was a rattle of metal, and once more the engine came to life. This time, however, the engine noise rose and kept on growing until it was a roar rushing away into the distance.

Then there was again only the soft creak of ropes, the lap of water and muted sobs coming from behind Miranda's gag.

THE WHITE DOG raced down the hill away from the mansion. Near the bottom she banked hard right, almost losing her balance. At the end of the next block she leapt off the cracked sidewalk and into the street without stopping. Car tires squealed and someone yelled, but Patsy Ann neither heard nor cared.

The next block was entirely taken up by a single two-storey building, one of very few in Juneau that were not built of wood. Patsy Ann galloped halfway along to a modest door set into the plain brick. She put her nose to the door and barked urgently.

Moments later the door opened.

"Why 'lo there, Pat ..." She pushed past a pair of legs in work trousers. "Hey, what's your hurry?"

But the white dog was already galloping away down the wide hallway. Her rough pads made poor footing on the polished floor. At the first corner she slid away sideways, banging off the far wall before gathering herself for another sprint.

When at last Patsy Ann did try to stop at a closed door, she slid right past it and had to scrabble back a few steps to stand in front of it. She barked.

Painted on the frosted glass were the words, "U.S. Marshal

— Alaska Southeast Division," in square gold and black letters.

Again she barked with a piercing urgency.

But the glass in the door was dark, the office behind it silent. The door remained closed.

With a last, annoyed bark the dog turned and ran back the way she had come. At the door, the same human let her out, then followed her into the street.

"Must be some ship coming in," he said to himself as he bent to turn a key in the lock behind him.

But Patsy Ann was already off down the block.

Five minutes later, heads turned up and down the counter and booths of the Gold Dust Café as the door banged open. Patsy Ann trotted in, breathing heavily. Pink tongue out and drooling, she made her way down the full length of the café, looking this way and that at the people perched at the counter or on the benches of the booths.

"Hey, girl," one or two patrons called, waving sandwich ends and fragrant french-fries in her direction.

But Patsy Ann only gave a short, frustrated bark as she came to the end of the narrow room, then turned and galloped back to the door. There she barked again, her grimy front feet bouncing right off the floor with urgent impatience.

"Okay, okay," the thin man in the stained apron grumbled from behind the counter. "Coming." He stepped to the door and opened it. Patsy Ann shot out like a scalded cat.

A young couple who had just finished a pair of malted milks got to their feet. "Must be a pretty important boat," the woman said, while her partner pulled two quarters from his pocket and dropped them on the table.

A large woman climbed down off a stool. "*Excelsior* was the only ship in the paper," she said, "but it was in hours ago."

"Never known Patsy Ann to be wrong though," said an older fellow in a faded suit, abandoning his half-finished chili at the far end of the counter.

All four went out the door.

The white dog showed up next at O'Doule's barber shop. But after a quick snuff at each pair of shoes along the row of chairs she scooted straight out the back and Billy O'Doule had to pop the piece of moose jerky into his own mouth.

It was the same story at the Red Dog, where Patsy Ann ducked under the swinging doors, made a fast circuit of the tables and barreled out the way she had come in without so much as a sniff toward the counter, where Pete's hand was already feeling around in the brine for the fat end of a pickled sausage.

On the small stage, Huk-sing and Pontch exchanged startled looks with a third man, who was tuning up a bass fiddle as big as himself. A moment later, Huk-sing slipped his clarinet back into its case and Pontch closed the lid over his trumpet. All three joined the growing train of Juneau men, women and youngsters following in the white dog's wake.

By the time Patsy Ann approached the waterfront, with its promenade and park bench deserted now, at least two dozen people were hurrying to keep up with her. Their excitement was equaled by their curiosity and mystification. "It must be some special boat," they told each other. "She hasn't taken a bite from anyone!"

But when the white dog turned away from downtown Juneau and headed up the road that led past the coal-yard and along the shore away from town, curiosity became confusion. "What's she doing out this way?" more than one voice wondered. "Nothing out here but B&P and the boat docks."

INSIDE THE dim boat shed, Jackson felt certain he could hear blood pulsing in his ears.

Two hundred ninety-eight thous'n'one... two hundred ninety-nine thous'n'one ... Three hundred thousand and one!

He breathed into the liquid silence. *Now?*

Jack had counted carefully to three hundred — one thousand and one at a time. But still he hesitated. Were they going to come back?

No, dumbo, they're headed for Canada. That's not so far from here. And they'll get there if you don't do something.

Wriggling and writhing, he scootched across the dusty deck on his side. At last he was in the corner where the canvas lay piled and smelling of mildew.

He squiggled around some more, getting his back to the stack of material. Over his gag, he could see Miranda, watching him now. She had stopped crying. Instead, her blue eyes blazed over the cloth covering her own mouth.

Tied as he was, Jack could not move his bound hands far from his ankles or easily reach his fingers under the canvas pile. He pushed harder against the mouldy material and began feeling blindly around.

His fingers met nothing but damp deck and crumbling canvas. *Jeez, how far back did I shove it?* He scootched over and stretched a little harder. Coarse rope dug into his wrists.

But then ... *there it is!* His fingers closed on the smooth, familiar bone curve of the clasp knife.

Wriggling a little more, he pulled himself back toward the middle of the cockpit. *Now ...*

But the next bit turned out to be much harder than he'd expected. He couldn't see what he was doing. He couldn't find the little groove on the knife blade that you used to pull it open. As he wriggled, the rope around his wrists seemed to get tighter, stealing the feeling from his fingers. Twice he dropped the knife and had to scrabble around until he felt it again.

But at last he had it open and in his hand. Turning his wrist painfully, he managed to saw through the rope tying his hands to his ankles. *Oh yeah ...* he straightened his body with grateful relief and for a moment just lay there.

Then he tried to get the knife blade into one of the cords around his wrists. He still couldn't see what he was doing and several tries just brought the sharp blade down onto bare skin. He felt something warm and slippery on his fingers that made it even harder to hold the knife.

Exhausted, Jack sagged back against the cockpit bench, breathing hard through his nose and biting down on the soaked gag. He was now facing Miranda. Their eyes met.

Muffled noises came from behind her own gag and the blonde eyebrows wriggled frantically. She dropped her eyes to her lap and raised them back to his. Then again, blue eyes flicking up and down, back and forth, again and again.

Jack followed her gaze to her lap. *Of course!* Miranda's hands were tied *in front* of her. If Miranda used the knife, she could see what she was doing!

A new energy flowed through him. He turned his back to Miranda and scootched across the cockpit until he felt her cool fingers on his. Not until he felt her take it from his hand did he release his grip on the knife.

A moment later he felt the back-and-forth pressure as she began sawing the blade through the thick rope. His new muscles bulged as he tensed, pulling on the knots.

First the rope loosened as, strand by strand, the brown fibres parted. Then it gave way altogether.

Yes! Jackson's hands were free!

His first act was to yank the filthy handkerchief out of his mouth. He spat it out and gulped in lungfulls of moist air. Even as he did, he leaned forward to undo Miranda's gag.

Then he was pulling at the knots on her wrists. As soon as her hands were free, he used the knife to free their feet.

The moment he was completely loose, Jack vaulted over the remaining boat to the dock. He raced up the gangplank to the small landing and wrenched at the door.

Yeow! He'd pulled so violently that when the door jerked an inch then held fast, his shoulder hurt. Too late he noticed the shiny brass padlock now looped through a very solid-looking iron bolt on the inside of the door. He was as thoroughly locked in as he'd been locked out earlier.

He looked down to where he had dived without difficulty under the submerged planks that formed the boathouse wall. He could no longer see the bottom ends of the planks, the gray wood simply vanished into emerald depths.

For a moment his head spun. *Is reality playing games with me again?* Then he noticed that the gangway no longer tilted so steeply down to the floats. He also noticed that the light in the boat shed was much dimmer.

Darn it, of course! He had learned about the tides while working at the docks. How the moon pulled the oceans up in a bulge that traveled right around the globe, leaving valleys in between the bulges. Depending on whether the tide was in or out ships towered over the wharf and or lay so far below it that Jack could stand on the edge and look down into them.

The tide must have been at its lowest point when he ducked under the submerged walls. Now it was rising again. It would be hours before they could get out that way.

He padded down the gangway and out to the end of the float where he had seen Ericson pull a chain and open the tall, hanging doors.

He reached up and hauled with his entire weight on the rusty chain. There was a brief squeal of rusty metal from somewhere overhead and the chain moved a little. The doors jerked but did not open.

Sunzabees, Jack cursed under his breath. *Thought of everything, didn't you?*

Thinking hard he retraced his steps around to the boats and clambered back across to where the blonde girl was throwing the last piece of rope over the side in disgust.

"Miranda?"

"Yeah?" She turned to him. Her blue eyes met his darker ones.

"You ever start one of these things?"

Twenty-Six

THE LAST WHALER

PATSY ANN was not built for marathons. By the time she pointed her nose away from downtown Juneau, her gallop had slowed to a walk. She was panting heavily, pink tongue lolling out the side of her mouth. Still, she did not stop: she was a dog on a mission.

Behind her, a Pied Piper's train of Juneau citizens found it easier to keep up — but even more puzzling where she could possibly be going.

Late afternoon sun slanted low across Gastineau Channel, bringing up the colours of buildings and setting windows afire with reflected light. As Patsy Ann rounded the corner of the first big warehouse painted with the "B&P" logo, the road ahead was bathed in clear light. Hurrying toward them were two tall figures and one shorter one.

Patsy Ann let out a sharp bark and her white shoulders lifted. Summoning some deep reserve of energy, she put her down head and again began to run.

The distance between them closed quickly and soon everyone could make out Deputy Marshal Al McMann and

Captain Ezra Harper, walking fast toward town. Behind them young Rose Baker trotted to keep up.

THEY MET where the largest of the whaling station's several warehouses came to an end at a gravel parking lot. Beyond it, the lowering sun shattered in a dazzling dance off the waves of Gastineau Channel.

Patsy Ann wove back and forth between Al McMann and Captain Harper, butting at their knees and barking non-stop.

The two men fended her off but kept moving, turning away from the road onto the gravel lot.

"Where do we start?" Marshal McMann wondered aloud.

"It's a big place," the Captain said doubtfully.

"Well, let's start by asking," said the deputy. "The office is over this way."

He had barely taken a step when a muted rumble began somewhere off toward the water. The two men broke into a run. Rose and Patsy Ann followed at their heels and the rest of the crowd brought up the rear.

As they sprinted past the end of the row of warehouses, an older shed came into view. Weathered gray sides sagged out over the dark blue channel waves.

In the next moment the rumble surged to a full-throated roar. The seaward side of the old building seemed to explode with a sound like the biggest axe in creation cracking open the biggest log imaginable. Something low, fast and loud shot from the boat shed and across the water. The roar became a thunder that followed the speeding boat out across the sunlit channel.

The two men at the head of the parade, the girl, the stocky white dog and all the men, women and children of Juneau following them, came to a sudden, astonished stop.

Out on Gastineau Channel, the speeding boat swerved and looped dangerously. It narrowly missed a slow chugging fishing boat, then terrified a young family out for a paddle in a small canoe.

Captain Harper and Al McMann began running again. Now they headed toward the long row of private floats belonging to the whaling station.

The crowd, not to be cheated of a single instant of the excitement, fell on their trail.

JACKSON HAD BEEN at the helm of a boat precisely once. That was Al's old aluminum skiff with its chuttering little three-horse outboard. It was nothing like the high-performance engine now rocketing the chase boat across the tops of the waves, bucking and kicking up great rooster-tails of spray as Jack fought with the steering wheel.

"Slow down!" Miranda yelled into his ear.

Yeah, right, but which lever? In the adrenalin rush of bursting through the boat-shed doors he had flat forgotten which of the two levers on the dashboard was the gas pedal and which threw the powerful boat into gear.

Jack looked up and his stomach went watery. Beyond the

deadly profile of the harpoon gun, bucking and rolling where it was fixed at the point of the bow, they hurtled toward a line of pilings that marched across the water like soldiers in close file. In thirty seconds they'd crumple against the pilings like bugs on a windshield.

Fifty-fifty either way! Jack grasped one of the identical black-knobbed levers and hauled back on it.

Half a second later the engine note dropped back to a low grumble. The boat quickly lost speed, then slumped into the water, slowed down even more. A moment later it shot forward again with an unsettling dip of its bow as the steep wake it had been churning up rolled forward and slapped at the boat's transom.

But now at least Jack could turn the thing without fear of flipping it right over. He spun the wheel and the boat turned sharply away from the oncoming line of pilings.

Still, it was another ten minutes of stop-and-go trial and error before they were nosing back in toward the B&P company floats. Al McMann and Captain Harper waited with Patsy Ann and Rose beside them. On the bank above them, looking on, was a large and growing portion of Juneau's citizenry.

With a grinding bump the boat hit the dock and slid along it.

"Neutral! Throw it in neutral," Al yelled, grabbing at the boat's side.

Oh, yeah. Jack pulled back on the other lever. From somewhere there was a double ka-thunk and suddenly the boat was moving *backward* as fast as it had been going forward a moment ago.

"Neutral!" Al shouted. "In the middle!"

Right. Jack pushed the lever partway back and heard it ka-thunk once. He felt the boat lose its momentum.

Jackson's heart thundered in his chest. *Wheee-haw!* He knew he must be wearing a silly grin. *I gotta do that again some time.*

He turned to Marshal McMann. The lawman wasn't smiling at all.

It took Jack several minutes to satisfy young Al that the dramatic breakout had been their only course of action. But with Miranda nodding at every turn of Jack's tale, the deputy's doubt soon turned to decisive resolve.

"So they're in a chase boat," Al summed things up when the two were finished, "and they've got a head start on us."

"They're gone, Marshal," called a voice from the bank above. "There's nothing on the coast can catch one of them boats."

"They'll be in Canada before anything else can touch them," said a man who appeared to have walked out of O'Doule's only partway through his shave.

Jack, Captain Harper and the deputy exchanged looks. Then, as one, they looked at the speedboat rocking beside the float, its engine ticking as it cooled down

"Except another chase boat," said Captain Harper.

Al McMann pulled out a notebook and scribbled something on a page. He tore it out and handed it to Rose, then helped Miranda out of the boat and onto the float.

"Rose, take Miranda and find Judge Burns," he said.

"Give him that note, and give him those envelopes of yours; Miranda, you tell him what happened in the boathouse. And tell him we need the Coast Guard — pronto!"

Then he climbed into the boat. Captain Harper followed him.

A moment later, they were again roaring down the channel, this time with the Marshal at the wheel.

THE POWERFUL engine rocketed the boat nearly out of the water, sending it skipping from wave-top to wave-top in a thrilling, jarring flight. They could barely hear each other speak, and for the first little while, they didn't even try.

Where Gastineau Channel opened out into a wider seaway, the waves became bigger. They were now truly flying from one curling crest to the next, the entire boat coming out of the water for seconds at a time. Each time it did, the propeller spun free in the air and the racing engine reached an eerie scream. Each flight ended in a bone-jarring "landing" that had all three passengers grabbing for anything in reach.

For what seemed like an hour — although really it was barely half that — they roared over and through the waves. Spray surrounded them like a white veil. Jackson's knees and back began to ache from the constant pounding. His wet clothes had begun to dry on his body, sticking to him where they did and chilling him where they hadn't completely dried. The constant thunder of the huge engine made his ears ring.

Then, as they lifted off the top of a wave bigger than the rest, in the blue distance they saw the white rooster tail of another speeding boat.

"There they are!" Jackson yelled, his words barely audible above the thundering engine. Al and the Captain just nodded.

For the next few minutes, no one said anything. The boat ahead was moving fast, but so were they.

"Can we catch them?" Jack shouted.

"All these boats are identical," the Captain yelled back. "Depends on the weight in them."

"They've got full tanks," shouted Al. "So for now, we're lighter and faster."

For a minute they were silent as their boat steadily narrowed the distance separating them from the fleeing fugitives.

The same thought occurred to all three of them at once. As one they looked down and found the glass gauge on the dashboard marked "Fuel."

The red needle quivered barely above "empty."

Jack's stomach clenched. *Weight.* He looked back. Heart in his throat, he stepped out of the cabin onto the boat's spray-slicked cockpit deck. The wind caught him just as the boat came down on another wave. Suddenly he was rolling across the cockpit.

"Jack! No!" The Captain's voice came from a million miles away through the engine noise. The thunder was much louder out here, mixed with the roar of wind and the rush of water under the hull.

But now Jackson was on his knees beside the pile of rotting canvas. *Sorry about this,* he whispered a silent apology to any sea creatures beneath them. Then he began to heave musty folds of heavy material overboard. It was like trying to work on a cold frying pan while the cook was flipping pancakes, but somehow he managed it without going over the side himself.

When he got back to the cabin, crawling and sliding on his hands and knees, he was soaked to the skin again. Purple bruises were forming on both arms.

Al looked over at the boy a moment. Then his head bobbed once.

Jack was suddenly warmer with a feeling he hadn't felt since he first looked in the young deputy's eyes and no answering recognition looked back. Despite the glow of Al's esteem, he began to shiver as seawater trickled in icy lines down his back.

But now they were gaining visibly on the other boat. As they bounced off the waves they could see right into its cabin. Now and again they caught the pale flash of a face looking back.

Then the sound they had all been waiting for — fearing, really — came: the engine's steady thunder faltered. The huge motor coughed and three hearts skipped a beat. It made a spitting noise, then roared back to life.

Not now! Not when we're so close! Jack leaned forward against the dashboard, as though that might help them go faster. For a moment the tall harpoon gun on the boat's bow hid the fugitives from view.

A thought exploded in his head.

"Hey, does that thing work?" he shouted, pointing to the cruel-looking weapon.

The Captain and the Marshal exchanged startled glances. Then the Captain was pulling open drawers and lockers, ransacking the tiny cabin.

His hand emerged from the bottom of a locker. He opened it to show them a single stained brass cylinder. It looked like gun cartridges Jack had seen on television, only much larger.

"It's been a long time since I fired one of these," Captain Harper shouted into a sudden silence as the engine coughed and caught again.

"It's all we've got," Jack shouted. "It's our only shot!"

"Use it!" Al yelled back.

A hinged section divided the boat's windshield. With Jack's help, the Captain undid a latch and swung it up. Immediately salt spray and cold wind filled the tiny cabin. In the next moment the wiry seaman crawled out onto the leaping foredeck.

Jack's heart pounded. *Don't fall ... please don't.* Then the captain was sitting, feet planted against the very edge of the foredeck. His back was to them and he seemed to struggle with the rusty breech of the heavy gun.

The Captain's voice whipped past them on the wind: "Close up ... As close as you can."

One ... two ... three ... four ... more wave tops crashed beneath them. Ahead, the wild ride had washed away the tape concealing the other boat's name. Now Jack could read it plainly: the *Hunter II*.

The engine coughed again ... then again. For a moment it roared back to life. But then it hiccupped one more time and subsided into silence.

A loud bang sounded and a puff of white smoke flew past them. Jack could actually see the short bolt of the harpoon fly through the air, rope whipping behind it.

In the sudden quiet they heard a distinct *thwack* as the harpoon struck home, smack in the middle of the name emblazoned across the other boat's transom.

Their own boat slumped into a trough between waves and began to turn sideways. Then the rope snapped tight and they began to move through the water again.

The other boat's engine still ran at full speed, but with the rope now binding the two craft together it had slowed considerably.

The Captain began hauling in on the rope. Jack scrambled forward to help. The line was wet and slippery. It snapped and jerked as the two boats fought for headway against the waves. Jack's shoulders ached as the rope threatened to pull his arms completely out of their sockets. But length by length and hand over hand, they slowly retrieved the line. With each yard, they got closer to their quarry.

Ahead of them, Captain Petric leaned desperately over the transom of the fleeing boat. He was trying to pull the harpoon loose, but it was buried deeply in the solid wood.

There would be no getting away.

"Stop your engine!" Al McMann bellowed. Looking back, Jack saw the Marshal in the window hatch. His hands were together in front of him, a pistol trained on the boat ahead.

For a moment no one moved and nothing changed. The two boats churned through the water held together by the vibrating cable.

Then the roar of the other boat's engine died away. It sagged deeper into the water and the tension went out of the cable. Petric retreated back into the *Hunter-II*'s cockpit and raised his hands. A moment later Ericson stood beside him, hands high.

Gotcha!

Nothing in Jack's entire life had ever felt this good.

Twenty-Seven

TIME CATCHES UP

JACK WAS once again at the wheel of the retired chase boat. Only now it slid silently through the water at a sedate pace on the end of its harpoon tether. Jack's only responsibility was to steer so that it followed the *Hunter II* in a more-or-less straight line.

It was Ericson and Petric who now sat in the other boat's cockpit, hands and ankles secured in rope bracelets.

After a short debate, they had decided that Captain Harper and Deputy Marshal McMann should travel together in the fugitives' boat — one to drive, the other to keep an eye on the captives. But as long as they were going to tow the second boat home, someone needed to be at the helm.

"At the helm." It had a nice ring to it. "Master of the ship." *Well, more or less.*

It was after nine o'clock now and the light of the long northern evening was finally fading to a pearly shimmer in the sky. Left to himself, Jack's thoughts wandered to what would come next.

They'll have to let Stanley go now, he mused. *Will Patsy Ann take me home? But if she does, will I ever see Miranda again? Or can I stay awhile, maybe gloat around town a little?* He grinned in the deepening twilight.

Will Al "recognize" me when I get back? And what'll Mom say when I turn up after being missing for three weeks?

Maybe I should *stay here! Make a living betting on stuff I know is going to happen.* Jackson laughed out loud at that one. "Yeah, right!" It was a little late to start getting better marks on every history test he'd ever punted. Besides, he was pretty sure the Captain wouldn't approve.

From outside the boat came a sudden *whoosh.* Jack craned to peer through the small side window.

Oh ... my ... God!

Yards away a vast gray hill emerged from the inky blue waves. Only it wasn't a hill: the dorsal fin that rose above it stood higher than the chase boat's cabin-top.

There was another deep *whoosh.* A fine spray of mist geysered up in front of the fin and blew away in the wind. A smell full of funk and barnacles and fish and wildness wafted across the water. Jackson's entire body tingled.

The gray hill sank under the waves. As it did an immense, flared tail rose from the water, the sea running off it in foaming streams. Then, with a slap at the liquid surface that Jack felt in his bones, it too vanished.

Jack breathed out. His heart raced and he felt his tears rise. *It's going to be okay ...* he found himself almost praying the words. *It's almost over ... You're going to be okay.*

Twice more the gray hill appeared. The great breath of

the whale *whooshed* into the night air. The vast tail rose up and slapped down on the surface of the sea in what Jackson could almost believe was a salute.

Then it was gone and the sea was an inky blue emptiness of restless waves. Looking up for the first time, Jack saw the first stars glimmering in of the late-falling darkness.

So, he thought, *that's why Patsy Ann brought me here.* A strange, fierce and wholly unfamiliar gratitude swelled in Jackson's heart, burst out and flooded through him.

THE LATE mid-summer night had settled fully by the time they chugged up Gastineau Channel. In the deep black bowl overhead a carpet of stars glittered like nothing Jackson had ever seen at home. He searched the mysterious twinkling depths for the constellation Cetus. But the great whale eluded him.

It didn't matter. Hidden or visible, he knew it was there — swimming deep and immortal, beyond the reach of any harpoon in the inky sea of space.

Sparkling lights strung like Christmas along the shoreline ahead told him they were nearly home.

As they approached the Bering and Pacific floats, Jack could see the shore lined with people. At the centre of the crowd a white dog seemed to glow under banks of powerful floodlights. Beside her stood the erect figure of Judge Burns. Next to him a tall man held his arm around a slender woman, who jounced a blanket bundle in her arms. Beside them were Sylvia Baker, Rose and Miranda.

Jack felt something catch in his throat. *Imagine seeing your own dad brought home in handcuffs.* He couldn't imagine what her life must have been like in that big sad house. *Money sure doesn't buy happiness.* He had a sudden longing to hug the one parent he had.

The *Hunter II* slipped smoothly in to the dock. At just the right moment Al McMann cut it into reverse so that Captain Harper could step ashore, rope in hand. A few seconds later, Jack's boat bumped up to the float.

"Hey kid, congratulations!" Clancy grabbed the edge of the boat. With something like shock, Jack saw that his pit-bull boss was flat-out grinning.

The next few minutes were a blur of grinning faces and pumping hands and hearty claps on the back.

Vera gave the baby to Stanley long enough to wrap Jack in a long, tight hug and say "Thank you" so many times he lost count. She seemed to have been crying again but now the effect was entirely different.

Stanley himself simply took Jack's hand, looked him straight in the eye and said, clear and loud, "Jack Kyle, I was wrong about you. You're a right guy. I owe you!" Then he gave Jack's hand a strong squeeze and a powerful shake.

Al wasted no time marching Ericson and Petric up to a waiting black panel truck. The blond man kept his head down, not even glancing up as he walked past his daughter. But she watched him, her face looking ready to collapse at any moment.

The truck pulled away. Sylvia slipped an arm around the

blonde girl's slight shoulders and Rose took her hand. "Miranda, honey," Sylvia said very gently, "you've always got a home with us, you know that don't you?"

"We're practically sisters anyway," added Rose.

Miranda sobbed and turned and then all three of them were wrapped together in a tight embrace. Then Patsy Ann was there as well, inserting nose between pairs of legs and pushing her thick self forward into the middle of the hug. For a moment, the blonde head came up and Jack saw tears and laughter all at once on Miranda's face.

JACK FELT something shove hard against him. He opened his eyes and saw the grimy white back of a small furry head and one sharp ear pointing up to the ceiling. He reached over and scratched around the ear. Patsy Ann gave a contented little sigh and stretched all out four legs in front of her, pushing him even harder into the small sliver of bed that remained to him.

Light poured in through the window. He smelled seaweed drying on the shore rocks across the road and leaves in the warm sun. A bee buzzed. *It must be waaay late ... like, after seven, even!* With a momentary panic he shoved Patsy Ann aside and swung off the bed. *Ohmigosh! Clancy's going to* kill *me!*

Then he remembered ... he was fired ... again.

Then, with a rush, it all came back to him. Everything that happened the previous day: Patsy Ann's sacrifice dive, the boats in the shed, Miranda and her father, blasting out of the boathouse, the desperate pedal-to-the-metal pursuit of the *Hunter II*. *The whale!* He closed his eyes and saw again the gray hill in the twilight sea, heard the *whoosh* and smelled that incredible smell of ocean.

He let the memory go reluctantly. The grin on Clancy's face at the float came back to him. So probably he wasn't fired any more.

Then again, maybe he didn't need to go back to work again either. Not yet, at least.

Jack leaned back again, resting on Patsy Ann's solid bulk. A shaft of green light angled in through the small window behind him. Its beam brought a blush to the roses and carnations on the papered walls. The burnished bone of his knife glowed in the sunlight that fell on the dresser.

If Captain Harper were right, he'd have to go home soon. Back to Brampton. Back to the future — the very idea almost made him laugh. *But I'm* here *... so* it *must be there,* he reasoned. *Unless I'm just crazy.*

He knew he wasn't crazy. *But when I get home ...* He'd have a secret no one would believe.

An idea began to form. He pushed off the bed.

On impulse Jackson dressed in his own clothes — the ones he'd worn the day he arrived.

"Coffee?" Al McMann greeted him in the kitchen, holding the blue enamel pot high.

"You bet," Jack answered on his way into the bathroom.

Five minutes later he sat on the Bakers' small back porch, a mug of coffee at his side and Patsy Ann stretched nearby in a bull-terrier size patch of sunlight.

Jackson's left hand cradled his pocket-knife, Al's — *old* Al's — knife, its folding blade closed. In his right was a nail scavenged from under the porch. Bending into the task, he ran the sharp tip of the nail back and forth into the yellow bone, doing it over and again until he had scored a small but unmistakable "X" deep into the smooth sheath on one side of the knife.

Behind him, the screen door slapped open. Footsteps sounded on the small porch. The door banged shut on its spring and Al McMann dropped to sit beside the tall youth, a steaming mug in hand.

Jack looked over and met the young lawman's eyes.

"Stanley's not the only one who was wrong about you," Al began. "Without you, I'd still be building a case against an innocent man."

"Sometimes people think they're doing right, it just comes out wrong," Jack said softly.

There was a wry edge to Al's chuckle. "Yeah, I've heard that somewhere." He sipped from his mug. "Say, you ever think of a job in law enforcement? It's sure an interesting life."

Jack nodded. "Matter of fact."

"Who knows," Al said. "You're not that much younger than me. Maybe we'll work together some day."

Jack couldn't suppress a grin. "Yeah, who knows?" He spun the nail into the long grass along the fence. "Listen, Marshal." He'd gotten used to it by now. There'd be plenty of time to call him "Al" later, back home. "I'd like you to have this." Jack held out the pocketknife. "Call it a souvenir of your first big case.

It was lucky for me. Maybe it'll be lucky for you."

For a moment, the young marshal was struck silent, mouth open. Then he stammered, "I ... I don't know. I don't think I can. It's yours."

"What goes around, comes around," Jack said lightly. "I'll get another one." *Or maybe, not exactly* another *one,* he thought to himself with a secret smile.

"Well ..."

A bark turned both their heads. Patsy Ann sat watching the two of them. The sunlight danced in her black eyes and a smile wrinkled the corners of her open mouth. She barked again, eyes on Al.

Reluctance gave way. Al's fingers closed on the knife as Jackson's hand released it. He pulled back the strong, sharp blade and admired its edge. Then he closed it again and turned it over in his hand. He ran a finger over the mark newly etched into the case. He gave Jack a long thoughtful look, then smiled. "Well, thank you! I'll let it be a reminder never again to rush a man to judgment."

Their eyes met. Jack knew it was a promise the young marshal would keep.

The door behind them slapped open. "Flapjacks are up!" Rose sang out.

Jackson fell on his food with a will. By the time they'd returned to the boarding house last night — really this morning — he'd managed only a cold sandwich before falling into bed. Now he tucked greedily into a thick stack of fluffy pancakes studded with ruby raspberries and swimming in butter and thick amber syrup.

"I still don't understand one thing," Sylvia asked over her own plate. "Mr. Ericson sent the radio signal that tricked the plane into landing. Captain Petric was the man in the boat who actually took the money — and later he put that bank wrapper aboard *Cetus* to lead you to Stanley. But I still don't know *why*? Why would they rob themselves?"

"I can answer that, Mrs. Baker," Al McMann said, hastily swallowing a bite of flapjack. "They weren't really robbing themselves, for starters. They were robbing their employees. Besides that, they both knew that time was running out for them — for the whaling, that is.

"You see," the deputy put down his fork, "Ericson owns his supply company outright. But he's just a small shareholder in the Bering and Pacific Company. When we searched his office last night we found letters from the company's directors. They were going to close it down at the end of the season. Said it was costing too much to find whales and it was too much trouble to fight the conservationists."

"So they faced a lee shore, the two of 'em," said Captain Harper. "No whaling, no fleet; no fleet, no captain's work. And no one to sell supplies to."

Somewhere outside Patsy Ann barked.

"What will happen to him now?"

Jackson looked over at Miranda. Her face was pale but she'd asked the question in a new voice — resigned, but calm. More curious than caring — as though the hurting part was almost over.

Patsy Ann barked again, louder than before.

Now Al was going on about the stages of a trial. But his voice seemed distant somehow. *Swimmy and ... strange.*

Jackson's gaze shifted and he saw the Captain looking at him. The old seaman had an odd look on his face, as though he saw something Jack didn't see. Then he tipped his head, indicating the door.

"'Scuse me," Jack mumbled, and got to his feet.

Sylvia gave him a nod and a vague smile, then returned her attention to the deputy.

Captain Harper also rose, retrieving a brown paper sack from below his chair as he did. He followed Jack out.

Once they were alone on the sunlit porch the Captain reached into the sack and removed Jack's Air Jordans. "I had a feeling you might need these today."

Another bark rang loudly into the quiet air. Jack turned. Patsy Ann stood facing them at the back of the garden, her head held low. As he looked, her white teeth flashed in another bark.

Through the screen door, he heard Miranda laugh.

Another bark — sharper now, urgent.

"Aye, lad," the Captain said. "It's time."

Jackson's heart skipped a beat. "But ..." Now it was really time to go, he wanted to stay. *Just a little longer ...*

"You've done what you came for."

The barking was non-stop now.

Jack dropped to the porch steps. He shucked off his almost-new 1935 boots. He he slipped into his Air Jordans and did them up, feeling momentarily strange in the space-age footwear. Standing, he handed the leather boots to the Captain.

"You said I'm not the only one she's brought back," he said. "Maybe you can use these sometime."

At the back of the garden now, Patsy Ann jumped and spun with impatience.

"Captain ..."

"Go, lad," the old man smiled.

"Thank you for everything." He turned and sprinted across the mossy yard. "Alright, I'm coming," he called, knowing the white dog couldn't hear him.

But she had already turned and disappeared into the bushes. Jack dropped to his hands and knees and scrambled after her. He felt the tug of barbed raspberry canes on his shoulders and in his hair. Ahead of him he saw Patsy Ann's white behind deke around thickets of canes. Then he saw the fence and the ragged hole where the planks were broken off.

Patsy Ann disappeared through the gap. Jackson threw himself to the ground and wriggled after her.

Twenty-Eight

WHAT GOES AROUND

IT WAS VERY dark beyond the fence, much darker than the thick foliage overhead could explain. Jackson could no longer see the white flash of the dog ahead of him.

Blindly, he pushed between barely seen branches and the grasping fingers of shrubbery. The salty, faintly fishy air he'd become used to these last few weeks was gone, along with the soft, constant murmur of the channel waves. He breathed in and smelled green, fresh-cut grass against a background of gasoline and fry oil. In the distance, traffic whined.

Then suddenly he broke through the last wall of leaves and felt the soft brush of mown lawn beneath his palms.

Jackson scrambled to his feet and looked around. Ahead was the green belt that wandered through Brampton. Beyond it were house roofs and the glow of the distant city. No narrow back trail, no trees towering to the sky, no wall of mountain rising through mist. He looked up. For some reason it didn't startle him that the bright daylight had vanished or that the sky overhead was black. Black and dull: only a few stars glimmered dimly.

Off to the left, streetlamps cast orange pools of light. Patsy Ann was nowhere to be seen.

Let's see, he thought. *It was Sunday when I left ...* But was it now Sunday night? With a jolt, Jack realized that he had no idea how long he'd been gone.

Everything looked familiar, just as he had left it *whenever that was.* Beyond the greenway, rooftops and the square bulk of apartment buildings made black silhouettes against the city's distant glow. Only one or two windows showed lights. The shortest path home was along the greenway, following the foot-trail that led to the ballpark and then to the neighbourhood of townhouses where the Kyles lived.

The air was cool and Jackson shivered. He shrugged his shoulders deeper into his jean jacket and set out. By the time he reached the trail that wound along the middle of the greenway, cold dew had soaked through his sneakers. He stepped gratefully onto the gravel path.

Jack had been walking about ten minutes when the path brought him to the playing field with its baseball diamonds and soccer pitch. Over there was the long grass where Patsy Ann had lain in wait for his wild flyball. He felt a tingle at the back of his neck. *If I ever feel that again,* he thought, remembering the strange electricity he'd felt at his first sight of the stray dog, *I hope I remember.*

He walked across the diamond, a flurry of sudden doubts tugging at his mind. He'd have to come up with *something* to explain his absence to Mom. And what would he say to Al?

He passed the dugouts and came to the curb, where he turned right toward home. Suddenly, he was bathed in a dazzling brilliance. Every blade of grass in the lawn and every leaf on the bushes stood out in high relief. He could even see the line of footprints behind him where his steps had disturbed the dew.

The light was coming from the parking lot across the street. Jack blinked and raised his hand to shield his eyes.

"Police!" A woman's voice. "Stay where you are."

A moment later he made out a uniformed silhouette walking across the pavement toward him.

"Are you Jackson Kyle?" she called.

"Yeah." *Oh, shoot ... How much trouble am I in now? Jeez — from hero to crook in ... well, seventy years I guess.* He suppressed a grin.

"Your mother's reported you missing."

"I ... didn't know." *But jeez, I kinda* hope *so. I mean, seeing I've been gone, like, weeks.*

The officer was at his side now. She flicked on a flashlight and shone it in his eyes, making him blink. Then she ran the beam over the rest of him.

"Have you been in a fight?"

Eh? "No!"

"Hold out your hands."

Handcuffs?

But the police officer merely focused her light on his palms. They were scuffed and scraped and stained red with raspberry juice. She examined him closely. "How did your hurt your hands?"

"Uh ... climbing on rocks. And those are berry stains."

The officer cocked her head at him skeptically. "Are you alright?"

"Yeah." *Just don't ask where I've been.*

"Your mother says you've been gone since Sunday morning," the officer said. "Can you tell me where you've been?"

Oh, I could tell you, you just wouldn't believe it. "I, um, met some people and I ... hung out with them a while."

The flashlight came back to his eyes. "Are you on anything? Have you taken anything? Any pills? Smoke anything?"

What is it about grown-ups today? "No ma'am." *Not unless you count coffee.*

"Do you need to see a doctor?"

"I don't think so."

She finally seemed satisfied. "Would you like us to give you a lift home?"

Jack had never seen the inside of a real police car. "Yeah, that would be great. Thank you."

"C'mon, then." The officer turned back toward her patrol car. The spotlight went out, leaving a ghostly blue dot to dance in front of Jackson's eyes.

The officer opened the back door of a cruiser. Jack got in. Perforated metal separated him from the front seat. There was the smell of coffee and disinfectant and old puke. And he noticed there weren't any door handles back here.

The male officer behind the wheel began a series of back-and-forth turns on the narrow gravel pathway running down the middle of the greenway. Jackson put his face to the metal grille and examined the front of the patrol car with interest. A laptop computer sat between the driver and his partner. At her feet, he spotted the butt of a rifle or shotgun.

A radio crackled. *Boy, would young Al love to get his hands on some of this stuff.*

Jack's eye drifted over to the car's side mirror. *Ohmigosh.* A white dog stood out clearly in the glass against the dark shrubbery behind her. Patsy Ann's mouth was open in a wide grin. Her tail beat back and forth. White fur shone with a soft brilliance in the mild night air. He whipped around in his seat and looked out the back window.

There was nothing behind the car but empty lawn and shrubbery along the distant fence line.

Jack's heart swelled with a strange mixture of wonder and loss.

"You sure you're okay, bud?" the driver said.

"Yeah, yeah. I just ... thought I saw something. Nothing." He sagged back into the seat.

The car turned onto the empty street and began to pick up speed.

Maybe I did just hit my head and I've been out for a while, he thought. He reached down and felt his pocket. His knife was gone. *Or did I just lose it?*

"Excuse me," he knocked on the metal grille. "What day is it?"

The female officer turned and gave him a sharp look. "You don't know what day it is?" she asked. "Are you *sure* you haven't been partying?"

"Really, no." *Not like you mean, anyway*. "I just ... don't have a watch and I ... I kinda lost track of time." *Boy, there's an understatement.*

"It's three-thirty Wednesday morning. Your mother reported you missing Sunday afternoon."

Huh. That out-of-body feeling he'd felt the first few days in Juneau hit him again. *So, almost three weeks in 1935 turns out to be almost three days in 2005. So it's true, everything* does *go faster today!* He caught the woman officer giving him another hard look. He'd been grinning and shaking his head.

Sheesh, I just clear my rep in Juneau and I lose it Brampton.

Ten minutes later the car pulled up in front of the familiar brick and stucco townhouse. A light was on in his mother's bedroom over the garage. The woman officer got out and opened Jack's door. As he stepped out, he saw the curtain flick aside in his mother's room.

From outside the door he heard steps flying down stairs. A moment later, Carla Kyle had Jack wrapped in a deep bear hug, almost lifting him off his feet. "Oh, honey, I thought you were dead." He could feel wetness on his cheek and realized with embarrassment that Mom was crying.

"We found him on the greenway," the policewoman said. "He says he wasn't partying and he doesn't seem to be on anything."

"Oh, thank you, thank you," Carla Kyle said over and over.

"But he hasn't wanted to tell us much about where he's been or what he's been up to." She tilted her head and looked from one Kyle to the other. "I think maybe you two need to do some talking."

"Oh, we will," Carla said with feeling.

With an effort, Jackson pulled himself away from his mother

and faced the officer. "Really, I know I can't explain everything, but believe me, everything's fine. You don't need to worry about me ... or her."

The officer looked far from convinced but after a moment she nodded. "I hope not. Have a good night now." The cruiser pulled out of the driveway and left them alone.

THE FAMILIAR kitchen smelled of burned coffee and microwave popcorn. Jackson was momentarily dismayed by the stack of take-out trays. *I gotta get Al to teach me how to make real biscuits,* he told himself as Carla busied herself making tea. *How hard can it be?*

Getting his mother to believe that he was really alright — and not on some kind of drug — took a little longer. He had to do rather a lot of fancy skating not to stretch the truth any more than necessary. It helped that he only had seventy-two hours to explain, not three weeks. Still, the sun was up by the time Carla Kyle accepted, with reservations, that Jack had simply returned the white stray dog to its "family" and then spent the past couple of days with them, afraid to come home and face her anger.

"Oh Jackson, honey, never be afraid to come home," she finally relented. "You know I only want you to be safe."

She was still Mom, Jackson couldn't help thinking — but she sure wasn't Eric Ericson. He put up with another long hug.

"But Mom," he said after extricating himself from her arms one more time. "You have to let me do something."

"What's that, honey?"

"You have to let me hang out with Al. He's a good guy, really. I like him and ..."

"Oh, honey," Carla cut him off. Her stricken face sent a blade of ice into Jack's chest.

"What?"

"Mr. McMann ... While you were gone ...

"What?"

"Well, he passed away on Monday."

Noooo! Jack pulled away from Carla and searched her face. *He can't be dead. He can't. He just* can't.

He leapt up and headed for the stairs.

"Jack!" his mother cried out.

He caught himself on the first step and looked back at his mother. "Don't worry, Mom, I'll be back. *Promise*. I'm just going to Al's. I'll see you later."

He took the stairs three at a time and raced out the front door into the clear morning light.

THERE WAS a car in Al's driveway, but it wasn't Al's. Jack ran up the steps to the front porch and pounded on the door. "Al!" he called. "Al!"

The sound of movement came from inside. A woman he'd never seen before opened the door. She looked older than his mother, but still quite a bit younger than Al — *old* Al. A man about the same age appeared behind her.

"Who are you?" Jack blurted out. "And what are you doing in Al's house?"

The woman gave him a searching look, then smiled. "My name's Amelia, but Al McMann was my father." She indicated the man now standing beside her. "This is my brother, John."

Jack stood in befuddled silence. The man in the door looked just like a cross between *young* Al and *old* Al.

"And who are you?" the man asked.

"Jack ... Jackson Kyle."

An odd look came over the two adults' faces. "So *you*'re young Jack," the woman said. "Dad used to talk about you. You meant a great deal to him. He said you 'brought back his youth'."

The icy knot that had gripped Jack's stomach let go. His knees felt wobbly.

Ohmigosh, "used to." "Is it ... Is he ..."

"I'm afraid so," the man said. "Monday afternoon. A stroke. He went peacefully."

"But come in," his sister said. "There are some things here for you."

Huh? Jack stepped inside the familiar hallway. It felt very strange to be here, everything looking the way it did, *smelling* the way it did, only Al missing.

"Come on through," John McMann said, directing him through to the kitchen. "Do you drink coffee?"

"Yes, please." *I was drinking coffee with him just ... just this morning.* He would remember that cup of coffee forever — a memory to reach for when he fell, to help him to his feet.

As he passed through the hall, Jack noticed something that certainly *hadn't* been there before. Glass in a frame protected a yellowing front page from the *Alaska Daily Empire*. "Harpooned!" a huge headline read. Below was a breathless paragraph about the high-seas capture of "prominent local businessman Eric Ericson" and Captain Jerry Petric, after a dramatic boat chase. A faded picture showed a tall young man with a badge standing between a leathery looking older fellow in a sea-captain's cap and a girl with dark hair in pigtails.

Jack felt that dizzy, *floor-moving-under-me*, feeling again.

John McMann stepped up beside him and lifted the frame from its hook. "He wanted you to have this," he said. "Said you reminded him of another Jack who helped him crack that first big case. There's a couple other things, too."

They went into the kitchen. Sheets of paper and an open file box were on the table where he'd eaten crusted, flaky perch and scones with black-currant jam.

Al's daughter poured coffee and put an open box of donuts on the table. Her brother disappeared upstairs, coming back a moment later with a small wooden box. This he put it in front of Jack. "Dad's will says this goes with the newspaper story."

A harsh squeal of brakes came from the driveway. A moment later there was a timid knock on the kitchen door.

It took several minutes to explain everything to Carla Kyle. But when she'd taken it in, she shook her head. "I feel so badly," she said. "I misjudged him so terribly."

Jack put his hand on her arm. "Mom, it's okay. He understood. He didn't blame you. He used to say, 'Sometimes people do the wrong thing for the right reasons'."

Jack reached out and pulled the box closer. "You should know," Amelia McMann said, "that there's also some money going into a trust. He wanted you to be able to go to college."

Her brother coughed. "Said he hoped you'd think about law enforcement, but that's up to you."

Mystified, Jack lifted the wooden lid. Inside, a silver metal star lay in blue velvet. Beside it was a clasp knife, its blade folded into a bone-covered handle. Heart beating, Jack lifted out the knife. On the other side of the bone handle, time had worn smooth the edges of a small incised "X." He grinned.

PATSY ANN

is a real Bull Terrier who lived in Juneau, Alaska, during the 1930s. Stone deaf from birth, she somehow "heard" the whistles of ships long before they came into sight and would trot purposefully to the wharf to greet them. She became so famous that her likeness appeared on postcards. In 1934, the town's mayor bestowed upon her the title of "Official Greeter of Juneau."

In 1992, on the fiftieth anniversary of her death, a bronze statue of Patsy Ann was erected on the Juneau waterfront. There the little dog sits watching and waiting with eternal patience, forever fulfilling her duties as "Official Greeter."

The authors are donating a portion of their royalties to the Friends of Patsy Ann Society, an organization set up in conjunction with the Gastineau Humane Society to promote understanding of and kindness to animals. Patsy Ann's statue was created by noted artist and dog show judge, Anna Harris.

For more about Patsy Ann, log on to her website:
http://www.patsyann.com

BEVERLEY WOOD is a writer and marketer. Her husband **CHRIS WOOD** is a journalist and author of fiction and non-fiction books. Their dog, Cato, is a bull terrier. After a decade of living afloat on a boat in Vancouver, they all recently moved ashore to a home within sight of the sea on Vancouver Island.

SIRIUS MYSTERIES

by Beverley and Chris Wood

Look for these adventures starring Patsy Ann

DogStar

Juneau, Alaska, 1932. This is where thirteen-year-old Jeff Beacon is stranded when his parents take him on an Alaskan cruise to help him get over the death of his beloved dog, Buddy. The problem is that Jeff is a twenty-first century kid, with a laptop computer and hightop sneakers. Why has he been transported in time to the Alaskan frontier? And how can he find his way home? Jeff must answer these questions quickly — and his only help is the town's Bull Terrier, Patsy Ann.

1-55192-638-5 • *Available*

The Golden Boy

Tomi Tanaka can take almost anything apart and put it back together again. But he can't seem to please his demanding dad. When Patsy Ann visits him, the two travel back to Juneau, Alaska, in the 1930s, where Tomi has a chance to make sense of a puzzling treasure that has the town stumped — and he ends up on the trail of a mysterious missing gold mine.

1-55192-711-x • *Coming in Fall 2006*